Novels by Reed Farrel Coleman
featuring Moe Prager:
Walking the Perfect Square
Redemption Street
The James Deans
Soul Patch
Empty Ever After

featuring Dylan Klein:
Life Goes Sleeping
Little Easter
They Don't Play Stickball in Milwaukee

as Tony Spinosa:
Hose Monkey
The Fourth Victim

with Ken Bruen:
Tower

INNOCENT
MONSTER

INNOCENT MONSTER

Reed Farrel Coleman

TYRUS
BOOKS

Published by
TYRUS BOOKS
1213 N. Sherman Ave. #306
Madison, WI 53704
www.tyrusbooks.com

Names, characters, places, and incidents in this novel
are the product of the author's imagination or are used fictitiously.

Library of Congress Cataloging-In-Publication Data has been applied for.

12 11 10 09 08   1 2 3 4 5 6 7 8 9 10

978-1-935562-20-7

Acknowledgements

I owe more than I can say to Peter Spiegelman for his editorial suggestions and his endless patience with me. Many thanks to Jonathan Santlofer for helping me navigate my way around the perilous fringes of the art world. Thanks to Marla Bayles, PhD, Ellen W. Schare, and Sara J. Henry. I also want to say that I am grateful to Tyrus Books, Busted Flush Press, and my agent David Hale Smith for finding a way to allow readers to once again walk the streets of Brooklyn with Moe as their guide.

Love to Rosanne, Kaitlin, and Dylan.

For Rory

If only it was a matter of the innocent and the guilty.
Too bad for us it's usually a matter of the guilty
and the more guilty.

—Israel Roth

ONE

Katy's blood was no longer fresh on my hands and after 9/11 people seemed to stop taking notice. I stopped trying to scrub it away. With all due respect to Lady Macbeth, there isn't enough soap or hot water to get those stains out and scouring brushes are impotent at guilt. Jews know from guilt. So do Catholics, but they know it differently. Jews know you can't pray it away or confess it away and that there is no number of good acts that will balance the ledger sheet. Guilt is a tattoo and, if you're lucky, it will fade. 9/11 faded my tattoo. Besides, in a world awash in blood, what's one life, give or take?

Even my daughter Sarah started talking to me again, if only once a week and then with a robotic detachment that hurt me more than her year of silence ever did. In the wake of 9/11 all of us New Yorkers were really just robots there for a little while. So it was that the pain of my divorce from Carmella and the dissolution of our partnership barely registered. It had taken twenty years of secrets to destroy my first marriage and about twenty minutes to destroy my second. I wondered if there were Las Vegas odds on how fast I could fuck up a third? I missed Israel, Carmella's son by another man and, for a very brief time, mine in every other way that mattered. But he was less than a year old when Carmella moved up to Toronto and I doubt he misses me. At my age, on the other hand, you start to spend a lot of your time missing people: some living, some dead, some just gone.

Although Carmella and I were no longer partners, I kept our firm, Prager & Melendez Investigations, Inc., open, at least until the end of our lease. And I couldn't see putting Brian Doyle and Devo on the street because my marriage fell apart. It turned out to be one of those rare things done with best intentions that paid unexpected dividends. Sometimes the road to profit and not just to hell is paved with good intentions. Business boomed in the months following 9/11, but it was an odd kind of business. Other than our contract insurance work, we continued looking for people. That hadn't changed. It was the nature of the people we were hired to find that had changed.

Suddenly our clients, especially the ones forty years old and up, had an urgent need to reconnect with people who'd fallen through the cracks in their lives. We had a lot of jobs finding old flames and first loves, childhood friends, teammates and coaches, even black sheep relatives from the "wrong" side of the family. National tragedy fucks with people's heads. And in those days when Chicken Little screamed that the sky was falling, no one seemed inclined to argue. But the sky didn't fall and, in terms of our once burgeoning caseload, the affection for reconnection waned.

That was six years ago now: our lease long expired, the office long closed. Brian Doyle and Devo have opened their own shop in lower Manhattan, scavenging off a better class of lice than on the Brooklyn side of the river. Currently, no one needs to pay to find anyone, not anymore. Well, at least not to find old flames or high school football heroes. You can find them where you find everything else in the world: on the Net. And if you don't find them, just count to ten, and they'll find you. Ah, the internet. Ten years ago I told Aaron to stop wasting our money on online advertising and building a topnotch website. He didn't listen. Now internet sales accounted for about twenty percent of our business. So much for my business acumen, but the Net wasn't all magic. If you want to find an ex who's skipped town and is two years in arrears on child support payments, you might still consider using a professional investigator.

These days I was a professional wine merchant. Period. I didn't even know where my PI license was or if it was still valid. Somewhere along the way I moved it out of my sock drawer and haven't seen it since. I think I might hunt it down one day and make a collage of it and my equally valueless shares of Enron stock. But for now, I was too busy being bored numb and sleepwalking through preparations for the summer grand opening of our second Long Island store—Sunrise and Vine in Bridgehampton—to worry about the toys in my attic. Tucked away there in the basement office of my favorite store, Bordeaux In Brooklyn, I was so enraptured by the details of the local ordinances concerning exterior commercial signage that I nearly forgot to breathe.

"Moe, pick up line one," a voice called to me from somewhere beyond the womb of my stupor. That it was the voice of the store's assistant manager on the intercom mattered little. To me, it was the voice of salvation.

Having depressed the speaker phone button, I said, "Good morning, Moe Prager."

"Dad?"

"Hey, kid—Sarah."

"Are we on speaker phone?"

"Don't worry. I'm in the office. No one's here. What's wrong?"

"How do you know something's wrong?"

"I don't want to fight."

"Why would we fight?" she asked.

"Because if I answer your question about how I know something's wrong, you'll get pissy with me."

"Risk it."

"I know because you've called me once a week, every Sunday morning at eleven, for the last six years. Whenever you break that schedule, something's wrong. That, and I can hear it in your voice. I guess there are still some things you can't hide from me."

She answered with silence, a noisy silence. I could hear her gears turning as she decided how to react. We had once been as close as a dad and daughter could be. No more. Sarah blamed me for her mother's murder. That made two of us. I hadn't pulled the trigger, but, in my way, I was just as guilty as the man who did.

She finally spoke. "Can you meet me for lunch?"

"Sure, but what's wrong?"

"I'm okay. It's not me. I swear."

"Then who?"

"I'll see you at New Carmens on Sheepshead Bay Road in an hour and we can talk about it."

Click.

North Shore Herald, Friday, July 14, 2000

Pint-sized Pollock Dazzles Locals

GABRIEL BYNUM

All of four years old, Sea Cliff's own Sashi Bluntstone is already a world-renowned artist. She first put paint brush to canvas at eighteen months of age and has yet to stop. She sold her first painting at age two to local collector and patron of the arts Sonia Barrows-Willingham of Glen Cove.

"I paid a mere five hundred dollars for 'Pistachio Sprinkles,'" said Barrows-Willingham, gesturing at a canvas on the brick wall at the Junction Gallery in Sea Cliff. "Best five hundred dollars I ever invested. Just last month, I was offered twenty-five thousand for it. But I wouldn't care if they offered me twenty-five million for it. I just love all of her work. It's marvelous. I have several of her works and plan to add more. Don't you just love them?"

Four-year-old Sashi, busy chasing her friends around the gallery, seemed completely unfazed by all the hoopla surrounding her first big showing. An apparently normal kid in most ways, the green-eyed and russet-haired prodigy is shy with most adults, but when she opens up, her favorite subject isn't art, it's her beagle puppy Cara.

The young Miss Bluntstone, whose work is most often categorized as Neo-Abstract Expressionism, is not without her detractors and doubters.

"At best, the child's an unwitting shill for her ambitious parents. At worst ... I don't even want to consider it," says Wallace Rusk, curator at the nearby Cold Spring Harbor Museum of Modern Art. "The child is being mercilessly exploited, which, if she were actually any good, might be understandable, if not forgivable. But it's just so much kitsch and finger painting in the guise of high art."

Yet in the face of withering criticism, nothing could dampen the palpable excitement in the crowded gallery. If there were any Sashi doubters or detractors on hand, they weren't very vocal. There were abundant smiles and sales seemed brisk as gallery owner and art agent Randolph Junction delighted in placing red dots—marking the pieces as "sold"—on the small, white name placards next to each painting.

TWO

December was never a favorite month of mine. Regardless of how good it was for the wine business, I found the season depressing on myriad levels. I wonder how many people were conscious of the subtle shift away from the phrase Christmas Season to the more mundane, palatable, and politically correct Holiday Season. *Holiday Season, my ass!* The older I get, the crankier I get, and nothing gets me quite as cranky as political correctness. Besides, who asked us Jews if we minded Hanukah being ignored? My questionnaire must've gotten lost in the mail. Now with the advent of Kwanza, there would be no going back. But there never is a going back, is there?

I had my own very personal reasons for hating December. Exactly thirty years ago, a handsome college student named Patrick Michael Maloney worked a shift at Pooty's Bar in Tribeca for a student government fundraiser. When he left Pooty's that night, he vanished into thin air. And while it's not quite factually accurate to say I was hired by his family to find him, it is essentially the truth, the truth always being more important than the facts. I found him, all right, when no one else could: not my former employer, the NYPD; not hundreds of volunteers; not the small army of private detectives hired by the Maloneys. I also found a trunk full of ugly secrets and my soon-to-be wife, Patrick's sister, Katy Maloney. What I kept was Katy. I kept the ugly secrets too, until they blew up in my face. I let Patrick go. If there was a going back wish, that's what I would spend it on. I would hold on to Patrick Michael Maloney with both hands and never let go. In his vanishing, the seeds of new lives were born. In my letting him go were born the seeds of destruction. Look closely enough and you can see the crooked and bloody red line that leads from one to the other.

New Carmens Restaurant was a diner at the bent elbow of Sheepshead Bay Road in Brooklyn. While there were restaurants that Katy, Sarah, and I once loved to go to as a family, New Carmens was a special place for Sarah and me, *our* special place. It was where the two of us went for onion rings and vanilla egg creams when we had something like a good report card to celebrate. It was where we went for banana splits and coffee when young knees got scraped and then later when teenage hearts got broken. Neither Sarah nor I had set foot inside New Carmens since Katy's murder seven years ago. That's how I knew that whatever Sarah wanted to discuss was serious business.

My daughter was waiting for me in the damp outside the front door, the curls of her long red hair undone by the rain. She might have been Sarah F.J. Prager, a newly minted Doctor of Veterinary Medicine to the rest of the world, but to me, at that moment, she was just my sad little girl. When she saw me, she smiled, then caught herself and stopped. She made to speak and, again, stopped herself. What was there to say, really? It was only right, I thought, that we go back in together. Yet when we walked in, things had changed. The restaurant had been remade. The old gold and grimy vinyl booths and speckled Formica countertops were gone, replaced with polished granite, cold brass, and black leather. The memories and quaintness had been squeezed out of the place like breakfast juice from an orange. I suppose there's no going back, not even in restaurants.

A cute girl no more than seventeen years old greeted us.

"Two?" she asked, thumbing a stack of menus.

"Two," Sarah said. "Is Gus here?"

The hostess crooked her head in puzzlement. "Gus?"

"Gus," I answered. "He used to run the place."

"Gus died three years ago," said a customer paying his bill at the register. "Massive stroke."

"Shit," I muttered.

Sarah shrank into her memories.

"This way," said the hostess.

We ate mostly in silence and a little bit in mourning for Gus and for the love Sarah and I once shared.

"So, you want to tell me what this is all about?" I said, no longer able to stand the dark cloud that had followed us inside and settled over our table. "Is there something wrong? Is the practice you bought into not working out or something?"

"No, Dad, the practice is great and I swear I'm fine. This isn't about me."

"Then what?"

"Do you remember Candy Castleman from down the block?"

"What a silly question. Of course I remember Candy. She was like a big sister to you until she got married to that shithead who got her pregnant: Max Whatshisname."

"Max Bluntstone."

"You were in her wedding party. Your mother and I were there. I remember thinking how you looked like such a woman that day even in that hideous bridesmaid dress."

"All bridesmaids' dresses are hideous. It's tradition. The bride is supposed to be the star of the show."

"Well, you were the star of the show that day. Your mom cried at how you looked." Oops! I'd strayed into dangerous territory. "I'm sorry."

"For what?"

"For mentioning your mom."

"This isn't about that, Dad."

"Yes, it is, Sarah. For the last seven years everything between us has been about that."

"Not this."

"Okay, then what is it about?"

Sarah reached into her bag, unfolded a newspaper article, and slid it across the table to me. I didn't want to look. I didn't want to look because this was how it started, how it always started. Whenever someone wanted to hire me, this was how it began: a newspaper or magazine article shoved into my hand or pushed across a tabletop. Inevitably, the article would be about Marina Conseco, a little girl who'd wandered away from her family in Coney Island and wound up in the hands of a predator. It was Easter of 1972 and I was working in the Six-O precinct, the precinct that was responsible for Coney Island. Although we weren't as sophisticated back then and didn't have milk carton photos or AMBER Alerts, we knew that once a few days had passed, we were more likely to find Marina's remains than to find her. But find her I did, alive, at the bottom of one of those old wooden rooftop water tanks that still dot the New York City skyline. Marina had been abused and beaten and thrown into the tank to die. Finding her was the only noteworthy thing I ever did as a cop and it got a lot of press. Well, what passed for a lot of press in 1972. From the day I found her, Marina and I have been inextricably linked together and in ways I'm still not sure I fully understand. Another story for another time.

"Sarah, don't do this."

"Dad, please."

"For you." I turned the article so I could read it.

NEWSDAY, FRIDAY NOVEMBER 16, 2007
Child Prodigy Missing

BY ALICE WANG [Alice.Wang@Newsday.com]

Nerves are frayed and tensions are running high in the little village of Sea Cliff on Long Island's North Shore. One of this close-knit community's most celebrated citizens, artist and child prodigy Sashi Bluntstone, has been reported missing by her parents to the Nassau County Police Department. When contacted by Newsday, police spokesperson Det. Mary Holt refused comment other than to say that the report was being investigated.

Sashi Bluntstone, now 11 years of age, skyrocketed to prominence at age four when her Abstract Expressionist paintings—most often likened to those of Jackson Pollock and Wassily Kandinsky—began selling for tens of thousands of dollars. She had several shows at prominent New York galleries, but serious art critics questioned Miss Bluntstone's talent.

More damaging perhaps, were the serious allegations that she didn't, in fact, author the paintings, and that they were done by her father, Max Bluntstone, a one-time performance artist. These charges led to an exposé done by Nathan Flowers of CNN. In the exposé, Mr. Flowers stated that "… while I cannot say who does do the work, I can tell you Sashi does not."

That statement caused a firestorm of charges and countercharges and a lawsuit is pending. After Flowers' report, Sashi Bluntstone's work began disappearing from gallery walls and Sashi herself withdrew from the public eye. Her last show and public appearance was nearly one year ago. Very little is known about the circumstances surrounding Miss Bluntstone's alleged disappearance, but it is clear this tiny village, one square mile in area, has been shaken to its core. Pradeep Patel, a physician and neighbor of the Bluntstones, summed it up well: "It is all most unsettling."

Although the article wasn't about Marina Conseco, it might just as well have been. The net result would be the same.

"Okay, I've read it."

"That's all you've got to say?"

"What do you want me to say, Sarah?"

"Haven't you heard about this? It's been all over the news."

"I've been busy with the new store. You know how crazy your Uncle Aaron gets when we're going to open a new store. Besides, since your mom ... I just don't pay much attention to the news anymore."

"That's Candy's daughter, Dad."

"I didn't need a PI license to figure that out, but what can I do about it?"

"It's been three weeks."

"Does anyone have a sense of what really happened?" I asked.

"They don't know. Candy and Max thought she was in her studio painting and when they went to get her for dinner, she wasn't there. First, they thought she'd just gone for a walk on the beach. She did that sometimes, but she didn't come home. When they called the police, the police said that she had probably just run away."

"Sounds reasonable."

"Not anymore."

"No," I agreed, "not anymore."

"The cops and neighbors searched for her and found nothing. Now the police think she was ..."

"Kidnapped?"

"Abducted," she said. "There's been no ransom demand."

"Listen, Sarah, it's awful. If it had been you, your mom and I would have been sick with panic, but we're back to my original question: what do you want me to say?"

"I want you to say you'll go talk to Candy about it. She wants to hire you to help find Sashi."

"I can't do that."

"You mean you won't do it."

"Okay, yeah, I won't."

"Why?"

"You, of all people, shouldn't have to ask," I said.

"I'm asking anyway."

"Because my getting involved with people's lives this way is what got your mother killed and I'm not going down that road again."

"Do it for me."

"You're precisely why I won't do it. I'll take the guilt over Katy's murder to my grave, but that guilt's just background noise compared to the hurt I've felt for the last seven years over what happened between us. Even in the worst of times, when your mom miscarried, when our marriage collapsed, when my friend Larry Mac committed suicide, I always had you and your love to hang on to. We were a team, me and you, kiddo. You were always the best part of me and as long as you loved me, I knew there was hope in the world. Well, the world and me, we've kinda parted ways since you parted ways with me."

Sarah was sobbing quietly, tears streaming down her face. I wanted to reach over and wipe the tears off her cheeks, to make it all better like I had many, many times in her life. All it used to take was a reassuring kiss on her forehead, a hug, and a confident whisper from me about how everything was going to be okay, but we both knew better than that.

There were things that could happen, that *did* happen, that couldn't be made right. Humpty Dumpty wasn't the only one who couldn't be put back together again. And, frankly, I wasn't at all sure that if I did reach out to her, my arms—long as they were—could span the distance between us.

"Please, Dad, do it for Sashi. She's just a frightened little girl who's had a very strange life."

"Do what? What could I do? I'm one person and I haven't worked a case in seven years. All my police contacts have died or moved to Florida."

"Isn't that the same thing?" she said, a hint of a smile peeking through the veil of tears.

"You always did have my sense of humor. Still, I don't even know where my license is, for chrissakes."

"You're good at this stuff."

"I was always just lucky."

"Right now, I think Candy would take lucky. Please, Dad."

"Let me think about it, all right?"

Sarah stood up, came around to my side of the booth and threw her arms around me. She put her head on my shoulder and whispered, "Thank you, Daddy. Thank you."

It was the first time she had let down the barrier between us since we buried Katy, and I knew right then there would be no thinking about it. I was back in the game.

Transcript from Nathan Flowers' investigative report "Little Genius or Little Grifter"

NATHAN FLOWERS: Hi, Sashi, my name's Nathan. Would it be all right with you if we talked about your paintings for a few minutes? (Unresponsive, silence)

MAX BLUNTSTONE: Sashi, come on, Mr. Flowers is from TV and came all the way here just to tell everyone about your paintings. (Camera cuts to Flowers. Smile gone. Expression hostile)

SASHI BLUNTSTONE: Hi. (Disinterested)

NF: So, can we talk a little about your work?

SB: No. I don't feel like talking. I want to take Cara for a walk on the beach. (Staring at her father)

NF: Cara?

SB: She's my dog. She's a crazy beagle and she eats everything.

NF: (Smiling) Does she eat your paintings sometimes?

SB: You're silly, mister. (Giggles) Cara doesn't like my paintings.

NF: I do. Lots of people do.

SB: I know that. (Frowns) Where's Cara, Daddy?

MB: I'll get her in a minute, but let's just answer Mr. Flowers' questions right now.

SB: Okay. (Still frowning)

NF: Thank you, Sashi. Do you like your paintings?

SB: (Shrugs her shoulders) Sometimes.

NF: When do you like them?

SB: When I make swirlies. I love blue swirlies. (Rotates her hand as if painting circles)

NF: When you do the blue swirlies, does anyone help you with the other parts of the—

MB: (Standing up) That's it! Stop filming, now. (Camera shakes, shows fingers covering lens)

NF: Why does that question irritate you so? (Audio only)

SB: Where's Cara, Dad?

MB: (Deleted) you, Flowers! Come on, Sashi. Let's get Cara.

THREE

I was still pretty much a Luddite, but in 2007 even Luddites with AARP cards know their way around certain corners of the internet. So it was no problem for me to find out more about Sashi Bluntstone than I could ever hope or want to retain. My daughter wasn't kidding when she said that Sashi had lived a very strange life. Fame and money are difficult enough to deal with when you're twenty or thirty. I can't even imagine how it messes with you when you're four. It's the precarious nature of child stardom. Where is there to go when you start at the top? Most parents tell their kids they're wonderful, though kids are usually smart enough not to believe everything they hear, especially when it comes out of Mommy or Daddy's mouth. What must it be like, I wondered, to have everyone in your world telling you you're wonderful and talented and a prodigy? How long would it be before you noticed that all the good things everyone was saying about you also made you a freak? No kid wants to be a freak, not at that age. Being a freak is what the teenage years are all about. And how would a little girl react to being the family ATM? Questions, I had lots of questions.

I started with the most recent stuff and worked my way back to that first article about Sashi, the one Sarah slid across the table to me. Then I worked my way back to the first articles about Sashi bursting onto the scene, the first mentions coming in local Long Island papers in the late '90s when she was around three. I saw the damning exposé done by that Flowers guy on CNN and watched several segments of a video the Bluntstones had produced of Sashi doing a painting called "Orange Meets Blue Swirlies." Christ, watching paint dry was more exciting than watching the kid paint. It wasn't must-see TV. More like torture. I've got to admit that the end product, the painting itself, was quite impressive, but what the hell did I know about art?

What's the old story?

One friend says to another, "I don't know art, but I know what I like."

And the friend says, "Yeah, but so do cows."

I'd taken two terms of art history in college before I took the police entrance exam. I liked art history, but did better on the entrance exam. Katy had been a graphic designer and schlepped Sarah and me around to art museums all over the place, so I guess I knew a little bit more about art than the average cow. At least I knew who Pollock and Kandinsky were. I knew some of their works and I could see how Sashi's paintings got compared to theirs. Anyway, as impressive as the painting done in the video was, it didn't exactly erase any doubts from my mind about the authenticity of the work. I had about as much faith in the production of this "documented proof" as I did in test studies paid for by the industry they benefited. *Ford Pinto Safe! So says a new study funded by the Ford Motor Company.* Then again, I was a born cynic. I didn't believe in the Tooth Fairy either.

Frankly, I didn't give a rat's ass about whether Sashi did the paintings or not. That's not why Sarah had come to me. If she wasn't already dead, there was a frightened little girl out in the world somewhere and it didn't really matter if she was the next Mozart or a future trailer park princess. She needed to be found and I needed my own daughter back in my life. Even I could do the math: doing the one would get me the other. Unfortunately, the newspaper articles and reports I found on various websites were incredibly sketchy and unhelpful. They repeated the same vague story about how the Bluntstones thought their daughter had gone for a walk on the beach and didn't come back for dinner. There was literally nothing beyond that except a lot of speculation. I was pretty good at speculation myself and wasn't in need of any help on that front.

I hadn't looked in a mirror for hours, but could feel my eyes were bagged and bloodshot. They burned in need of sleep, but I couldn't sleep, not yet. I kept flicking through the web images of Sashi. At three, she was a lovely girl with fire and mischief asparkle in her green eyes. They were eyes much like her mother's. Sashi also shared Candy's reddish hair, yet she didn't look like Candy. Over the years, I'd forgotten what Max Bluntstone looked like, but Sashi's face refreshed my memory. Except for her eyes and hair, Sashi had Max's face. She had her father's granite jawline and high cheekbones, both kind of odd features on such a little girl. Still, she managed to pull them off. As she aged, Sashi's looks softened, but her eyes grew old, older even than mine. The mischief seemed to have been extinguished, but not the fire. The fire raged. Maybe I was just seeing things that weren't there. Tired old eyes do that. When I let sleep come to me, I was wondering about Sashi's old tired eyes.

FOUR

Sea Cliff is one of those tiny villages on Long Island that even most Long Islanders have never heard of. Across Hempstead Harbor from Port Washington and just south of Glen Cove on the cusp of the Gold Coast, it is a place contentedly trapped in a narrow swath of the past. And that swath was marked on the one side by the village's rather grand and fanciful Victorians, some, like the Bluntstones', overlooking the harbor and Long Island Sound beyond. The other edge of the swath was drawn in a line of classic '60s ranches and splanches. It was the kind of place where you could imagine freckle-faced boys in stiff, cuffed blue jeans and canvas sneakers, eagerly clamping baseball cards to their bikes so that they clickity-clacked along the spokes as the wheels turned. It was a place where people set their clocks to the pealing bells of the Russian churches, and those bells were ringing when I pulled up to the Bluntstone house.

The house was a Queen Anne Victorian, its design as busy as a beehive and its seven-colored paint job nearly as noisy. It must have taken a forest full of trees just to supply the stock for the spindles and gingerbread work on the wrap-around porch alone. No doubt a second forest had been sacrificed for the shakes, clapboards, fish scales, and row after row of diamond-shaped accent shingles. I more admired this kind of architecture than liked it. The house called too much attention to itself for my taste, screaming "Look at me! Look at me this instant!" It was nearly impossible not to. As I stood out of my car and beheld the behemoth before me, I couldn't help but think that Candy had come a long way from the basement apartment in Sheepshead Bay that she shared with her long-divorced mother and two Siamese cats.

I patted the .38 I kept holstered between the waistband of my pants and the small of my back. Nervous habit, I guess. It felt like a fifth limb. I didn't anticipate having to use the damned thing, but I'd carried it in that same spot for many decades, initially as my off-duty piece and then as a kind of conceit. When I got my PI license, I fooled myself that it was a necessary piece of equipment for a man swimming alone in dangerous waters. Figures that the first time I really needed it—a quarter century ago in an abandoned hotel in Miami Beach—I didn't have it on me. If I had, rather than the pea-shooter automatic I was forced to borrow from a friend, history might've been very different. Not world history, my history, my family's history. With my .38, I'd've killed the man who ambushed me on that long ago night. Instead, I just wounded him and he escaped. Seventeen years later, seven years ago, he helped murder my wife. These days my .38 was a shopkeeper's gun because, until Sarah convinced me to take this case, that's what I'd been for the last several years, a shopkeeper.

The steps of the porch creaked slightly under my weight. Funny, the creaking added a kind of character and an air of authenticity to the place. This was an old house and all the pretty paint in the world couldn't hide that. Somehow those creaking steps made this case real for me. This was Sashi's home and suddenly that mattered. It mattered a lot. Candy stepped out onto the porch before I made it to the door. She didn't say a word, but came to me and hugged me. I hugged her back. I hadn't seen her since her wedding day. How strange, I thought. Candy had been a semi-permanent fixture at our house back in Brooklyn.

Christ, I think we fed her more meals than she ever ate at home. Life is like that, though. People fall away when you're not looking. People fall away.

"Mr. Prager. Mr. Prager," she kept repeating. "It's going to be all right now, isn't it?"

"I hope so, Candy. I hope so. Let's see."

Candy wasn't crying. I suppose she'd cried herself dry during the last three weeks, but I could tell her nerves were raw. She was ashen faced, her eyes flitting from place to place. When I let her go and she hooked her arm in mine to show me into the house, Candy walked as if on a high ledge. It seemed that any loud noise or unexpected movement would split her in two. I'd been to that place. It was a very lonely place, empty but for guilt and self-recrimination.

Paying a visit to someone's home under these circumstances was an odd thing. It wasn't entirely business and it wasn't exactly social. I'd learned long ago that at the beginning of a case it was best to treat people like water and let them find their own level. Besides, people reveal all sorts of things if you just give them enough space and silence. Candy and her husband had no doubt gone over the story of their daughter's initial disappearance a hundred different times with the police and the press. Problem with that was, once you've repeated a story several times, it takes on a life of its own beyond the facts, a life that often has a fast-diminishing connection to reality. The story becomes the reality and your mind naturally embellishes and alters it. I was interested in what really happened, not in what three weeks of anxiety, worry, and guilt had done to change the truth.

Inside, Candy took my coat and hung it on a hook in the etched glass and oak paneled vestibule. It was toasty inside, but Candy, dressed in a white cable-knit sweater, kept her arms folded around herself as if she were on the verge of chills.

"Come on, Mr. Prager, I want to show you something," she said, leading me into the house, past the curving front staircase, and to a door that led to the basement.

"You're gonna have to start calling me Moe."

"That's not going to be easy for me, Mr. Pra—Moe. I know I never said anything back when I was a kid, but I used to wish you were *my* dad too. I was always really jealous of Sarah that she had you."

"That's a lovely thing to say, Candy. I'm honored."

"All I ever had was the assembly line of worthless boyfriends my mom slept her way through. Sarah was really lucky to have you."

"I'm not so sure she would agree with you anymore."

"God, I'm sorry, Mr. Pra—Moe. Moe, I'm sorry. I didn't mean to bring that up. I know that you and Sarah … I mean, since Mrs. Prager was …"

"It's okay, Candy. Let's not worry about my hurt feelings and let's concentrate on finding Sashi, okay?"

"I'm just not thinking real clearly these days."

"That's understandable. You're doing fine. Come on and show me what you wanted to show me."

One steep and narrow set of stairs later we were down in Sashi's studio. It was a brightly lit, almost sterile room. I don't know how else to describe it. The place had a kind of movie set vibe. The walls were painted in white semi gloss and the ceiling was covered in those ubiquitous white drop-in tiles. The flooring was a kind of spongy blue material and it was only the floor—stained here and there by colorful splotches from where Sashi had dripped, drizzled, or splattered paint over the edges of her canvases—that felt broken-in or touched by human hands. Blank canvases of varying sizes were lined up in neat rows at one corner of the studio. One wall was covered with low shelves and on some of these shelves were quart-sized Chinese soup containers half-filled with myriad colored paints. Another shelf was stacked with tube after tube of acrylic paint and another shelf was for jars full of brushes. No easels here. Candy explained that Sashi preferred working on or close to the floor so that she could look down at her work. Good. This confirmed what I'd seen in the video the night before.

"This room doesn't look familiar to me," I said, wanting to see how Candy would react.

"So you saw the video we did?"

"Some of it."

"And?"

"It bored the hell out of me, Candy. Sorry."

"That's okay. It can take Sashi weeks sometimes to finish a painting. It bores me too. She works best when we just leave her alone."

"Like the day she disappeared."

"Like that day, yeah," Candy said, and began hugging herself again.

"The room," I said, "what about the room?"

"Oh, sorry ... what?"

"I didn't recognize the room from the video."

"We were living in a rented house then on the other side of town."

"I'll want to see that house," I said.

Candy seemed not to hear me. "We bought this place three years ago and Max had this studio made just for Sashi."

I let the thing about the old house go for the moment and I noticed there were framed photographs on another wall, but no paintings. Most of the photographs were of Sashi and a sad-eyed beagle.

"That was Cara," Candy said, following my gaze.

"Was?"

"She died last year. She loved that dog. Cara meant everything to her."

"Do you think Sashi could have run away?"

"Because of Cara?"

"Because of anything: Cara's dying, the pressure of creating ... anything."

"She didn't run away!" She was emphatic and there was more than a little anger in her tone. That was fine. I wouldn't have liked the maybe-you're-bad-parents implications of the question either. "Someone took her."

I dropped it and pointed at a lone canvas on the floor. "And this ..."

The entire canvas was covered in a thick, textured coat of black acrylic paint. Looking more closely, I noticed a fine mist of crimson among the textured waves and folds of the black base. It was as if Sashi had put blood-colored paint in an atomizer and sprayed the air over the canvas, the tiny droplets falling where the air currents in the room took them. Christ, it was bleak.

"That's what Sashi was working on when Max and I came downstairs to get her for dinner. We thought she went for a walk on the beach across the way, but she didn't come home. When she didn't come home, we went to look for her on the beach. Then we called the police. They said she probably ran away, but they came and we looked for her. Our neighbors helped, but we couldn't find her. There were no signs of forced entry and there were no fingerprints that didn't belong."

I didn't like that. I didn't like that at all. Candy was repeating the story verbatim. Her recitation had an eerie *Manchurian Candidate* feel to it. *Raymond Shaw is the kindest, bravest, warmest, most wonderful human being I've ever known.* I didn't ascribe any specific negative judgment to it beyond my original misgivings about a frequently repeated story taking on its own reality. I didn't, for instance, think she was lying to me, though I suppose she might have been. Candy's canned response had an upside, though. It would serve as a reminder to me to count as fact only those things I knew to be so. There had been too many times in the past that I had trusted too quickly, believed too easily. Watching my ex-wife get murdered before my eyes cured the shit out of that problem for me. Katy had been killed as much by my easy trust as by the bullets that severed her arteries.

"Where's your husband?" I asked as we walked back up the stairs.

"I sent him out to do some errands."

That set off some alarm bells. "He doesn't know about my being here, does he?"

"No," Candy confessed as we reached the first floor. "Come on upstairs. I guess you'll want to see Sashi's room."

"I do." I followed Candy up the more grand and beautifully restored main staircase. "Why didn't you tell Max?"

"Because we've already hired three other investigators and it's costing us a fortune. Max worries about those kinds of things."

"And …"

"And because he remembers you hated him."

"I didn't know him. I hated him getting you pregnant and rushing you into marriage. I hated that."

That stopped her in her tracks. Candy turned on her heel to face me and planted herself on one of the carpeted steps.

"*He* didn't get me pregnant, Mr. Prager."

"Come on, Candy."

"I got me pregnant." You could have knocked me back down the steps with a whisper. "I needed to get out, to get away from my mother, away from … I knew Max would do the right thing. He loved me. He *really* loved me."

"I can't be hearing—"

But she wasn't finished. "He was happy, Mr. Prager. He didn't run because he knew he could have me forever."

"Did you love him?"

"Enough, I guess. Enough to let him get me out of there."

"I did the math last night, Candy," I said. "Sashi isn't that baby."

She hung her head. "There wasn't a baby. I went off my birth control pills and when I had my next heavy period, I told him I miscarried. Don't hate me, Mr. Prager." She was crying now, finally, for a baby that never was and a lie that would live forever.

"I couldn't hate you and believe me, I'm in no position to chastise people for their secrets. Does Sarah know?"

"Oh, God, no. Please don't tell her."

"Listen to me, Candy. I won't tell her, but this is where it ends. From this point on, I won't keep any secrets for you except if they help me find Sashi. So don't tell me anything else that doesn't have to do with Sashi. She's who I'm here about. Do we understand each other?"

"Yeah."

"I'm gonna have to talk to Max eventually, you know?"

"I know."

"And this isn't going to cost you anything, so you don't have to worry about the extra money."

"But—"

"—nothing. I have my reasons."

"You want Sarah back," she said.

"That's right. You're not the only one here who wants to bring a daughter home."

FIVE

Detective Jordan McKenna of the Nassau County PD agreed to meet me for lunch at the Caan's Kosher Deli on Glen Cove Road. Once nearly as ubiquitous as pizzerias, kosher delis were now headed the way of the passenger pigeon and the Sony Walkman. I loved the smell of Caan's, the perfume of sour pickles and pastrami, but I loved it as much for the memories of my childhood it evoked as for its aromatic siren's song. Yet the reason I picked Caan's had far less to do with my desire to reminisce than with convenience and pragmatism. Not only was it less than ten minutes away from Sea Cliff, it also happened to be in the same upscale shopping plaza as our first Long Island wine store: Red, White and You.

Although RWY, as we called it, was a big money maker for Aaron and me, it was my least favorite store. It was the kind of store where most of the customers took more interest in a wine's cachet than its bouquet. They always wanted what was hot, what was trendy, and that usually equated to overpriced, but what did they care? If you could afford to live in this area, it didn't really matter. When Beaujolais Nouveau became the rage in the early '80s, our RWY customers were willing to pay absurd amounts of money to make sure they got the first off-loaded cases. Then later, when Pinot Noir and Zinfandel and then Malbec got hot, it was much the same. And the prices our customers would pay for the best years of Opus 1 … my god, it was insane. To paraphrase my late friend and former Chief of Detectives of the NYPD Larry "Mac" McDonald, the parking lot here often resembled a Porsche dealership. The odd thing is that even though I could now afford to live out here and to drive a Porsche and to pray at the altar of Long Island's holiest of holies, The Church of Conspicuous Consumption, the thought of it turned my stomach. No matter how much money was in my bank account or how much stock was in my portfolio, in my heart I would always be just a poor schmuck from Brooklyn, a broken down ex-cop and the son of a failed businessman. I guess I wouldn't want it any other way.

The other reason I chose Caan's was that I knew my brother Aaron would be at RWY all day and I needed to tell him in person that I'd taken a case. That was part of our deal. As far back as 1978 when we opened our first store, City On The Vine on the Upper West Side of Manhattan, it was agreed that I could take on private cases at my leisure. I never wanted to be a shopkeeper and I certainly never intended on getting into the wine business. That was Aaron's dream. All I did was hitch my cart onto it and go for the ride. Frankly, I hated the wine trade. As I've often said, there's only so many times you can explain the difference between champagne and methode champenoise without going utterly mad. When I was on the cops, I was sure I was going to be a lifer, one of those guys you'd have to force off the job at gunpoint. Then in 1977, when I got back to the precinct house after doing crowd control at Son of Sam's arraignment, I slipped on a piece of carbon paper and tore my knee to shreds. So much for the impact of my aspirations on a cold and random universe.

"What's wrong?" Aaron said when I walked into the store. Some people say hello; Aaron says what's wrong. It is his nature in the same way as having stripes is in a zebra's nature. "Did the zoning board in Bridgehampton turn—"

"Nothing's wrong and no, everything is going smoothly with the zoning board. Sunrise and Vine will open on schedule on budget."

"Then what?"

"I'm taking a case."

"Of what, Sancerre Rouge?"

"No, shithead. I'm working a case … as an investigator."

I braced myself for the inevitable backlash. Although my right to take on cases was part of our partnership agreement, Aaron rarely gave in without a fight. Even when I opened Prager & Melendez Investigations with Carmella, splitting my time between the two businesses, Aaron never tired of browbeating me for trying to be the PI Peter Pan, of not wanting to grow up. He was right, of course, but his tirades couldn't stop me. I wasn't easily stopped.

"What's the case?" he asked.

"What?"

"What's the case? Is your hearing going now?"

"Sarah spoke to you, didn't she?" I said.

"No, she didn't."

"You're a lot of things, big brother. A good liar isn't one of them."

"Okay, yeah, we spoke. She told me about Candy's kid and everything. Besides, when could I ever refuse my niece anything?"

"I think maybe this time you should have."

"Why?"

"Because I got a bad feeling about this one."

"A week, ten days tops," he said in a feeble attempt to play the heavy.

"If the girl isn't dead already. I doubt she'll last that long."

Aaron had nothing to say to that.

● . ●

Detective McKenna was in his late thirties. Dressed in an unbuttoned black trench coat, Payless shoes, a blue Sears suit, and an ill-matching Father's Day tie, he was busy checking his watch when I walked up to him. I recognized his face from a photograph of him I'd seen online. I would have spotted him anyway. McKenna had cop written all over him. He looked tired, but as I got older I thought everyone looked tired. I think maybe I was tired.

"Detective McKenna?" I said as if I didn't already know the answer, and offered my right hand.

"Mr. Prager." He shook it, but with little enthusiasm. I recognized the vibe. This had all the ingredients of a bad first date, and there are few things as unpleasant and awkward as a bad first date. "You're late." He had the second generation map of Ireland on his puss and the first generation Long Island twang in his voice.

"Actually, I was early."

I pointed at the wine store and explained. He rolled his eyes. I couldn't blame him. McKenna probably thought this was all a waste of time, time better spent tracking down leads or knocking on doors than paying a courtesy call on some shopkeeper playing at Sherlock Holmes. No professional wants to deal with a hobbyist.

"Let's have lunch," I said, gesturing at Caan's entrance.

Inside, the lunch crowd had waned and we were pretty much alone in the back room. I ordered pastrami and he ordered corned beef. A real shocker, that.

"For chrissakes, McKenna, give it a rest, it isn't St. Paddy's Day. You could've ordered some kishka or kasha varnishkes or maybe beef tongue on club."

He stared at me blankly, a bit taken aback at my willingness to break his balls. Then he seemed to get it and the blank expression broke into a half smile.

"That's better," I said. "You know, I didn't always own wine shops.

I was on the job once too. I have a gun with real bullets and everything."

"I know who you are. I read up on you. You got a hell of a track record. I respect that. That's why I'm here. You think I'd waste my time dicking around with every schmo a missing kid's parents want me to see? You'd be amazed at some of the clowns these people come up with. I call 'em the psychics and psychos."

"Desperation makes people do desperate things."

"Stupid things."

"Yeah," I agreed, "stupid things."

"Like maybe involving an old family friend in something he shouldn't be involved in."

"Are you worried I'm too close to the situation to see what's in front of me?"

"There's that," he said. "There's also that your track record, as good as it is, is old. You ain't been in the game for a long time. Kinda tough to hit a home run as a pinch hitter when you haven't seen a good fast-ball for a while. And there was that thing with your ex-wife."

"I can't argue with you there, but look, I'm in the game whether you want me to be in or not. You can boo like an armchair manager or you can help me so I can help you. Anyway, I'm not a stupid man. Talking with you now, my guess is that if you had anywhere to go with finding Sashi, you wouldn't be here, respect for my record or no respect."

"No, I guess you're not stupid. We've hit a wall."

"Well, if the info in the newspapers is correct, you didn't have much to go on."

Hey, a little sympathy never hurt.

"We got some stuff to go on, but …"

"Some stuff, like what?"

He didn't answer right away and spent the next few minutes eating his sandwich, so I ate mine too.

"Look, Prager, I can't afford you getting in the way with an ongoing investigation. Do we understand each other?"

"Okay, Detective, you've given me my warning. I'll keep out of your way and I'll pass on anything I learn immediately. The only thing I'm interested in here is finding Sashi alive."

"Fair enough," he said and handed me his card. "Those are all my numbers. I'm available 24/7. I'm taking you at your word. If you find out anything at all, I want a call."

The waitress came by and I took the check. "What now?"

He stood and threw his trench coat back on. "You go on over to your store. I'll be over in a few minutes. I gotta get some stuff outta my car."

I'd had much worse first dates, I thought, as he disappeared into the main dining room.

Back in the office of RWY, I spread out the paperwork McKenna gave me on one of the desks. I knew this wasn't all of it, maybe not even most of it, but given that I was three weeks behind the curve, it was a lot to digest. It was no mystery to me why Detective McKenna had let me in the door without making me run the gauntlet. Good detectives have the knack of being able to balance their own necessarily strong egos against the public interest. McKenna's equation was a simple one: his goal was to find Sashi and he didn't give a shit what it took to do the job. He wasn't interested in who got the credit and the kudos. He'd worry about bows and curtain calls after the girl was found and the smoke had cleared. It was always the weaklings and the climbers that put themselves ahead of the case. I'd known my share of the good, the bad, and the indifferent over the years. For now, at least, McKenna rated high on the list. I felt sure the detective would get through the night without worrying over my opinion of him. He had more important things to lose sleep over. We both did.

SIX

I set back out to Sea Cliff before sunup. I'm not exactly sure why I got such an early start. Maybe it was the buzz from working a case again or maybe it was that I wanted to travel under the cover afforded me by the veil of pre-dawn darkness. In the dark I could fool myself that I was going somewhere, anywhere other than Long Island. Long Island's never been my favorite place. I suppose my antipathy started when I was around six or seven and some of my best friends disappeared from class and from the schoolyard; it was whispered that their parents had moved them to exotic places like Oyster Bay, Great Neck, Massapequa, and Ronkonkoma. Might just as well have been Siberia as far as I was concerned. In my kid's mind, Long Island meant exile and punishment, a forbidden zone where friends went never to return. I mean, who would ever want to leave Brooklyn besides Walter O'Malley? Sometimes I think that prick's only saving grace was that he didn't move the Dodgers to Long Island.

But my rocky relationship with Long Island transcended my childhood visions of it as the briar patch. For almost nothing good beyond profit has ever come of my setting foot over the Queens-Nassau County border. Patrick Maloney went to school at Hofstra University on Long Island and I spent too much time there uncovering things about him, about his family and his relationships with women, one in particular, that made my skin crawl. It was five years later, however, after Katy and I were married and Sarah was just a little girl, that the first tentative steps in the long slow dance that led to Katy's murder were taken.

It was at the wedding of a former wine store employee. She was a rich girl from Crocus Valley and her father, Thomas Geary, a star maker, bullied and extorted me into taking the case of one Steven Brightman. Brightman, a state senator, was the next fair-haired boy with Kennedy charm and working class credentials, but he had a big problem. One of his interns, a young woman named Moira Heaton, had disappeared from his community office on Thanksgiving Eve 1981. Although there was no evidence tying Brightman to Moira's disappearance and in spite of his fully cooperating with the authorities, the whiff of scandal and suspicion put a hold on his once-meteoric ascendency. After two years in political purgatory, he needed someone to prove him innocent, to plunge him in the waters and have him come up pure and saved. That someone was me.

It almost worked too. I cleared him, but he came back up out of the purifying waters a little too clean and a little too easily. I found what had been planted for me to find: a patsy in a nasty package by the name of Ivan Alfonseca or, as the press had dubbed him, Ivan the Terrible, a convicted serial rapist. Already going away for life, he was paid to confess to Moira's murder, clearing Brightman's path to the Senate, if not to the White House. But I was no patsy and I kept digging. Problem was, the brother of one of Ivan's real victims killed him in jail and with Ivan dead, I had a case as solid as air. So instead of going to the cops, I set Brightman up to spill his guts in front of two witnesses— his wife and Thomas Geary, the people in his life who could hurt him most. His wife left him and Geary withdrew his money and backing. Moira got whatever scraps of justice and shreds of revenge she was ever going to get. Then, seventeen years later, Brightman got his. He and his flunky, Ralph Barto, the man I wounded in Miami Beach, murdered Katy in front of me.

So here I was again, heading back to Long Island, the sun rising up before me, blinding me. I felt in my bones only darkness lay ahead. There were a lot of people I needed to speak to, people whose names appeared in the paperwork Detective McKenna had shared, and there were things I needed to see for myself. The day before, Candy had been with me, showing me Sashi's room, the rest of the house and the property, walking with me along the length of the little beach across the road from the big Victorian, but when you've got a guide it's hard to see things for yourself. You see things through their eyes. I didn't know that I'd find anything or notice anything new. Nothing had jumped out at me, nothing got under my skin. Still, I had to look.

I stopped off at a deli and got myself a large coffee and a cholesterol special: two eggs scrambled, bacon, and cheese on a buttered roll. A steady diet of these had killed more cops than all the skels and mutts who'd ever lived. I laughed to myself thinking about the NRA's PR team creating a new lobbying campaign. *Guns don't kill cops. Egg sandwiches do.* I took my time eating, scanning the paper, waiting for a phone call I hoped would come before I got all the way into Sea Cliff. Whether Candy realized it or not, when she hired me—if you want to call it that—she got more than she bargained for. I was playing catch-up and if I needed to take on some paid help or to call in some old markers, so be it. My job was to find Sashi and it wasn't anybody's business, not even her parents', how I did it. That's why I'd called Brian Doyle.

Brian Doyle wasn't ever going to be mistaken for a theoretical physicist or a McKenna type of detective. He had been one of those cops who managed to hang on to the job by his fingernails. Back in his day, the NYPD wasn't in as much of a rush to cut people loose as they currently seemed to be. A dumbass with a smart mouth who was too eager to use his fists, Brian depended too heavily on shortcuts to get the job done. He had no use for nuance or subtlety, but he was effective. Turned out that some of the things that worked against him on the job were pluses for him as a PI. Much to Carmella's dismay, I took a chance on the dumb prick and we made him into a hell of a good investigator. He'd turned himself into the boss at his own firm. I hadn't spoken to Doyle in years, but there were bonds that held regardless of the passage of time. Besides, he owed me. He owed me big time. The call came in just as I was pulling out of the deli parking lot.

"Hey, bossman, I just got your message."

"That's ex-bossman. You drove me into retirement."

"Yeah, sure. Whatever you say. So what can I do you for?"

"You got room in your busy schedule to do some real work?" I asked.

"This gratis?"

"Gratis! Jesus Christ, Doyle, you been reading the dictionary or what?"

"Funny thing about owning a company instead of just working at one, you learn the word gratis quick. Everybody comes outta the freakin' woodwork asking for all kinds of shit on the arm. Fuck that! You wanna play, you gotta pay."

"You don't have to lecture me on the subject. And no, this isn't gratis. It's pay for play."

"Then what's the play?" he asked. "Wait, just let me grab my pen here. Okay, shoot."

"Max Bluntstone. That's Bravo-Lima-Utah-November-Tango-Sierra-Tango-Oscar-November-Echo. And his wife, Candy Bluntstone nee Castleman—"

"Not for nothing, Moe, but is this about that missing girl, the artist?"

"Yeah, why?"

"You working cases again? I thought you was gonna—"

"Gonna what?"

"I thought after Katy and all … And then when you and Carm split up, I thought you were through with this shit."

"Look, Brian, you want the job or what? I don't need to get lectured to by you."

"For fuck's sake, Moe, take it easy. You don't gotta bite my nuts off."

"Sorry."

"No biggie," he said, not meaning it. "What you need?"

"Everything."

"That all?"

We both had a laugh at that.

"No, what I need is for you to get me all you can on their finances and their sheets. Put Devo on it."

"Hey, Moe, you're the client here, remember. No need to tell me who should do what."

"You're right, Brian. Forgive me?"

"No, but I'll pad your freakin' bill for that, ya hump."

"Fair enough, but I need it as soon as you can get it, okay?"

"Sure thing. So, you think the kid's still alive?" he asked, worry in his voice. "I got kids now too. I don't know what I'd do if anything happened to one of 'em."

"I'm with you there," I said. "I'm with you there."

"You know, Moe, while I got you on the phone …"

"What?"

"Maybe it's nothing, but a few weeks ago we had kinda a weird phone inquiry from a PI in Vermont someplace."

"What's so weird about that?"

"It was about you and the guys you used to run with at the Six-O."

"What did you tell him?"

"*Her.* She had a sexy voice, too. Anyways, I told her nothing that she didn't already know about us working together and your police career. Nothing too personal. Didn't give her any addresses or phone numbers or nothing. I never heard back from her and that was that. I put in a call to one of your stores to let you know. That's why I thought you were calling me, but I guess you never got the message."

"No."

"What do you make of it?" he asked.

"Who the fuck knows? I got bigger troubles now."

We chatted some more about sports and business and anything else other than what he really wanted to talk about. Brian Doyle was one of the few people who was close to me during the period stretching from the end of one marriage to the end of the other. Those were bad years: the steady drip, drip, drip of pain and disappointment interrupted only by thundering tragedy. When I got off the phone with him, I realized I resented Brian for knowing me then. It was irrational, but there it was. And the thing about it was, he knew it.

Although Detective McKenna had been generous in sharing information, I wasn't operating under any illusions. I knew he'd left a lot of stuff out of the mix. Of course the stuff that was missing was conspicuous by its absence. Was that intentional? Did he just want to get my attention? I don't know. More likely, it was unavoidable. For instance, there was almost nothing on Max and Candy: not a word on their finances, nothing about confirmation of their alibis for the day Sashi went missing, no transcripts of or notes from their interrogations. I mean, any novice knows that parents and/or siblings are the immediate and primary suspects in these situations unless there's obvious evidence pointing in another direction. Physical evidence. That was something else McKenna had conveniently omitted. From what he gave me, I had no idea if there was any significant physical evidence or, if there was, what it might indicate. The only assumption about evidence I could safely make was that there wasn't enough of it to arrest Max or Candy, or anyone else for that matter.

What I did have were several transcripts of interrogations or, to use the euphemism preferred by nine out of ten law enforcement officers, *interviews*, done over the course of the last three-plus weeks. Basically, these were the interviews that, for one reason or another, hadn't gone anywhere. Detective McKenna gave me the transcripts because he knew I would probably reinterview all of these people and that I might shake something loose he'd been unable to. PIs do have certain advantages over the police when it comes to evidence gathering. PIs can ask the types of questions that cops might get called on the carpet for asking and we could ask them in a manner that cops couldn't risk. Let's just say that when Brian Doyle worked for me, he got a lot of answers even the best NYPD detective wouldn't have been able to get. Being a cop has its limitations, shield and gun notwithstanding.

It was a little darker on the beach than the surrounding area because the cliff where the Bluntstones' house was perched blocked out the rising sun. The absence of full sunlight didn't actually make the beach any colder. That's the trick of December, though, isn't it? The sun looks just as bright and blinds you equally well, but it doesn't warm your face or fulfill the hope it hints at. There was no hope to be found here anyway. At first, when I'd heard the story of an eleven-year-old girl going for a walk on a beach alone, my radar went up. I wouldn't let Sarah go to Manhattan or Brighton Beach alone until she was fifteen and even then I was nervous as a cat, but this wasn't New York City in the '80s. There weren't two thousand homicides a year out here. Bernie Goetz wasn't playing shoot 'em up on the subway. No bands of roaming gangs were out *wilding* nor was Robert Chambers lurking at the local pub. This was still Howdy Doody-ville and the beach was literally just across the street from Sashi's house.

I was about to leave when I caught sight of someone coming up the beach in my direction. He was an old man dressed in washed-out jeans, a faded Mets hat, and sweater against the cold. White-skinned, thin as a sheet of paper, he walked along the water's edge seemingly searching for something, something I could not see. Trailing behind him was a dog, a bleached-out retriever even more ancient than the man himself. I hesitated to approach him or to call to him for fear of breaking his concentration, but then he looked up as if sensing my presence and gave me a snappy wave.

"Morning," he said, turning to me. He had bright blue eyes, a crooked mouth, and cigarette teeth more yellow than his dog's coat. "Chilly day."

"Cold, yeah."

"I don't know you."

"No, you don't." I pointed back at the Bluntstones' house. "I'm looking into the little girl's disappearance."

His yellow teeth disappeared behind taut lips. "Shame, that. I used to see her here all the time with that goofy beagle of hers. Sad little girl."

"Moe Prager," I said and thrust out my right hand.

He gave it a short, firm shake. "Ben Schare."

"So, you guys talked."

"Not really. We just used to sort of walk together along the beach with our dogs trailing behind us. We said hello and all and sometimes she might say that something was pretty or ugly, but not much else. Sometimes she'd be out here talking on her cell phone to her friends."

"But you said she was sad. How do you know that if you didn't talk?"

"Come on, son, you've lived a little. You know. It's a feeling. She just seemed lonely and sad. Nothing I can point to directly, but when that beagle of hers croaked …"

"What about that?"

"Then it wasn't guessing about her being sad. She was positively abandoned. I used to see her sometimes walking alone down here and when I would wave, she'd turn and go. I don't think she could bear seeing me and the old lady back there." He turned to look at the slow-moving dog behind him. "She don't have much time left, but she still loves to be near the water. It's a comfort to her, I think, even though she don't go in anymore."

"She remembers, you think?"

"She remembers. Come on, old girl," he said and turned to head in the other direction. "Nice meeting you, son."

"Take care, Ben."

I watched Ben and his dog retreat slowly down the beach in the opposite direction. As they went, I thought about how Ben had described Sashi, how everyone seemed to describe her: a sad little girl. Thinking about that erased the thirty years that had passed since I was looking for Patrick Maloney. The thing of it is is that when you're looking for someone, anyone, you get to know them only through other people's eyes. As it was with Patrick, so it would be with Sashi: other people's eyes. Yes, I'd watched the video of her painting, but I had seen too much in my life to mistake a snippet of someone's life as their life or to believe that a camera has no point of view. There's always someone standing behind a camera. When my vision blurred and Ben and his dog became indistinct shadows, I left the beach too.

East Village Vox February 21, 1994

Maxed Out
"Wagner's Ring Ding" A Must Miss

BY EVANGELINE MANHEIM

Touted as the next great performance artist by devotees of the emerging Williamsburg scene, the rather unfortunately named Max Bluntstone lived down to his name and proved to be yet another Brooklyn import not quite ready for the bright lights of Manhattan. In fact, he proved not quite ready for the dim lights of Camden.

At last night's premier of "Wagner's Ring Ding" at the Out House on the Bowery, Bluntstone even failed at failing. No mean feat, that. I suppose the audience might have booed had Bluntstone given them a chance to react to his boorish, amateurish, and scarcely original rants. Instead, the crowd of unfortunates were left to ponder in abject silence about what mortal sin they had committed that they might be punished in this way.

Using a pastiche of canned still images, movie, and video clips of battle sequences, sex, simulated and real executions projected onto the walls of the small theater and onto large screens suspended at the rear of the stage, Bluntstone sat strapped into an electric chair. The artist, and I use the term generously, would lead into his various diatribes by reciting well-known poems. Then, with a single phrase, he would veer off, launching into poli-psycho-pop culture-babble at the top of his rather grating voice. Oh, many were the moment I prayed the electric chair were not a prop.

Bluntstone's only glimmers of success came at those points during his performance when he stopped raging and took to playing a variety of uncanny homemade instruments. This critic suspects that he could go much further opening a one-man fix-it shop than with his dreadful one-man show. He would almost certainly make more money and more fans.

SEVEN

I didn't want Candy around if I could help it, so I sat down the block from the Bluntstones' place and waited. This was the part of the job I didn't miss, the waiting. Although there were many days I would have preferred sitting alone in a too-hot or too-cold car—and having to piss into the coffee cup from which I'd just been drinking—to tying frilly ribbons around the necks of gift bottles wrapped in flimsy silver foil. I especially hated it when customers would come rushing in, throw their black AmEx cards down on the counter, and demand, "Just get me something red and expensive. I'm in a hurry." Nothing like a five-hundred-dollar bottle of wine in a two-cent gift bag to impress your friends. *Good night! Fuck you very much!*

But whether Candy left the house or not, I was going to have a chat with Max, for whom I still had no use, in spite of his wife's confession about using a fake pregnancy as a pretense for marriage and a means of escape. Max was just one of those people I took an immediate dislike to. Other than knocking up my kid's best friend, role model, and babysitter, I mean, what was there to dislike about the guy, right? Okay, so the pregnancy was bullshit and maybe I felt more paternal about Candy than I realized, but that wasn't all of it. Max was Eddie Haskell: handsome enough, charming, polite, and poison. Sometimes the way you feel about people has nothing to do with rationality, maybe most of the time, but that was only part of it when it came to Max. The minute I met him, my cop radar switched on and the arrow on my bullshitometer jumped into the red numbers. I just knew that nothing the guy said or did was pure. He was always performing; there was always a shadow motive, a hidden, less obvious agenda. Always. He was an emotional pickpocket and you had to watch both his hands, not just the one he wanted you to look at.

Candy did me the favor of leaving. Though she was made-up and well-dressed as she left the house, she looked broken and old as she made her way down the porch steps. I could relate. Her steps were robotic and it seemed to take all her strength just to pull open the door to the blue Honda CR-V parked on the stone driveway. I ducked as she drove past, though I needn't have. She stared blankly, straight ahead. Stress had temporarily blinded her.

Max Bluntstone smirked when he answered the front doorbell, and didn't seem surprised to see me.

"The Great White Father has arrived," he said, showing me his back, but leaving the door open. "I knew you'd show up sooner or later. I'm in the kitchen."

I closed the front and vestibule doors behind me and followed him into the kitchen. And as much as I wanted to continue to dislike him, the look of him made me heartsick. For as tired and broken and stress-blind as his wife was, he was worse. He wasn't broken. He was defeated. He was pale, gaunt, vacant. The bags under his eyes were bloated and purple, the corners of his eyes were crusted, and the eyes themselves were shot with blood. He hadn't shaved in a while and his sweat stank of bourbon. His clothes were wrinkled as if he had slept in them for several days. I recognized the signs. Max Bluntstone was grieving. His hope was gone. In his head, in his gut, and maybe in his heart, he knew Sashi was dead. Candy wasn't there yet.

I'd seen this happen before. People were simply different from each other. Just as they aged and grayed and gained weight at different rates, they reached emotional crossroads at different times. For as beat-up and old as Candy looked, there was still some hope in her tone, in her facial expressions, in her words.

"Coffee?" Max asked.

"Sure. Just milk."

I watched him pour my cup, spilling some, adding milk and sugar. He wasn't there.

"Here."

"Thanks." I hated sugar in my coffee, but I wasn't going to piss and moan about it. "But if you're gonna add some bourbon to yours, save some for me."

He laughed, hollow as a carved pumpkin. "How'd you know?" he asked, pulling a half-empty bottle of Maker's Mark out of a drawer and topping off my cup.

"I used to be a private detective, remember? Besides, you stink like the floor at a Kentucky distillery."

Max shook his head in agreement. I decided to gut punch him and watch his reaction.

"You think she's dead, don't you?"

First, briefly, he swelled up defiantly, but he didn't have energy or anger enough to fight the good fight and he caved in on himself before he said a word. "It's been over three weeks. The cops try to be hopeful, but I can see it in their eyes. What do you think?"

She's probably dead. "I don't know enough yet to have an opinion. That's why I want to talk to you. I talked to Candy yesterday."

"I figured something had happened."

"How's that?"

"She was a little upbeat last night. It didn't last."

"Yeah, I saw her leaving the house. What was she made up for?"

"You mean who, not what," he said.

"Okay, who?"

"Randy Junction. He owns the gallery in town that shows Sashi's work."

"I know the name. I came across it in some stuff I was reading, but why go see him this early in the morning?"

"For a little comfort." I purposefully kept my mouth closed and Max obliged my silence. "That's right, Moe, comfort. The kind I don't seem able to supply to my wife anymore, not that she'd want it from me. She's been fucking him on and off for years. Until Sashi ... Until lately, it had been off. I learned not to mind it so much when she would throw me a bone too every now and then. I suppose if I had the heart for it, I'd be looking for the same kind of comfort. Candy doesn't want to face the reality of things yet, but it won't last."

I let it go because that was a time bomb I wasn't prepared to dig around just yet. "Tell me about the day Sashi disappeared."

Raymond Shaw is kindest, warmest, bravest ... It was the *Manchurian Candidate* all over again. Max's story was nearly word for word what Candy had told me. Not only that, but his movements, his hand gestures, his intonation pattern were all startlingly similar. I didn't like it any better this time than when Candy told it to me. There was definitely something they both knew that they weren't telling, but badgering Max or Candy wouldn't lead me to what it was. No, they would only circle the wagons and gird themselves. Now I was certain I knew what had motivated Detective McKenna to let me in on the case without having to jump through fiery hoops. He was hoping my presence might rock the boat a little and get Max or Candy to either confide in me or to tell an obvious lie. So far, the strategy was a failure, but it was early ... for me. Not for Sashi. According to her father, it was late for her. Too late. I hoped like hell he was wrong and I hoped it was just a feeling he had and not something he knew for sure.

"Tell me about Sashi's friends."

"She didn't have many friends."

Didn't. Past tense.

"In a lot of the stories I read about her, there were often mentions of her playing with friends at shows," I said.

"When she was little ... Yeah, she had lots of friends, but she really became very much a prisoner of her work. I'm to blame for that. I encouraged her, maybe pushed her too hard. Most ten- or eleven-year-olds aren't working on their version of the Mona Lisa. I was such a complete fuck-up at my art, I wanted her to succeed so bad. I guess I wanted it too much. Her friends just sort of fell away. And the criticism and exposés didn't help. We tried to shield her from that, but you can't protect kids, not when some guy on CNN calls you a fraud, not with the Net and social networks. She heard it. She felt the pressure."

"She had to have some friends."

"There's Ming," he said.

"Ming?"

"Ming Parson. Her and Sashi have been buddies forever, but in the last year or so ..."

"I'll want her address."

"Sure." Max scribbled something out on a pad, ripped the top sheet off, and handed it to me.

"Thanks. How are you guys doing financially?"

You throw enough punches, some are bound to land. This one landed square on his jaw and the Max I disliked suddenly reappeared out of the past. He shook his head in disgust and that familiar cocky curled lip returned, the grief and mourning vanishing as if I'd taken an eraser to his face.

"Fuck you! You and that cop, you're both the same. Get the fuck out of my house. Now!"

Now it was my turn to oblige him. I left. Staying wouldn't have done anything for either one of us and it almost certainly would have done my cause harm. I'd pissed the man off. I might have been pissed off, too, had someone implied my precious daughter's disappearance was somehow about money. Clearly, McKenna had done more than imply it.

● . ᵔ

The Parsons' house was rather more modest than the grand Victorian on the cliff. It was a cute, slightly worse-for-wear little bungalow on the same block as one of the two Russian Orthodox churches in town. The bungalow was on a small lot with a tiny front yard and a gravel drive-way barely big enough for a full-size car to park on, but it looked cozy and lived in, comfortable as a pair of old jeans. I knocked on the front door and a woman answered. She was forty, on the short and heavy side, not pretty, yet attractive in the way her house was.

"Hello there." Her voice was warm and welcoming. "How can I help you?"

"Hi. Mrs. Parson?"

"Dawn."

"Dawn, my name's Moe Prager. I'm an old friend of Candy Blunt-stone."

That took the warmth and sparkle right out of her. She stepped out of the house, closing the door behind her. "Look, mister, I've talked to the police about this several times and I don't want to discuss it any-more. My daughter talked to them too. She hasn't slept well since Sashi disappeared. At this age they know enough to understand what might have happened, but not enough to make sense of it."

"I don't think we ever get old enough to make sense of it."

"I'm sorry for Candy and I'm scared for Sashi, but I have my own child to protect."

I didn't say a word. Instead, I reached into my wallet, removed two items, and handed them to Dawn Parson. One of the items was an old card I kept to remind me of what I used to be. The other was a photo of Sarah that was taken when she was in fifth grade and was about the same age as Ming and Sashi. It was as manipulative as hell, but I'd worry about paying that bill later.

"She's a beautiful little girl. My god, such amazing red hair."

"Her name's Sarah and she's grown into a beautiful woman. The hair's a little darker now," I said. "Candy used to babysit for Sarah. She was like her big sister."

"Like I said, I feel for them, but I have to worry about me and mine."

"I know. How about you give me a few minutes and I'll get out of your way?"

"I don't know what I can tell you that I haven't already said to the cops."

"Different sets of ears hear different things," I said. "I was a cop once myself a long time ago and, like the card says, a private investigator. Sometimes it's not what you're saying that makes the difference, but who's hearing it. Please."

"Sure."

"Did Ming see Sashi that day, the day she went missing?"

Ming's mom frowned, looked at the welcome mat, and rubbed her hands. "They hadn't seen each other for a while. So, no, they didn't see each other that day."

"I heard they were really good friends."

"They were. We adopted Ming from China and she was older than most of the kids who come over. She'd been in the orphanage a long time. It was very bewildering for her at first and she was sort of the odd man out. I guess Sashi kind of felt like that too. They both didn't quite fit in and they became immediate allies, if you know what I mean."

"I do."

"Well, they just took to each other. Went to dance class together, summer day camp, you know, all the stuff little girls do together. If it wasn't for Sashi, it would have taken Ming much longer to learn English. They actually became pretty popular, the two of them, and had a whole group of friends."

"What happened?"

"Sashi stopped being a little girl and started having to be a grown-up somewhere along the way. She stopped doing the stuff the other girls did. Eventually, only Ming was left."

"But something happened."

"Well, no, not really. There wasn't a fight or anything like that. Sashi became, I don't know, more and more withdrawn. She stopped calling Ming and Ming got tired of trying to do all the heavy lifting. My girl's got lots of other friends and ..."

"I understand. When was the last time they saw each other?"

"A few weeks before Sashi disappeared. We were in town at the dentist and Sashi was there too."

"Did they talk?"

"Not much. It was awkward and kind of painful to watch."

"What do you think of Max and Candy as parents?"

That question caught her off guard. She hemmed and hawed.

"Listen, Dawn, my old relationship with Candy isn't as important as finding Sashi, so please don't hold back."

"I like Candy. She was always friendly and was really good with Sashi, but Max is ..."

"Is what?"

"He pushed her too hard."

"Dawn, I don't like Max much myself, so don't worry about it."

"Kids grow up too fast anyway these days," she said. "And Max, he just didn't seem to understand that Sashi was just a little girl with a grown-up talent."

"Thank you."

I turned to walk away. I did it slowly, hoping Dawn Parson might call after me with some forgotten tidbit of information or an offer to talk with her daughter. Instead, I heard her front door open and close.

I drove slowly down Sea Cliff's main street and saw that the Junction Gallery was closed. As it was just nine o'clock, the place probably would have been closed even if Candy weren't looking for comfort and distraction in the arms of the eponymous Mr. Junction. I wasn't going to judge her. That was somebody else's job. Besides, judgmental people gave me a rash. You ever notice how judgmental bastards are always so fucking sure of themselves? Me, I stopped being sure of anything a long time ago.

I pulled to the curb and got out of the car. I cupped my hands around my eyes and peered through the plate glass windows. Sashi's work covered the walls. In fact there was so much of her work on the walls, it looked like the Sashi Bluntstone Outlet Store. Displayed in one of the windows was an enlarged reproduction of a collection of very self-serving reviews. It was all breathless stuff:

Sashi Bluntstone is a genius!

Sashi Bluntstone is the Second Coming!

Sashi Bluntstone cures cancer!

And it now seemed not only ridiculous, but morbid as well. I'd come back some other time.

EIGHT

If it sounds like I know what I'm doing, it's bullshit. I've never really known what I was doing, certainly not in the wine business and not as a PI. What I said to Sarah at the restaurant was true: I'm more lucky than good. I'm a stumbler. Always have been. I fall into things, sometimes the right things. It isn't in my nature to follow a set of rules even when I know the rules to follow. I'm the musician who plays it by ear, by feel, and once I get a sense of things, I stick with it. The only two places I ever felt comfortable or like I really understood how to do my job was on the basketball court and on my beat in the Six-O. My ankle having been shattered by a bullet when Katy was murdered, it had been seven years since I set foot on a basketball court. I'd been off the job since 1977.

When we went into business together, Carmella tried to show me how real investigators worked a case. She knew. She had learned the hard way, from the bottom up. And her bottom was several sub-basements below the detectives she learned from. Starting out, she had more strikes against her than a tall lightning rod in a flat field. She was young, female, Puerto Rican, and beautiful. Advantages in many lines of work, but not in the NYPD in the '80s. As she was wont to say, "It's not about whether you stand or squat to pee. My gold shield is about being a good detective, not about my pussy or being Puerto Rican." And she *was* a good detective, but I never learned to do it her way. I was always going to pee standing up and I was always going to be a stumbler. The one aspect of the process I was good at was people. I understood people. That's why I didn't ask the questions everyone else asked. And what good would it have done me to ask Candy or Max or Dawn Parson if they knew anybody who might want to harm Sashi? If they knew, the cops would already be on it. If they didn't know, my asking wasn't going to make them give a magical answer.

Frustrated by the lack of information from Max and Candy, I decided it was time to go off the map, to stray from the list of people McKenna intended for me to reinterview. That's why, when I walked away from the Junction Gallery, I headed east, even more deeply into the enclaves of the rich and richer. The Cold Spring Harbor/Lloyd's Neck area of Long Island's North Shore was physically beautiful and a bit more isolated than the Sea Cliff/Glen Cove area I'd just come from. It was all little hidden inlets on the Sound, twisty private roads, hills, and old majestic trees. This was Movers-and-Shakersville, where, as my mom might say, all the big *machas* lived. Around these parts, the maids had their own cleaning ladies. Along the way I passed the Cold Spring Harbor Laboratory—run by that brilliant lunatic and co-discoverer of the DNA double-helix, James Watson—a fish hatchery, a few exclusive marinas, and a horse farm or two.

The Cold Spring Harbor Museum of Modern Art was located on a bluff overlooking Long Island Sound on one side and a small, tree-lined cove on another. It was a very dramatic structure that looked like a series of glass and steel blocks piled atop one another at odd angles. Too bad it was nearly impossible to find and harder to get into than Skull and Bones. You've got to love the rich. The museum was for the public, but their notion of the public and my notion of the public didn't seem to overlap much. The parking lot was nearly empty but for a classic gull wing Mercedes Benz and a five-year-old Honda Civic parked in the spot furthest away from the main entrance. I parked close to the Mercedes, but not close enough to clip its wings.

When I tried to push in the front door, I nearly unhinged my wrist. Neither my cursing in pain nor the noise at the door seemed to rouse anyone's attention, so I rapped hard on the glass with my good hand. That stirred the beast. A security guard who looked like an escapee from the Arnold Schwarzenegger School of Acting loomed before me. He was dressed in a neat blue blazer, gray slacks, and shiny black shoes. His impassive white face looked familiar to me, but I couldn't quite place it. He pointed a huge index finger at the intercom to the left of the door.

"Are you a town resident, sir?" he asked, his deep voice only adding to his already serious intimidation factor.

I pressed the talk button. "No."

"Do you have an appointment, sir?"

"An appointment? No. This is a public museum, right?"

"Yes, sir, but to town residents only at this hour. Non-residents do need an appointment before noon." He had a bit of southern cooking in his voice, southern Brooklyn.

"I'm here to see Wallace Rusk, not the art."

"Do you have an appointment, sir?"

"You're kidding me, right? Don't you have any other lines in this play?"

"Excuse me, sir, but do you have an appointment?"

I thought I saw the corner of his lip curl up a little.

"Funny man, huh?" I reached into my back pocket and did something that was either going to get me a face to face with Rusk or arrested … maybe both. I clanked my old NYPD badge hard against the door glass. "That's my appointment, motherfucker. Now open the fucking door!"

His face remained impassive, but he unlocked the door and held it open for me ever so politely.

"Sorry," he said, "just doing my job, you know?"

I didn't push it. First, because he was right. Second, because I didn't want him to take a closer look at my tin.

"Forget it."

"I'll get Mr. Rusk for you. What's your name, Officer?"

"Prager, but I'd rather go surprise him."

"He's not gonna like that."

"Too fucking bad."

"Hey, I need this job and trust me, that man'll can my ass if you go in unannounced."

Then it hit me. "You're Jimmy Palumbo, offensive tackle out of Rutgers," I said, snapping my fingers. "The Jets drafted you third round ten years ago, right?"

But instead of smiling, the big man's expression turned sour. "Eleven years ago. Might as well have been a million."

"You went to New Utrecht High, right?"

"Lafayette."

"I went to Lincoln when Lafayette was our big rival ... a long time before you went to school. Really rare for a local guy to make it in the NFL."

"Yeah, I guess."

"You fucked up your knees, didn't you?"

That didn't improve his mood any. "Both of 'em, yeah. You got a good memory for bad things, Officer."

I rolled up my pants and showed him the maze of scars that covered my knee. I would have also showed him the scars on my ankle, but that was a road better left untraveled. Besides, these days, I only limped on the inside.

"Holy shit!"

"No arthroscopic surgery when I went down," I said. "They used to cut you open like a fish and see what they could see. I had three surgeries, four weeks of PT with each one, and a pain script."

"Sorry to hear that."

"Me too. So why you working this gig?"

"Divorce," he said as if it explained everything.

Maybe it did. My two trips down that path had been amicable, but that was more rare than you might think. Some of the work we did at Prager & Melendez had been for divorce lawyers. We didn't handle the slimy end of things. We didn't videotape or tap phones or entrap spouses out for the night with the boys or girls. No, we were usually hired after the papers were served, when motel bills, fancy gift receipts, and hidden assets needed to be tracked down. Divorce tended to get ugly and very expensive, emotionally and financially, for everyone involved.

"Kids?"

"Yeah," he said. "Twin girls. The bitch moved 'em out of state. Like cutting the heart right outta me, taking them from me that way. Things are a little better now."

I was a big football fan and this was all very fascinating, but I didn't drag my ass up here to get Jimmy Palumbo's autograph or to discuss his past domestic woes. He did seem like a nice enough guy, though, and I thought he'd be fun to have a beer with.

"You ever work any private security?" I asked.

"Used to, not so much no more. Why you wanna know?"

"While I'm in with Rusk, write your contact info down on a piece of paper for me. I have some connections and maybe I can get you some outside work."

"That would be great. Thanks."

"Okay, you can call Rusk now. Which way to his office?"

"Walk through the galleries and take the elevator down to the lower level, turn left and you'll see his office door."

As I walked across the stark, hardwood floor, Palumbo spoke my name in hushed tones. Made me smile to hear it. It had been thirty years since someone called me Officer Prager. I'd worry about how to explain away my lie when I got to Rusk's office. For the moment, I was busy admiring the views through the floor-to-ceiling glass walls that let ambient natural light flood into the gallery space. The views were nearly as impressive as the Lichtenstein and the Warhol, the Wesselmann and the Rauschenberg I passed on my way to the elevator.

Rusk met me at the elevator door and looked pretty much how I expected him to look. He was small, in his early sixties with delicate features and a ring of neatly groomed gray hair around a bald pate. He wore a blue camel hair blazer—gold buttons et al—with a gold and red family crest embroidered on the pocket. There was a red silk hanky in the pocket that matched his French-cuffed shirt. His tie was a perfectly knotted and textured piece of gold silk. His teeth were white and straight, of course, and the crimson-framed glasses he wore over his blue eyes cost more than the Honda in the parking lot. I couldn't tell you the cost of the antique Patek Philipe watch he stared at impatiently as he waited to see who would get things going. I guess he got tired of showing me his watch.

"What can I do for you, Officer Prager?"

"This visit isn't official," I said, trying to sidestep the lie I'd told upstairs.

He furrowed his brow. "Then I'm afraid I don't—"

"Sashi Bluntstone."

"Oh, dear. Has there been some awful news?"

"What makes you say that?"

"Nothing in particular. It is simply that the child has been missing for some time now and I could think of no other reason for a police official to come to me."

"That's reasonable," I said. "Again, Mr. Rusk, my visit isn't official. I've been hired by the Bluntstone family to investigate their daughter's disappearance, to make sure the police are doing all they can."

"Investigate? Why on earth would you come see me? You couldn't possibly think I had anything to do with her disappearance."

"Well, you are one of Sashi's most vociferous critics."

"Vociferous ... my, my, no dumb cops on this beat, eh?"

"I also know how to tie my own shoes and everything."

"Please, Officer Prager, I've been rude. Come into my office and let us discuss this."

Rusk's office was startling. The back wall was a huge pane of glass not unlike those on the gallery levels upstairs and it looked out onto the Sound and the southern shore of western Connecticut. The furnishings themselves were all very austere, almost industrial, and there was not a stitch of art on the walls or anywhere else in the office. Rusk gestured at a metal chair in front of his desk and when I sat in it, he retreated around the desk and sat in a metal mesh desk chair.

"As you were saying ..."

"No, I don't think you had anything to do with Sashi's disappearance. If the cops did, they would have been here already."

"Forgive me, Officer Prager, but I now find myself even more confused by your presence here."

"First, Mr. Rusk, please call me Moe or Mr. Prager, if that is more comfortable for you. Second thing is that although the case is over three weeks old, I'm new to it and playing catch-up. The police do things their way and I do things my way. Why I'm here is to try and get some understanding of why Sashi's work and Sashi herself seem to make people like yourself, serious people involved in the art world, so incensed and crazed."

"That, Mr. Prager, is a very easy question to answer. Art, in this case, painting, is more, much more than what appears on the canvas. Art is also what goes on in the artist's mind before and during and after putting brush to canvas. Art is a continuum that stretches from conception to reaction and beyond."

"Okay, let's say I buy that. On the other hand, I've seen a lot of Sashi's work," I said, "and I know this is going to upset you, but it's pretty good. I'm no art critic and certainly not the curator of a museum, but I know a little bit about art. Her work is undeniably reminiscent of Kandinsky and Pollock."

Rusk clapped his hands together and laughed. "Ah, Mr. Prager, for an artist to produce work that is reminiscent of her forebears, mustn't she be aware of those forebears? Jackson Pollock didn't pull his art out of …"

"His ass?"

"I was thinking thin air, but your phrasing makes the point more emphatically. Pollock understood European Surrealism and had studied Jung in order to gain access to his unconscious processes and to free himself of conventionally constructed art."

"Okay, then what you're saying is that he knew what he was doing."

"Exactly. The very concept of an unschooled prodigy doing abstract expressionism, a style that merged two sophisticated art styles—surrealism and cubism—with automatic process is absurd, simply impossible. Look, Mr. Prager, had Sashi Bluntstone made exquisite realistic paintings beyond her years, maybe she would be taken seriously, but

anyone can smear paint on a canvas and say they are aping Pollock …
including an ape!"

"Don't you think her paintings have any merit at all?"

"Yes, I suppose, but not to a serious artist and not in the serious art
world. I don't so much object to the paintings as much as I do to where
fools and uneducated critics place them. And in all honesty, Mr. Prager,
I am not close to being Sashi Bluntstone's most vociferous or mean-
spirited critic. Here …" Rusk tapped something out on the keyboard
of his wafer-thin laptop and spun it around so as to face me.

I could scarcely believe what appeared on the screen. It was a ren-
dering of three crosses on a hill under an ominous black sky. There
were bloodied and brutalized bodies crucified on two of the crosses. To
the far left was a naked man, hands amputated, his torso speared in so
many places he looked like a pin cushion. The plaque behind his head
read *Kinkade*. On the far right cross was a young girl's body, her vagina
afire, an arrow through her head, and her torso covered in blood splatter à la Pollock. The letters on the plaque behind her head spelled out
Bluntstone. On the middle cross was the body of a frail young man
wearing a thorny crown and the mutilation to his body was meant to
replicate the damage done to Christ. His expression was beatific. His
plaque read *Martyr*. I'd seen enough and turned the computer back
around to Rusk.

"You see my point?" Rusk asked.

"Who is this guy?"

"Nathan Martyr. About ten years ago he was a hot new commodity, but his work quickly fell out of favor and he devolved into a very
bitter man. He has a particular distaste for Thomas Kinkade and Sashi
Bluntstone. But he's not alone. There are many such sites."

"Do you happen to know where I can find Mr. Martyr?"

"I don't have an address for him, but he used to show at the Brill Gallery on West Twenty-third Street in Manhattan. They should have an address for him."

I stood up. "Thank you for your time, Mr. Rusk. It's been enlightening."

"My pleasure, really," he said, shaking my hand. "I do hope you find the child. Maybe you can get her away from those exploitive monsters she was born to so she can get a real artist's education."

"I'll settle for finding her alive."

"Yes, of course, I'm sorry. That was insensitive of me."

"That's okay."

He walked me to the elevator and wished me farewell. Upstairs a few visitors—older women—were roaming about the museum. They were perfectly put together, tanned from weekends in the sun, every stitch of their clothing and every accessory just so. I guessed they were about the same age as my mom when she passed away. Yet my mom had looked so much older. My late friend Israel Roth once said that money was a retreat, not a fortress, and that the rich suffered as much as any of us. Some days that was easier to swallow than others. Today it was going down hard.

Jimmy Palumbo stopped me on the way out and handed me his contact information. He thanked me, but didn't seem encouraged.

"Don't worry about it," I said. "I'll call."

"Yeah, no offense, but I heard that before. Last coach I had told me he cut me so another team could pick me up, that a few teams had shown interest in me. He told me not to worry. That I'd get a call from somebody. Yeah, well, I'm still waiting for the call."

"No sweat. I understand."

"And I'm sorry for going on about my kids," he said. "It's just that I miss 'em."

"My daughter didn't talk to me for a year and it still hasn't stopped hurting, so no need to apologize."

I waved the paper at him and waved goodbye. Nothing I had to say was going to make him feel any better. I'd been cut by the NYPD. At least they'd had the good sense not to promise me anything but my pension as they shoved me out the door.

NINE

The Brill Gallery was less impressive than a brown paper bag and the art inside less interesting. Basically, it was a rectangle of four white walls, a white ceiling with tiny halogen spotlights, a blond hardwood floor, and a few white pedestals for sculpture. There was a small white table in one corner for brochures and a white desk in the opposite corner. A curveless woman of thirty with heavy-framed black glasses, cropped black hair, and lip, nose, and eyebrow piercings sat at the desk. The best and most colorful art in the place were the tattoos that covered her exposed flesh. Unfortunately, she was as interested in me as I was in the art. She paid far more mind to whatever was flashing on the laptop screen.

"Excuse me."

"Yes," she said, not gazing up.

"Are you the owner of the gallery?"

Still not looking up. "Do I look like the owner?"

"I don't know. What does the owner look like?"

She raised her eyes, unamused. "Not like me."

"Can I speak to the owner?"

"If you have her cell phone number and know what time it is in Bali, I imagine you could."

"So you're it?"

"Tag, what fun," she said, returning her gaze to the screen.

I snapped the computer closed without removing any of her fingertips.

"Fuck! What did you do that for?"

"To get your attention. That's what this is for too." I showed her my badge. I figured I should put it to good use, having aired it out once already today.

"Are you like the art police?"

"If I was, this place would be a crime scene. This stuff is crap."

She smiled. It was actually a pretty and welcoming smile. "I know. It's dreadful, isn't it?"

"Let's start over."

"I'd like that," she said. "My name's Lenya."

"Moe."

"What can I do for you, Moe?"

"I need an address for Nathan Martyr."

"Why, are you actually going to arrest him for this stuff?"

"This is *his* work?"

"In all its vapid glory."

"As my mom used to say, *feh!*"

"Double *feh*. It's putrid."

"Then why does the owner bother?" I asked.

Lenya leaned forward conspiratorially. "The truth?"

"Nothing but."

"I think she's hoping he drops dead. Then his new crap becomes valuable crap and his old crap becomes extremely valuable crap."

"Why?"

"Because if he's dead, he won't be able to produce any more crap. They'll do retrospectives and the critics will reevaluate him and he'll become in death what he wasn't in life. Nothing like a little death to raise your profile in the art world."

"But what makes the gallery owner so hopeful about Martyr kicking?"

"His habit."

"Heroin?"

"Yep."

"Bad?"

"He's the man on the monkey's back, not the other way around." She frowned. "Damn. I don't suppose I should have told that to a cop."

"Don't sweat it. I'm not interested. Do you have an address for him?"

She hesitated. I didn't jump on her. If she needed a push, I knew how I'd push, but bullying wasn't the way to go.

"Swear to me it's not about the drugs," she said, flicking a Rolodex card with her fingers.

"Cross my heart and hope to die."

"Here."

I wrote the salient information down and thanked her. She smiled that smile at me again, only this time her intentions were a little more obvious.

"You've got a beautiful smile, but I'm old enough to be your father."

"I love my father."

"He's a lucky man. Bye, Lenya."

●　　•　　 ●

Given what Rusk and Lenya told me, I half expected Nathan Martyr to be living down a rat hole and sleeping on a bed of used needles. Some rat hole! The address Lenya gave me turned out to be a converted factory building in DUMBO—Down Under the Manhattan Bridge Overpass—not more than a ten-minute walk from Bordeaux In Brooklyn. The bricks had been repointed and the terra cotta work around the huge arched windows had been beautifully restored.

Anyone living above the fifth floor would have spectacular views in any direction.

The doorman was an ex-cop. I didn't recognize him by face, but by attitude. He gave me the you're-not-getting-past-me stare when I came through the wrought iron and glass entrance. His "Can I help you, chief?" sounded more like a threat than a question. I guess if I lived in this joint and shelled out what the residents paid for the pleasure, I'd want this guy as my gatekeeper too. But from where I stood, he was just an annoyance, an obstacle to get around that wasn't going to make it easy for me.

"Relax," I said. "I used to be on the job too."

There were two ways he could go with that. Either he would give up the hard-ass stare and ask me about where I'd served and how long ago and who did I know that he knew, or he'd harden and get defensive. I hoped for the former, but was betting on the latter. I wasn't wrong.

"Yeah, you and thousands of other guys," he said. "If I got a stiffy every time an ex-cop stepped through that door, I wouldn't need Viagra. Whatchu want?"

I learned a long time ago, before I ever got on the cops, that backing down to a guy like this was a big mistake. I met a hundred guys like this prick when I was on the job. Some people become cops because it's in their blood. Some, like me, stumble into it. Then there are assholes that want the gun and badge, guys who want the power of the state to sanctify their bullying. Bullies are bullies, in uniform or out. Truth be told, I hated the bullies much more than the people I arrested.

"Take it down a notch on the heavy routine," I said, staring back at him with unfriendly eyes. "I'm here to see Nathan Martyr, 6E."

"Is he expecting you?"

"Not unless he reads minds."

"Name?"

"Moe Prager."

"What should I tell him this is about?" the doorman asked, his tone a tad more mellow.

"Sashi Bluntstone."

"The missing kid?"

"Yeah, her. I'm working for the parents."

"I already talked to the Nassau cops," he said. "He was here the day the kid disappeared. They got my statement."

Okay, that took some air out of my balloon, but not all of it. I was just as interested in the crazies who visited Martyr's website and blog as I was in Martyr himself.

"He's got an alibi, good. Then, when I go up, Martyr and I can talk of Michelangelo," I said. "You gonna ring him or what?"

The doorman pulled the phone off its wall cradle and punched in 6E.

"Yes, Mr. Martyr, there's an ex-cop here to see you ... Moe Prager ... about the missing Bluntstone kid ... yes, sir, I told him ... very good, Mr. Martyr." He replaced the phone. "He doesn't want to see you."

"Those his words?"

"No, Prager. His words were 'Fuck him! Tell him to get the fuck out of here.'"

"Nice guy."

"A real charmer," the doorman confessed. "Personally, I think he's the biggest dick I ever met, but he's the boss in this, so it's time for you to hit the road."

"So you vouched for him for the day Sashi Bluntstone went missing?"

"I did. He went out for breakfast. Came back in here about ten thirty and didn't leave for the rest of the day."

"No offense, but how can you be so sure he didn't slip past you or go out through another entrance?"

He waved me over to his desk and gestured for me to take a gander. There, hidden behind the wall of the desk, were eight video screens, one of which was currently featuring a shot of my thinning hair.

"Even if I'm away from my desk to drain the dragon, everything is kept on tape for review and it's digital. The minute I get back, I review all the camera footage from the time I was away. Martyr was in his loft from the time he came back from breakfast to the time I got off shift."

"Thanks, I appreciate the help."

I turned and left. Oh, I was going to come back, but there was no need to piss anyone off or to get any more unwanted attention.

I sat outside the place in my car, hoping Martyr might leave the building to score some drugs. While I didn't know what he looked like, I did know what drug-sick junkies looked like. I decided to take my chances with that. After about an hour and a half, I'd had enough. Truth be told, I was getting too old and impatient for this shit, though not nearly as impatient as my bladder. Sitting down the block from the Bluntstones for ten minutes was one thing. This was something else. I put the car in drive and set out for the nearest bar. Unlike almost every other kind of business establishment in the five boroughs of New York City, bars tended not to bust your balls for wanting to use their restrooms. More often than not, they figured you'd wind up buying a drink anyway.

Down the block from Grimaldi's Pizza and in the shadow of the Brooklyn Bridge, I found a bar. I was so happy, I nearly got religion. It didn't last. Just as I parked the car and reached to open my door, there was a bang and my car lurched forward.

Fuck!

I got out of my car ready to take a swing at the idiot who'd just rear-ended me. Much easier to take a swing when you have a gun on you … just in case. I don't know, I guess maybe I was a little more frustrated at not making immediate headway in finding Sashi. It had begun to sink in while I was parked outside Martyr's building that I was further behind than I imagined, that three weeks in a missing child case was an eternity and that if I ever did catch up, it would be far too late. My fists were clenched when I turned around and saw her standing there.

"Oh, my god. I'm so sorry. I don't think I did any damage to your car," she said, her voice raspy and on the deep side. She pronounced *car* and *god* like a New Englander.

She wasn't beautiful, but not by much. Forty, give or take, she possessed that deadly combination of dark blue eyes and black hair. Forty! Christ, I remember when I thought forty was old. I remember when I thought it was ancient. Now *I* felt ancient and forty seemed as far past me as fifteen. Her hair was bob cut and had some gray filtering through it. She had a plush mouth, nice cheekbones, and was impeccably made-up, but not so you couldn't see the lines at the corners of her lips and eyes. I liked that. She had lived a little and wasn't trying to hide it. She wore a black leather coat, black stockings, and heels. The heels were high without being ridiculous. I found myself staring at her ringless left hand. I don't know if she caught me staring.

"I'm so sorry. It doesn't look like there's any damage," she repeated. "Come look."

I did and she was right. There was no damage. "It's fine. Don't worry about it. If the car's scratched, I'll just throw it out and buy a new one."

"You're funny."

"Sometimes."

"I'm new to the city and it's been kind of hard getting adjusted. Now this … not my day, not my month."

"Really, don't worry about it …"

"Mary, Mary Lambert."

"Moe Prager." We shook hands. "No offense, Mary, but if I don't get to a restroom soon …"

"Go on. I'll wait for you in case you decide you want to exchange information."

"Fine."

When I came out of the bar, she was still there.

"It's nice that you waited, but I think we're okay."

"Well, Moe, here's my business card anyway."

I put it in my wallet, but didn't offer her one of mine.

"So, Mary Lambert, can I ask you what had you so preoccupied that you missed the fact that my car was sitting right there in front of you?"

She blushed. "I got lost and I was pulling to the curb to try and get my bearings. I had an appointment on Court Street and when I left I got all turned around." She looked at her watch. "And I have to get back to my sublet in Greenpoint in about a half hour."

"You're okay. You've got plenty of time and you're not that lost. I'll show you the way, but if you're going to do a lot of driving in this town, invest in a GPS. Manhattan is easy to get around in because it's laid out on a grid, but the other boroughs, not so much. You could ride around forever and never find your way to or from your destination."

"I know, but I'm just a stubborn Bostonian. We figure if you can navigate those streets, you can find your way around anywhere."

"Boston, huh?"

"Oh, Christ, don't tell me you're a Yankees fan."

"Mets fan," I said. "We're united in our loathing of the Yanks."

"There was '86, but I'll overlook that."

"I appreciate it."

"So what kind of appointment did you have on Court Street? I used to have an office at 40 Court."

"You're joshing me! That's where I had my appointment," she said. "I'm an IT consultant to law firms. My company moved me here for a few months because we've landed several contracts with big firms throughout the area. Don't tell me you're a lawyer."

"God, no. I'm a retired cop and I was a partner in a security and investigations firm—40 Court is where we had our offices."

"A PI?"

"That was years ago, Mary, and it's a lot less exciting than you'd think."

She looked at her watch again and frowned. "Moe, I'm sorry, but I have to get back to my place and do a conference call with the home office."

Shit! "That's okay. I'll get you back onto the BQE."

When I approached her to point the way, I noticed that she smelled as fine as she looked. Her perfume was grassy with grace notes of musk and honey. I pointed out how she should turn around, go left under the Brooklyn Bridge, and follow the signs to the BQE East. "Get off at McGuinness-Humboldt and you should be okay from there."

"Thank you, Moe Prager. You're a gentleman."

I held my hand out to her. She took it, but held on to it a little longer than I would have expected. "Listen, Moe, I still feel like an idiot for hitting your car. Let me take you to dinner. My treat. I could use a friend in this city. Us New Englanders, we like to think of ourselves as a hardy bunch, but this city will test you."

"How could I say no to that offer? And we can all use another friend."

She smiled and it lit up the afternoon. "Tonight?"

"I can't," I said, "not tonight."

"Then call me. You've got my numbers."

"I will. I promise."

With that, Mary Lambert let go of my hand and got back into her car. I watched it disappear under the Brooklyn Bridge and I suddenly felt very lonely. I wasn't a monk by any stretch. I'd dated a lot since Carmella and I split, but the walls I'd built around myself were thick. Closeness was no longer part of the equation for me, which meant my relationships with women had a very limited shelf life. I only felt the loneliness when I met someone like Mary, someone with whom I felt immediately comfortable. It reminded me of what I no longer had and would probably never have again.

TEN

Jimmy Palumbo was happy for the extra work, even if this wasn't exactly what either of us had in mind when we spoke at the museum. I met him in front of the same bar where I'd met Mary Lambert. It was easy enough to find and convenient to where we were going. The ex-jock came into the bar as quietly as possible, but it's kind of difficult to fly under the radar when you're six foot six, 270 pounds. People are just going to notice you. I was familiar with the phenomenon from walking the streets with my old running buddy, Preacher "the Creature" Simmons. Preacher was a former New York All-City basketball player who got caught up in a college gambling scheme and wound up throwing away his basketball career. He landed on his feet, running the security detail for several large housing projects in Queens. Believe me, when he walked in a room, everyone stared. Preacher was now retired and spending his time playing golf in Myrtle Beach.

Jimmy and I sat down at the end of the bar. I halfheartedly sipped a beer while he went with Diet Coke.

"Alcohol and me ..." His voice drifted off. "My impulse control is for shit when I've had a few. My wife used that against me in court to take the kids."

"Fine. So you understand what I've got in mind?"

"I got it."

"If you're having second thoughts, now's the time to tell me."

"No, I'm cool. Let's get to it."

We took my car over to the converted factory building and frankly, I wasn't encouraged at our prospects for success. My plan, such as it was, involved lighting a diversionary fire in the Dumpster at the rear of Nathan Martyr's building and getting the doorman—whoever was on duty—to vacate his post while Jimmy and I dashed up to the sixth floor. There was only one way it could've worked and ten ways it could've gone wrong, a few of them involving felony charges. This kind of stuff wasn't one of my strengths. Carmella, now she could always come up with a way to get a guy out in the open and it was almost always a simple plan. It was never simple for me.

Then, just as we turned onto Martyr's block, I caught sight of him coming out the maw of the old building. Planning might not have been one of my strong points, but at least I'd had the good sense to have found pictures of him on the internet so I wouldn't get the wrong man. My original scheme was flimsy enough without us strong-arming the wrong person. But seeing him there under the streetlight only confirmed my initial thoughts about the guy. He was drug sick. He was skinny to the point of hollow, sweating so that his face fairly shined, and walking like he had chains around his ankles. He kept wiping his nose with the back of his coat sleeve and bending over in pain. It didn't take a rocket scientist or even an ex-cop to figure out where he was headed.

"That's our boy," I said.

"You're kiddin' me."

"No, Jimmy, that's him. The stork couldn't have done a better job of delivering him. Now all I've gotta figure out is whether it's better to take him before or after."

"Before or after what?"

"He makes his connection. He's going to score drugs."

"How do you know that?"

"Never mind how I know it. I just do."

I followed well behind him for a few blocks and decided it was better to take him before he scored than after. Before allowed me to use Martyr's own sickness to pressure him. Jimmy wouldn't even have to do a thing except keep him in the car while I questioned him. If we took him afterwards, things could get a little more complicated. Once he bought the skag, it was the prospect of getting caught carrying narcotics by two nasty-dispositioned cops—hey, I wasn't going to tell him otherwise—and the prospect of jail time that would work the bad magic on him. But sometimes, if the connection and the user were cozy enough, the junkie would shoot up in the dealer's place. No, before was better.

Then, just as I put my foot down on the accelerator to catch up to Martyr, he stopped, turned, walked down the steps of a non-descript two-family house and disappeared through the basement apartment door. So much for taking too much time for deliberate thought. Now we only had one option open to us and that was to wait until he came back out. I wasn't about to bust into the basement and play Cops and Robbers: The Drug Bust Edition. Dealers had a lot to protect, including their lives, their stashes, and their money. That meant they usually had security in the form of hired help or guns or dogs: sometimes all three, but at least one or two. And as the minutes went by, I knew he was doing his business in the dealer's apartment.

About a half hour later, Nathan Martyr floated up the stairs and back onto the street. While he didn't look the picture of health, it was clear he'd gotten healthy. His zombie walk was now airy and free, the shackles off his ankles. I waited until he turned the corner and passed by an old church and an adjacent schoolyard. We were on him before he knew what was happening and we dragged him into the back of the dark playground.

I stuck my badge in his face and Jimmy shoved him to the ground. "Nathan Martyr, you're under arrest." I put my old cuffs tightly around his wrists. "You have the right to remain silent. Anything you say can and will be used against you in a court of law. You have the right to an attorney. If you can't afford one, one will be provided for you. Do you understand these rights?"

The asshole actually started humming "Singing In The Rain."

I patted him down and sure enough, he had an ounce, maybe two, of powder packaged in a knotted red balloon in his right front pocket.

"That's a lot of weight, Nathan," I said, cocky as could be.

He stopped humming long enough to tell me to go fuck myself.

Using one hand, Jimmy yanked Martyr up in the air by his wrists, and the asshole squealed in agony. Even at his junkie weight, getting lifted up that way must have felt like his arms were being ripped off his body. I shed no tears.

When Jimmy put him back down, I asked, "What did you say to me?"

"I said go fuck yourself, but what I should have said was good evening, Mr. Prager."

Talk about stopping the show. I didn't bother trying to plug ahead. He had me. I knelt down, uncuffed him, and helped stand him up. I held on to his heroin. It was the last card I had to play.

"The doorman, that asshole ex-cop, he showed you my picture," I said.

"Not two minutes after you left, he buzzed me and told me to come to the lobby, that he had something I might want to take a look at. Thompson's a dick, but he knows how to make tips and do his job."

"Yeah, well, you got me, but I got this." I held the balloon up and dangled it. He made a weak stab at snatching it away from me, but he was hopelessly slow. "Good thing you didn't get it," I said, "because then my only option would be to let my partner here have his way with your scrawny, pitiful ass and he'd make you hurt a lot more than you were hurting a half hour ago."

As if on cue, Jimmy brought his big paw down on Martyr's shoulder. He collapsed like a three-legged card table.

"Hey, man, there's no need for that. Just tell me what you want and maybe we can come to some understanding," he said, surprisingly little fear in his voice.

"I want your mailing list and I want all the data your webmaster has gathered about incoming emails, etc. I want—"

"Chill, Prager," he said, rubbing his wrists. "That's no way to negotiate."

"Negotiate?"

"I want! I want! I want! Didn't your mother teach you that saying *I want* won't get you what you want? It's pretty obvious what you want. You want to know which one of the people that visit my blog and site are sick enough to have abducted that little cunt Sashi Bluntstone."

The next thing I knew, I was pulling Jimmy Palumbo's fingers from around Martyr's throat. Jimmy got up, but Martyr stayed down.

"That won't get it done either, Prager," he rasped. He sat up, resting on an arm outstretched behind him. "You don't need to sort through all the shit you'd get from my webmaster. It's already been over three weeks. Time's running out on little Sashi. Tick … tick … tick …" He tapped his skull. "I have the names you want right here."

"You motherfucker! I'm gonna—"

This time Jimmy grabbed *me* and held me back. "Don't be stupid," he said. "Listen to this prick and let's get out of here."

"I'm okay." Jimmy let me go and I asked Martyr, "What do you want?"

"First thing I want is a gesture of good faith," Martyr said, pointing at the balloon, which was lying on the ground near Jimmy Palumbo's feet.

"I'll think about it. What else?"

"I want her last painting."

I couldn't believe what I was hearing. "What?"

"You heard me," he said, standing up, brushing himself off. "I want the last painting she was working on."

"Why?"

"Because the little bitch is probably dead and the last thing she worked on will be worth a fortune."

I wanted to rip this guy's head off. Jimmy did too. I think anyone would have, but I bit the inside of my cheek hard enough to taste blood and continued as calmly as I could. "But you hate her and her work."

"But I love money. I love it best of all. What, you think art is for art's sake? Don't be a rube, Prager. It's a commodity like gold or oil or pork bellies. And just like those things, art has no inherent value. It's about what the market will bear. You think when I kick that all the assholes who delight in pissing on my stuff now won't be clamoring for a piece of it? Sure I hate that little twat and her awful smears and finger paintings, but I want one and I hope she's—"

Jimmy Palumbo slapped Martyr so hard it split his lip. I thought the junkie's body would snap in two. I couldn't blame Jimmy, but I didn't want to have to answer for manslaughter charges either. I stepped between Jimmy and Martyr.

"That's it! Stop. Enough. You, back off!" I pointed at Jimmy. "Here, toss me the balloon." He did so, if not enthusiastically. "And you," I said, picking Martyr up in pieces off the playground, "keep your fucking mouth shut for two minutes. I'm gonna give you your drugs back and I'll get you that painting, but it'll be a day or two at least. First, I want one name and an address as a sign of good faith."

His right cheek was scraped and bleeding, his left swollen from where Jimmy's hand had landed, but Nathan Martyr smiled and looked at me with an odd mixture of contempt and pity. "You want a name? All right, Prager, I'll give you a name: Sonia Barrows-Willingham. Now give me my medicine."

"Sonia Barrows-Willingham … I know that name from somewhere," I said, still gripping the red balloon in my fist. "Does she visit your website?"

"No, Prager, but she's the one with the most to gain if little missy winds up dead."

"Who is—"

"She is the biggest collector of that little—of Sashi Bluntstone's *work*." He put finger quotes around the word work. "You want to know who had motive, look at her."

I handed him the balloon as promised. Martyr shoved it back into his pocket.

"When you get me the painting, you know where to find me."

"And when I bring you that painting, I want names I couldn't have found on my own or so help me, I'll stick my gun down your throat and blow that collection of pus you call a brain out the back of your skull."

He tried not to look rattled and failed. Jimmy Palumbo and I watched him recede into the night with the rest of the rats and roaches.

ELEVEN

I didn't play hide and seek with the sun as I drove back to Long Island. There was no fooling myself or anyone else for that matter about where I was headed or how this would end. Until meeting Nathan Martyr, it hadn't really occurred to me that there were people who actually had a rooting interest in Sashi Bluntstone's death. I'd met some repulsive human beings in my life, but none more so than Martyr. Being around him made me want to be able to molt like a snake and shed any piece of me that touched him. Yet, hours later, after I'd taken Jimmy Palumbo out for steak and paid him two hundred bucks in cash, after I showered and laid sleeplessly in my bed, I realized Martyr had done me a favor. Anyone who opens your eyes is doing you a favor. It was one thing when Lenya at the Brill Gallery mentioned the correlation between death and the value of art. It was something else when that junkie piece of shit gave me the lesson.

Martyr planted a seed in my head and it had blossomed overnight. Although I was still operating under the premise that Sashi Bluntstone had been abducted by a predator, possibly one of the resentful and twisted wack jobs who visited Martyr's website or the others like it, I could no longer ignore the chance that she had been taken out of sheer greed. Sure, I thought Max and Candy were hiding something from me, but I didn't really think they had somehow manufactured the disappearance to drive up the value of Sashi's work. Yes, they too would surely benefit financially from Sashi's death, at least in the short term, but neither Max nor Candy struck me as a criminal mastermind. Nor could I believe either of them was that cold-blooded. Candy couldn't even hide her affair from her husband and Max's grief was too real. Okay, maybe I was too close to Candy and maybe I was being naïve, but it was the cops' job to be objective and unsentimental, not mine.

I'd put in a call to McKenna and we'd agreed to talk at some point during the day, though he refused to be pinned down about timing. That was fine by me. He couldn't accuse me of keeping information from him if we couldn't manage to reconnect. Even if we did, I planned on being as vague as possible. I hadn't been on the job for decades and I was now pretty much just a civilian, but old resentments persist.

I spent my entire ten years as a cop in the bag, in uniform. Uniforms do the grunt work. It's their lives that get put on the line with every traffic stop, with every domestic violence call, but at crime scenes they're afterthoughts, blue window dressing there to string up the yellow tape and to say, "Please stand back." Even now it eats at me that I was treated as a stalking horse, that I was the first one through the door to find the body of a woman beaten to death or the rag doll body of a baby dangling head first from its crib, but that I was shut out completely once the detectives had taken my statement. McKenna had been fair with me up to a point and I wasn't going to do anything to risk Sashi's life. Beyond that, however, regardless of the promises I made to him, that was as far as I was willing to go. This case was as much mine now as his.

Then my phone rang and the load on my shoulders lightened.

"Moe? Is that you?" asked the raspy voice on the other end of the line.

"Mary Lambert, how did you get this number?"

"I have my ways."

"Apparently."

"You don't mind, do you?"

"Mind? Not at all. So you got back for the conference call all right?"

"Your directions were perfect. I found my way just fine. Thanks again."

"No problem. What's up?"

There was a hesitant silence and then, "I hope this doesn't put you off, but I haven't really been able to concentrate since yesterday."

"You've popped into my thoughts once or twice yourself," I confessed.

"Do you think we could have dinner tonight? Until you say yes, I'll be worthless to my employer and our clients."

Now I hesitated. I wanted to say yes, to stop the car and pump my fist, but I couldn't help but think about Sashi Bluntstone locked up in a dark, musty room, scared to death, waiting to be sodomized again or, worse, her cold body rotting under a pile of moldering leaves by the side of a highway somewhere. On the other hand, unless a major break fell into my lap, there would be no value in my sitting home alone in my condo. Mary misread my hesitation.

"I knew I shouldn't have called. I'm sorry. Please for—"

"It's not that. Believe me, it's not that at all, but I can't explain right now. Can I give you an enthusiastic but tentative yes?"

"I'll take it."

"I'll call you later."

"That's perfect." Her voice smiled. "Bye, Moe Prager."

"Bye, Mary Lambert."

● . ●

The Junction Gallery was open this time and I strolled in like a curious passerby. I don't know, regardless of what Wallace Rusk and the Nathan Martyrs of the world had to say, I liked Sashi's paintings. They were vibrant and whimsical and free of the constraints of European schools of thought and unconscious processes and whatever other rules the "serious" art world wanted to accuse her of breaking. If this was heresy, sign me up. Wouldn't be the first time I was on that side of things.

The Junction Gallery wasn't anything like the Brill. The Brill, in its stark whiteness, was nearly devoid of a sense of commerce. And with the junkie's crap on display, it was downright anti-capitalist. The Junction Gallery, on the other hand, with its exposed brick walls, neon signs, colorful brochures and flyers, Kenny G soundtrack, and small DVD/CD and framed poster section, felt more like a Disney Store at the mall. Of course nearly all of the original paintings, framed prints, and DVDs were either produced by or were about Sashi Bluntstone. The only missing items were stuffed Sashi dolls.

There were six other people in the gallery with me. A young Japanese couple seemed to be engaged in a serious debate over the aesthetics of a Sashi painting that featured bright orange swirls, bold black streaks, and layers of yellow drips. An elderly couple just walked the gallery shaking their heads as they hesitated briefly by each painting. I wasn't sure if their head shaking was commentary on the paintings themselves or on Sashi Bluntstone's fate. In a corner by another of the paintings—this one predominantly textured shades of green and blue—stood the two remaining souls. She was a woman in her late fifties, thinset and lock-jawed, who looked like she just stepped out of a Talbot's window display. She was so WASPy I thought I might have to check for wings beneath her tweed blazer. At her left shoulder was a tall, athletic man of forty with longish, slicked-back salt and pepper hair. Dressed in pine green corduroy pants over trail boots, a light green flannel shirt, and sweater vest, he struck me as an L.L.Bean man. By process of elimination, I pegged him as Randy Junction. I ambled casually over to where I could catch something of their conversation. As soon as he opened his mouth, he confirmed not only his identity, but the woman's as well.

"Come on, Sonia," he said, "you know the market for Sashi's stuff is back through the roof. Don't come in here and try and cut me off at the knees. We've been doing business with each other too long for that."

"Thirty is as high as I'm going to go for this."

He laughed, but not because he was really amused. "Sonia, Sonia, Sonia ... I happen to know you paid fifty last year for 'Red Waves' to that collector in Ojai."

"That was last year, Randy."

"And this isn't 'Red Waves.' 'Lime Ocean Blue' is the real thing and the subtlety of it shows Sashi was maturing as an artist."

Randy Junction's "was" stuck in my craw. They were talking about Sashi Bluntstone as if she were already dead and they were picking over the prime cuts of her carcass. I could have smacked him and kicked Sonia Barrows-Willingham in the ass. I chose to bide my time instead. Martyr was right: the vultures were circling, darkening the sky, ready to cash in on Sashi's death. And while I wasn't ready to write Martyr any love letters or apologies, he suddenly seemed less detestable somehow. At least his loathing and cynicism were on display for the world to see, not hidden in whispers in the corner of a low-rent art gallery.

"All right, Randy. Forty."

Junction couldn't have hidden his smile with an iron mask. "Forty-five." His heart wasn't in it, but he figured it was worth a try.

"Forty." Sonia reached into her million dollar handbag and pulled out her checkbook and Mont Blanc. "Shall I start writing or walking?"

"Writing, of course."

There would have been some advantage to surprising them and confronting them in public, but surprise can be overrated. I wanted a little more information before I went after them and I wanted them separately. Besides, I'd overheard their conversation and they could no more retreat from it tomorrow or the next day as they could today. Junction would have her money and she would have the painting and they could both rot in hell.

"Here's your check," she said, tearing it off and handing it to him. She didn't look particularly pleased, but she looked like the type of woman who never seemed particularly pleased about anything. She probably blinked when she orgasmed … if she orgasmed.

"Thank you, Sonia. Your paintings will be delivered tomorrow as always."

Paintings? When Sonia Barrows-Willingham left, I watched Junction place little red "sold" stickers on the white description placards next to three of Sashi's paintings. Randy Junction was practically floating as he walked from painting to painting with his red stickers. I thought I'd use his good mood to my advantage.

"Excuse me, are you the gallery owner?"

"I am indeed. Randolph Junction. How may I assist you?"

"I'm not much for art myself," I said. "One bunch of glops and drips is much like any other to me, but I'm an investor. I've got a nice portfolio, but that's not the thing that gets me going. No, I like investing in things: diamonds, stamps, wine … I got a tip from a friend that I should check out some of this kid's stuff."

I thought Junction was going to ring like an old-fashioned cash register. "Your friend has a good eye."

"My friend is color-blind and knows less about art than I do. What he knows is money and investments. So sell me, Junction."

"All right, you seem like a man who wants to cut to the chase. The fact is that if you had walked in here a month ago, you could have bought every original in this gallery for about a hundred grand. Today, you couldn't buy any three of them for that little."

"Why's that?"

For the first time since I entered, Randy Junction was off balance. He didn't answer right away and nervously brushed his palms against each other.

"Don't clam up on me now. I know the kid is missing," I prodded.

"Well ... look, if she doesn't turn up," his voice cracked, "the value will go sky high."

"Okay, I appreciate your honesty. Have you got a card and some literature?"

Junction obliged, but he didn't try to close me. There was no sales pitch with the handshake, no, "Maybe you want to buy one now, because if they find her body this evening ..."

I gave him some credit for that, but not much. I told him we'd speak again soon and we would. Only the next time, it would be on my terms, terms he was bound not to like.

● . ●

Someday I'd get Max and Candy home together, but it wasn't going to be today. Today it was Max's turn to be gone when I showed up and that was probably a good thing, because the time had come for me to explain about my needing Sashi's last painting. But just before the thought was translated into nerve impulses and then into muscle commands to move my tongue and lips, I was struck by a second notion. It was something that was kicking around in my head since the night before. It occurred to me that *I* might not give a shit if Sashi or her late dog Cara or the UPS man actually did her paintings, but it might matter to someone else, someone who might be very pissed off if they found out, or someone who might have an interest in keeping the secret. Dead men tell no tales nor do little dead girls.

Candy seemed to be sliding down the hill lubricated by grief. The faint signs of optimism I'd seen in her face and heard in her voice were gone. Her eyes were red on red and the makeup she'd managed for her lover was nowhere in sight. Max may have gotten there before her, but she was catching up. Who knows what set her off, what finally made her take a stark look at the reality of things? Was it something Randy Junction whispered in her ear as he put himself inside her? Was it that I hadn't been able to magically deliver her daughter to her in a matter of days? Or was it simply that she could read the calendar and there was no more fight left in her? Sometimes the why doesn't matter in the face of what is.

"What is it Mr. Pra—Moe?"

"I found a source who might give me an opening. It's the first real lead I have."

But the grief had taken hold, so not even the hope I was offering, as faint and vague as it was, did much to lift Candy up.

"Might," she said, "you said might."

"My source wants his palms greased."

Her eyes got wide. "Money?"

"No, honey. If it was as simple as money, I could take care of that. He wants paintings, four of Sashi's paintings."

She stared at me blankly as if I'd just spoken to her in a language she'd never heard before. Then she said, "Paintings?"

"Four: one from her early period, one from a few years back, a more recent one, and the one down in the basement ... the last one she was working on."

"Moe, I ... we don't have ... I have to talk to Max about it."

"Candy, I know this is hard for you, but I think we've got a real shot here to make some headway."

"But we don't have any of Sashi's stuff anymore. I—"

I grabbed Candy's forearm to get her full attention. "Listen to me. Go to Junction and go to Sonia Barrows-Willingham if you have to, but get those paintings for me by tomorrow."

"How do you know about Sonia?"

"I used to be a PI, remember? That's why you went to Sarah to come to me."

"I don't know if Sonia—"

"Then tell your boyfriend Junction to kick in the other three paintings." That got her attention all right. "And no, I didn't figure that out on my own. Max told me."

Now it all came out in one awful rush: the tears, the grief, the vomit, the horror and relief of being found out. I got on the floor with her, rocked her, and held her head the way I used to with Sarah when she was sick. Only this kind of sickness, the sickness of a dying marriage and a missing child, wasn't going to get better in a few days. I cleaned her up and put her into bed.

"I'll be by tomorrow afternoon to get those paintings. Get them any way you have to, Candy."

Then I kissed her forehead and closed her door behind me. Yeah, I lied to her, but I had a feeling the walls of this house had seen a lot of lying before I ever walked up those front porch steps.

TWELVE

Mary Lambert, flush with pride over having purchased a GPS at her firm's expense, fairly demanded that she come to my end of Brooklyn for dinner. I wasn't going to argue with her. The thought of seeing her again gave me that happy nervousness I hadn't experienced since I'd been with Carmella. Like I said, I was no monk and there had been no shortage of women to warm the other side of my bed, but there hadn't been any buzz with them beyond the buzz of bitterness. Dating always sucks, but dating in middle age sucks a whole lot worse because everyone involved has baggage, usually in the form of ex-spouses—either dead or divorced. You have no idea how much fun I had explaining that I had one of each. And even when the bitterness quotient was low, dinner conversation usually degenerated into a discussion of kids and grandkids or comparing whole-grain cereals and doses of Lipitor. Then, if dinner was nice enough, if there had been sufficient alcohol consumption, I'd wind up falling into bed with my dinner companion. You want to talk about baggage … Bed is the Broadway stage of baggage. *No, don't turn me over. My husband always forced me into that position and even when I liked it I hated it.*

I tried the younger woman thing for a while. That was even less successful because then most of the baggage was mine, and mine included a murdered ex-wife whom I still loved, an ex-wife I'm not sure

I ever loved but still wanted, and enough secrets to choke the Trojan Horse. Besides, it was nearly impossible to find common ground with women my daughter's age. And inevitably, within an hour or two, I wound up sounding paternal and/or professorial. I found out soon enough that no one finds it dead sexy when you utter the phrase, "Don't worry, when you get to my age you'll understand." There were times, I confess, I yearned for those whole-grain cereal discussions and photos of the grandkids. Modern pharmacology notwithstanding, there are issues for men of a certain age beyond just staying hard. The nature of desire itself changes with time.

I made three phone calls while I waited for Mary Lambert. I put Jimmy Palumbo on alert that his services might be required in the coming days. He was eager for the work, for the two hundred dollars, and, he said, for another steak dinner. The next call was to Palumbo's boss at the museum, Wallace Rusk. I didn't figure to get him in the office, not if his security guard was already home. I left a message anyway. What I needed from him could wait until Candy got me those four paintings. Then I put in the call I was least looking forward to, the one to McKenna. Not that he'd kept his promise either—I'd checked my cell phone all throughout the day—but cops can have funny notions of whose job it is to do what. Hallelujah! I got his voice mail and left a message. I'd have to talk to him sooner or later. Every minute later was better.

I found myself looking out the front window of my condo at the moonlight reflecting off the black waters of Sheepshead Bay and beyond to Manhattan Beach. I'd lived here for a lot of years now. I had intended to move Carmella, Israel, and me into a nice house, but I never got the chance. The marriage started to crumble almost from the second we took our vows. Given that we were business partners, that she was pregnant with another man's child, and that I was still reeling from Katy's murder, it was a miracle we lasted fifteen minutes. And Carmella had a rage in her that dated back to a time before her name was Carmella or Melendez, to when she had been abused as a little girl. One time I asked her why she chose to spell her new first name with a double l, a very untraditional spelling for a Spanish speaker. She told me it was a final *Fuck you!* to her mother who had reacted with shame to the abuse. Talk about baggage … I should have known our marriage was a mistake. She should have known. We did know, both of us knew, but we did it anyway. Sometimes I think our stubbornness in the face of the facts is what defines human behavior.

The bell rang and the spell was broken. No more staring into the black waters, not tonight.

I pressed the talk button. "Hello."

"It's Mary."

I buzzed her in and when she came up, I took her coat.

God, she looked spectacular and without trying. Or maybe that was the trick, to seem like you're not trying. She wore a blue silk blouse that perfectly matched the shade of her eyes over loose fitting black slacks that still somehow managed to accentuate her curves. There was a little bit more makeup on her face than yesterday, but not too much. Between the makeup and the blouse her eyes made the rest of the room seem positively unlit.

"You look nice," I said. I could be so articulate.

"As do you."

"Come in. Red or white?"

I'd already selected one of each and had them waiting. They were both ridiculous, of course. It's funny how I resented our customers who bought wines just to impress and here I was ready to pour a perfectly chilled Montrachet or the Château Mouton Rothschild I'd already decanted—purposely leaving the emptied bottle in plain sight for her to see. But until she stepped through my door, it hadn't occurred to me that she might not drink wine or that if she did, her taste might run to Glen Ellen white zinfandel or strawberry wine coolers. My fears were allayed when she walked slowly past me and carefully inspected both bottles.

"My god, Moe, you don't skimp on a girl. That's several hundred dollars of wine there on your counter."

"Don't worry about it, I get a big discount."

"How's that?"

"I know the owners of a few wine stores. Well, what's your pleasure?"

"I'll go with the Rothschild."

"Excellent choice," I said like a gleeful waiter calculating his twenty percent tip. "I was going to have some of that myself."

"I thought you might. You strike me as a red wine man."

I poured a finger of the wine for her to taste. "I do? Why's that?"

She didn't answer immediately, instead focusing her attention on the contents of the glass. She handled the task expertly, though she dispensed with swishing it around her mouth and sucking air in through her lips. That part of the tasting process is a surefire romance killer. It's like going for ribs on a first date. Then I remembered that I took Katy for ribs at the Buffalo Roadhouse on what was essentially our first date. So much for shoulds and shouldn'ts.

"Oooh, this is amazing," she whispered. "As to reds and whites and you—whites, even the best whites, are what they are. They tend to be about one thing. Reds are more complex. They have more depth and character, more texture, subtlety, and nuance. Like you, I suspect, more than what they seem."

I poured some for myself and added more to her glass. "I'm not sure how to take that."

"As a compliment."

"And you reached this conclusion how? From spending a few minutes talking to me in the shadow of the Brooklyn Bridge? I didn't think there was much subtext in my giving you directions back to Greenpoint."

"Between men and women, there's always subtext."

We both drank to that. I might have been a little smitten, but I wasn't ready to let it go just yet, not on the strength of answers any man would want to hear.

"Seriously, Mary, how did—"

She cut me off. "I asked about you. I had to go back to 40 Court Street again today," she said, blushing a bit and taking a prodigious gulp of wine, "and I mentioned your name to one of the lawyers and he …"

"What lawyer? What firm?"

"I'd rather not say, Moe. He's a client and …"

"Okay. What did he say?"

"I'm sorry, Moe, I wasn't checking up on you. I was just curious."

"It's fine."

She felt compelled to explain. "Like I told you yesterday, I'm new here and I never expected to be quite so overwhelmed as I feel by it all. I'm a grown woman, for goodness sakes, yet it's gotten to me. For a solid month now I've had lawyers hitting on me every day and I'm weary. Lawyers, Jesus, like I'd date a lawyer ever again." She took another gulp and held her glass out for more. "People don't realize how hard it is to make friends when you're near fifty and in a new city and you don't really want to socialize with your clients. Then I hit your car and you were so sweet about it and here I am. I guess I'm feeling vulnerable."

"I understand. I do. So what did this lawyer tell you?"

"A lot of things," she said, turning away. "About your first wife being murdered and your divorce from your business partner. He said you did good work."

"And the wine stores?"

"That too. I'm sorry."

"Cut it out, Mary Lambert. No more apologizing. Deal?"

She pecked me on the cheek. "Deal."

I poured us both a little bit more wine and Mary, feeling relaxed, went back to sipping and began walking around my living room, staring at the photos on my wall and the ones on the coffee table. That unnamed lawyer had actually done me a huge favor. I now felt spared from the pressure of choosing my words carefully when explaining about the faces in the photos.

"My goodness, your daughter is a beauty."

"I think so." I *kvelled* a little about Sarah being a vet.

We went through all the pictures: Katy, Carmella, Israel, Miriam and her family, Aaron and his, Mr. Roth, Wit, Preacher "the Creature" Simmons and me at an Over-50 two-on-two b-ball tournament, Klaus, Kosta, and ten others. Then Mary found a partially hidden photo I'd forgotten was there and wished I'd taken down years ago. It was of three uniformed cops, arms around each other's shoulders, in front of Nathan's Famous in Coney Island. The three cops all had shaggy '70s haircuts and bad brush mustaches. They all seemed happy and more like brothers than just colleagues. Now two of them were dead.

"I'll be damned," she said, "that's you at the end there! Jee-sus, will you look at that hair and those whiskas? These days, you'd be charged with a Class A misdemeanor for that look."

"Ah, the '70s …"

"Who are these otha two happy fellas here?" The wine was definitely bringing out the Boston in her speech.

"That guy there on the right's named Larry McDonald and the other guy's Rico Tripoli. The guys in our precinct used to call us the Three Stooges."

"Moe, Larry, and … Rico?"

"Rico had wavy hair, so he was Curly."

She asked, "Where was this picha taken?"

"Coney Island, in front of Nathan's Famous Hot Dogs."

"I've heard of that place."

"Yeah, well, famous *is* in the name."

"Wise guy!" She slapped my arm. "Come on, let's go there fah dinner. I've always wanted to see Coney Island fah myself."

"It's freezing out and it'll be deserted."

"Even betta."

● . ●

It *was* freezing out and Coney Island *was* deserted, at least the amusement park was. Nathan's Famous, on the other hand, was bustling with activity. That was the amazing thing about the joint. It was nearly always busy: day or night, no matter the season. Years ago I came to the conclusion that it wasn't about the food, not really. It was about what the food and the smells and the sight of the place represented. I mean, the hot dogs were okay and the fries were the best on earth, but Nathan's was about so much more. It was a touchstone, a safe place where people could time travel, where they could return and relive, if only briefly, their happiest childhood memories. For so many people, Nathan's represented comfort and security and, sometimes, sadly, the one good thing in their fucked-up lives. I can't tell you how many suicides ate their last meals at Nathan's. I didn't mention that last bit to Mary. She was having too good a time and I wasn't about to break the trance.

Noticing two couples dressed in tuxedos and killer gowns, she said, "We're not close to being the best dressed folks here, are we?"

"Nope. This place is a kind of crossroads. When I was in the Six-O, I used to think that someone standing with a camera on that corner over there," I said, pointing to where Surf and Stillwell Avenues met, "could capture the essence of human experience if he stood there long enough and had enough film. Now he wouldn't need film, just memory."

"I was right about you, Moe Prager. You're a complicated fella."

"Why's that?"

"Because I didn't know cops were so philosophical."

"Ferguson May, he was our precinct philosopher. I guess he rubbed off on me a little."

"Ferguson May, where's he nowadays?"

"Dead. Got stabbed through the eye during a domestic violence call in the projects more years ago than I can count. He was a good guy. Weren't many black guys on the job back then and he suffered through all the bullshit by being philosophical about it."

"C'mon," she said, looping her arms through mine, "show a girl the sights."

We walked out of Nathan's, our bellies full of hot dogs, fries, and watery beers, and turned right onto Surf. We went up the steps onto the boardwalk, the moon high above, the soft roar of the invisible ocean and the wind whistling in our ears. I drove past Coney Island nearly every day on my way to work, but the days of my stopping by, of my coming here for comfort and to think things through were gone. It had been many years since I'd stood on the boardwalk in winter, looking out at the white-haired waves and the hibernating dinosaurs of the amusement park rides. I'd spent so much of my childhood in this place and walked countless miles on the boardwalk as a cop. In a parallel universe somewhere you could probably still hear the echoes of the warped and pitted boards squealing under the weight of my ugly black cop shoes.

"What's that there?" Mary asked, pointing up at the orange super structure looming over our right shoulders.

"That's the Parachute Jump. It used to be part of Steeplechase Park, but it hasn't worked in years. That enormous Ferris wheel there is called the Wonder Wheel. It has enclosed cars that swing and ride on rails as it turns. And that roller coaster over there is the Cyclone, the most famous wooden roller coaster in the world."

"And this was your precinct?"

"In some ways, I guess it always has been. I grew up around here too."

"Let's walk." She tugged me towards Brighton Beach. "So tell me about the bad old days. When you were a big tough cop with bad hair. What about you and the other two stooges? What were they like?"

"Larry was a shrewd customer. To call him ambitious was like calling Hitler mildly anti-Semitic. He was always working an angle, but he never climbed up over the bodies of his buds, never threw us under the bus to clear the path for himself. He nearly made it to the mountain top too. He was top brass when …"

"When what?"

"He committed suicide. Gassed himself in a car by the old Fountain Avenue dump."

"Oh … I'm so sorry. What about Curly?" she asked.

"Rico? God, I haven't thought about Rico in years. I think he was the closest friend I ever had, but he threw our friendship away."

"How?"

"He had ambitions too, but he wasn't as clever as Larry Mac. Rico never understood that wanting isn't worth a thing in this world and that there's a big gulf between wanting and getting. Larry, he always understood the difference and was good at paying his own way up the ladder. Rico paid his bills too, but with other people's sweat and blood. I guess I wouldn't have minded if he didn't pay so much for so little in return."

"What do you mean?"

"Rico wanted to make detective. We all wanted to, only Rico was impatient about it. The city was in bad financial shape back then and you practically had to be the second coming of Christ to get your gold shield. So Rico made a deal with some political hot shot, which wouldn't have been so bad, I guess, if the deal hadn't involved me. He set me up to bring a powerful man to his knees, a man who turned out to be my future father-in-law."

"Oh, no."

"Oh, yes. And the ironic thing is that if Rico had only waited a few months, he would've made detective on his own merit. He was on a joint task force that broke the biggest murder-for-hire and car theft ring in this city's history. Every uniform connected to the case got his shield and every detective got a bump up in grade."

"That's sad."

"It gets worse, but do you mind if we skip this conversation?"

"Of course not," she said, stopping to slide her arms around me. She kissed me, softly, tentatively. It wasn't an invitation for more, but rather a kiss of possibility. It wasn't a thanks-for-dinner-and-goodbye kiss either. It was kind of sweet, not hungry or bitter. Those kinds of kisses were rare to come by these days.

"What now?" I asked.

"Let's go back to your place, try the white, and make out a little bit. I have to give you a reason to ask me to dinner again."

"I already have reason enough."

"Jesus, Moe Prager, for such a bright and complex fella, you're slow on the uptake. You mind if a girl gets to have a little fun?"

"Perish the thought."

"Then come on."

When Mary Lambert left my condo that night, lipstick smeared, but most of her clothes intact, I was a little lightheaded. I hadn't had a good make-out session since my freshman year at Brooklyn College. Back then, making out used to leave me more frustrated than anything else. I was feeling a lot of things as I watched Mary's car pull away. Frustrated wasn't one of them.

THIRTEEN

I woke up feeling a little less giddy than I had when I went to bed. Not because I wasn't still into Mary Lambert. On the contrary, a night of sleeping on the memory of the way her skin warmed to my touch and how the scent of her perfume changed as we kissed, and the way her nipples stiffened when I brushed my hands across the front of her silky blouse, had done nothing to dampen my enthusiasm for her. But too much expensive wine on a hot dog and french fry stomach wasn't a prescription for a happy morning. I used to be able to drink, but these days hangovers didn't just vanish with a few sips of water and a fistful of aspirins. *Clint Eastwood stars in Sergio Leone's A Fistful of Aspirins.* Ah, the joys of growing older.

Just after I crawled out of bed, breakfasted on two bottles of water, Pepto, and painkillers, the house phone rang. House phone, now there's a quaint idea about to go the way of the front yard water pump and the transistor radio. No one I knew under the age of thirty even had a house phone.

"Yeah."

"Prager. Detective McKenna."

"I don't usually date men who blow me off when they promise to call."

"Very funny."

"What's up?"

"You got anything?"

No beating around the bush with this guy. He asked the big questions right away. The thing is, I didn't want to answer. If he found out about where I was going with Nathan Martyr, McKenna might step in and do things his way. And while the detective didn't strike me as a hard-ass or strong-arm type of cop, there was a girl missing for over three weeks now and his patience was probably at low ebb. Hard-ass or not, I doubted McKenna would approve of my agreeing to Martyr's extortion demand. Paying off a no-talent, scumbag junkie with the last painting of a lost girl whose abilities he ridiculed and reviled was utterly perverse, but there was a kind of twisted symmetry to it. I just didn't want to waste time by trying to make McKenna see it. I also doubted he would have thought much of my manipulating Candy to get the extra paintings. He would think that what I planned to do with them was beside the point. Again, I didn't want to waste time convincing him it wasn't.

"Nothing, not really. Just reinterviewing people you've already spoken to. How about on your end?"

He wasn't buying. "That's it? You got *bubkes*?" Only in New York did people named McKenna speak Yiddish.

I didn't want him to pursue this any further, so I played one of the two cards I still had in reserve and said, "I got a feeling."

"What feeling?"

"Max and Candy aren't telling us something. It's something big, but I don't know what it is."

"I'm with you on that, Prager. But I don't think they're lying. More like they're—"

"—holding back," I finished his sentence.

"Exactly. That's it. From day one, I felt there was a part of the puzzle they had that they weren't showing me. Any ideas?"

"Not really."

"You're an old friend of the mother's. Work on her."

"I will. How about you?"

"It's cold out there, very cold and very fucking dark. Three weeks and counting ..."

"Okay. If I get anything or make any progress with Candy, I'll let you know."

He didn't bother with goodbye. That worked for me. My head and gut were feeling a little better, but McKenna's words stayed with me. We needed to make some progress soon or the real mourning would soon begin.

• . •

I went back to bed thinking that it would be a waste of time. Wrong. I woke up three hours later with the phone trilling at me like a pissed-off cricket.

"Mr. Prager?" It was Wallace Rusk. "Are you quite all right?"

"Sorry, I'm not feeling great today."

"You left a message ..."

"I did. I don't know if you'll be able to help, but I figured it couldn't hurt to ask."

"Ask?"

"I might need some paintings authenticated," I said.

"That's not an issue. I'd be glad to recommend someone and if she's not to your liking, any of the major auction houses—"

I cut him off. "They're Sashi Bluntstone's paintings."

"Oh, I see. That *is* a bit more problematic. Let me think ... Okay, yes, I have someone for you. His name is Declan Carney. Wait, let me get you his number."

"Is he any good?" I asked, scribbling down the number and address.

"For what you want, yes, the best, but I should warn you his services will not come inexpensively and he's a bit … let us say … idiosyncratic."

"I don't care if eats mosquitos on toast for lunch as long as he can do the work."

"Now, Mr. Prager, if that is all …"

"One last thing."

"Yes."

"Is Nathan Martyr a liar?"

There was a sudden and profound silence on the other end of the line and it spoke well of Wallace Rusk. He was actually thinking about the question and not dismissing it out of hand.

"I don't think very highly of his work and I think he's a detestable human being, but in my thankfully limited dealings with the man I have never known him to lie or renege on his word. Why do you ask?"

"He's promised me something and I just wanted to make sure I wasn't being jerked around."

"Very well then. Good morning to you."

I liked Wallace Rusk in spite of himself. I didn't think we'd be going to a sports bar to catch a Jets' game together any time soon, but he seemed an honorable sort. Old-fashioned as it may be, I admired that in a person. Honor seemed to be a commodity in very limited supply these days.

FOURTEEN

Candy said she had the paintings for me, but didn't exactly sound happy about it. Tough shit for her, I thought. Besides, a little anger never hurt anyone and stuffing her guts with feelings other than guilt, panic, and grief would do her good. I didn't question her about how she managed to get the paintings because I didn't care about how. Nor did I ask her if there was any fallout from my telling her that Max knew about her affair. No matter how any of this turned out, even if we somehow managed to find Sashi alive and relatively well, their world was never going to be the same. Whether they chose to blow it apart or to plow it over and begin again was up to them and them alone. But when I told Candy I would be over in an hour or two to collect the paintings, she said I should get them from the gallery, that Randy Junction had them wrapped and ready for me. She hung up on me before I could ask why he was involved. That was just as well.

It was a particularly bleak day, cold and threatening, gray clouds churning, snow showers here and there. So when I walked in, the gallery was empty except for Randy Junction himself. He was busily dusting dust that wasn't there and straightening already straight paintings. He gave me a big smile when he saw me and that knocked me off my game there for a second. Then it occurred to me that he didn't know who I was, not really. He thought I was that investor come back to snatch up some of Sashi's works at pre-death prices.

"Hello again," he said with dollar sign eyes and a glad hand. "You've come back for some paintings."

"That I have, but not any of these." I gestured at the walls.

"I'm afraid I'm at a loss."

"That's probably true."

His glad hand turned frigid and his smile went nearly as cold. "Look, I don't know what you're playing at, but—"

"I'm not playing at all. My name's Moe Prager. Candy sent me over to collect some paintings."

If I expected him to get all weak-kneed and weepy, I had something else coming.

"You're a prick, you know that, Prager? Why the hell did you tell Candy that Max knew about us?"

"Because I needed her full attention. I've got my eye on one thing here and that's getting Sashi back. What you and Candy and Max do is up to the three of you. But I'm gonna do what I've gotta do and I don't give a shit whose feelings get hurt in the process."

"Very nice."

"Nice! Are you fucking kidding me? You think I wasn't paying attention to your sales pitch yesterday? You think I didn't see you nearly come in your pants after Sonia Barrows-Willingham handed you that check? Give me a break, Junction, all right, and get down off that high horse. It doesn't suit you."

He opened his mouth to say something, but just turned on his heel and disappeared. When he returned he was carrying four bubble-wrapped paintings.

"What do you need these paintings for?"

"For kindling." The guy actually grimaced. "Take it easy," I said. "I'm kidding. Let's just call it bait."

"Do you think they could—"

"I'm not thinking anything right now except about getting Sashi back. If I somehow manage to do that, you and me, we can sit down and have a chat. Right now, just give me the paintings."

He did without hesitation. "You know, Prager," he said once I had the paintings in my arms, "you are walking into a situation you don't understand."

"That's true. I'm always late to the party and too stupid to get the inside jokes. I'm always playing catch-up because people come to me late in the game. But, you know, sometimes it's a big advantage not to be on the inside."

"Nice speech. You ought to get it carved in stone and put on your grave, but you don't fool me."

"How's that?"

"You don't even know Sashi and you haven't seen Candy in a hundred years. No, there's something else at play here. There's something in it for you. I just can't see what it is."

"Candy came to me," I said, sounding defensive as hell.

Junction smiled at that. "I know all about how Candy came to you. Moe Prager *ex machina*: you were going to come in out of the blue and save the day. You were going to come in off the bench and hit a walk-off home run. What a load of crap. You're just going to make it all worse. What am I saying? You already have."

I wanted to disagree with him, but he was right, up to a point. I had walked into a situation I didn't understand. I didn't know Sashi except through videos and I hadn't seen Candy since her wedding day. I did have a separate agenda in wanting to regain my daughter's love and, as far as Candy and Junction were concerned, I had made things worse. I took the paintings and left.

As was the norm with this case, I didn't get very far. All four of my tires were slashed and the driver's side window was smashed to bits. I found a stuffed brown teddy bear propped up on my glass-covered front seat. Its head was missing, its legs and arms hog-tied behind it. The words STOP NOW were stenciled in red spray paint across the passenger seat. While I may not have known what I was doing, there must have been someone else who saw it differently.

I didn't want to call McKenna, but I had to. There was no way I could leave the cops out of this without risking obstruction charges and further endangering Sashi's life. This was evidence of something even if the vandalism turned out to be just some bullshit stunt. I'd managed to piss somebody off. No surprise there. I had a talent for it, but it wasn't necessarily the person who had Sashi. Still, I couldn't take that gamble. Before I called the cops, I brought the paintings back around the corner to the gallery. I warned Randy Junction not to talk about the paintings to the cops if they came asking questions, that mentioning them would ruin the one good lead I had. He may have been a bit of an asshole, but he seemed to care about Candy and Sashi enough to play along. After I called McKenna and the rent-a-car company, I rang Jimmy Palumbo and told him we were on for a visit to Nathan Martyr that evening. My back was in need of some serious watching.

FIFTEEN

I hadn't even bothered calling for a tow as there was little doubt my car would be impounded before it was released back to me. Detective McKenna was fairly humming with perverse joy when he showed up and beheld the wrecked glory that was my car and the crime scene boys fussing over it like nervous ants attending the colony's newborn. I couldn't begrudge McKenna his newfound joy. It is the harsh reality of police work that bad news is sometimes the best possible news, that a new crime is a welcome event as it might shed light on an icy cold case. I remembered when I was in uniform and got assigned to do grunt work for the Son of Sam task force. Confounded as they were by the .44 Caliber Killer, the detectives let out a silent somber-faced cheer every time Sam struck again because it meant fresh evidence. Every new killing meant there was a chance to find that one fingerprint or shell casing or witness that would break the case wide open. And in the end, that's what happened. On the mid-summer night Sam shot out the eye of Robert Violante and snuffed out the life of Stacy Moskowitz, he got a parking ticket and was spotted by a woman walking her dog. So I understood why McKenna looked about ready to click up his heels.

"You got somebody's attention, Prager."

"Sure as shit looks that way."

"Any idea who?"

"No."

"Bullshit."

"You want a list of the people I've spoken to?"

"That would be a start," he said. "Go ahead."

"Max and Candy."

"Yeah."

"Nathan Martyr, but he was alibied by the ex-cop doorman."

"David Thompson."

"He's an asshole."

"He may be, but it's airtight," McKenna said. "Martyr didn't do it. He was home that day."

"Junction, the gallery owner. Wallace Rusk."

That got McKenna's attention. "Who's this Rusk guy?"

"Not your man. He's an art critic and the curator of the Cold Spring Harbor Museum of Modern Art."

"You don't mind if we talk to him anyway, do you?"

"Be my guest."

"Anyone else?"

"Dawn Parson. She wouldn't let me talk to her kid."

"Okay. You need a lift or anything? I can get one of the uniforms to take you."

"No thanks, McKenna. I got a rental being dropped off for me."

"Keep in touch."

It was an order, not a suggestion.

The rental was dropped off at the gallery and I loaded the paintings into the backseat of the Japanese generic-mobile. Man, I was old. I still recalled a time when one car looked different than the next. "Not no more," as my old friend Crazy Charlie Rolex used to say. Those days, like the majority of mine, were past. I was relieved that McKenna was still around the corner salivating over the crime scene. It would have been a bit awkward trying to explain to him what I was planning to do with the paintings. Many years had passed since I'd come anywhere near working a case, but the lying came back to me like riding a bike. You work a case, you start lying to everyone. More often than not, you even wind up lying to the person or persons who hired you. Sometimes especially them. The one person you can't lie to is yourself.

As I drove out of Sea Cliff, away from the fussy Victorian houses and the quaint little shops on the main street, I thought about what must have been going through McKenna's mind. He couldn't have been any more confused by what had happened to my car, the hog-tied and headless teddy bear, and the cryptic warning than I was, because it didn't seem to make any sense at all. I still had no idea what had become of Sashi Bluntstone or who had taken her or why. My stumbling around had only just begun and it had netted me very little in the way of progress. I hoped that was about to change.

●　·　　◦

When the earpiece to my phone beeped that I was getting a call, I felt myself getting more than a little aroused at the memory of holding Mary Lambert in my arms. I imagined I could still smell the intoxicating scent of her sweat and perfume and I rubbed the tips of my fingers together, recalling the feel of her hardened nipples beneath the lace of her bra and silk of her blouse.

"Hey, there," I said in the best bedroom voice I could manage.

"What the fuck's the matter with you, you sick or something?" It was Brian Doyle.

"Or something, yeah. What's up?"

"The Bluntstones are broke, Moe."

"Broke broke or just broke?"

"Broke broke. They're mortgaged to the balls and their only assets are the kid's paintings."

"How about the house?"

"The thing cost two million and my bet is they're still paying off the closing costs. I got more equity in my baseball card collection."

"You collect baseball cards?"

"No, but I'm just saying."

"How about available cash?" I asked.

"Less than ten grand and that ain't gonna get them too far. Maybe the next time you're over there, you should check if they're hiding scratch in coffee cans or flour jars 'cause they ain't got shit elsewheres."

"Thanks, Brian, and thank Devo for me."

"No sweat, boss."

"Fax the stuff over to my house, okay?"

"Sure."

"Look, just send me the bill ..."

He was gone.

● . ●

Declan Carney's studio was in an old loft building within shouting distance of the Fifty-ninth Street Bridge on Vernon Boulevard in Long Island City. This Queens neighborhood, just across the East River from Manhattan and Roosevelt Island, had undergone tremendous change and gentrification in the last decade or so. As Manhattan became even more unbearably expensive, people looked for places to live where they could still have a short commute to work and ready access to the city. Like Williamsburg before it, Long Island City was now an increasingly hot part of town. The thing about LIC, though, is that it was more industrial in its previous incarnation than Williamsburg, and not all of its factories and warehouse buildings had been converted into fabulous living spaces for expatriate Manhattanites.

Carney's building was as yet untouched by the shifting tides of the churning real estate market. It was covered in a coat of soot and dirt so thick that it was nearly impossible to tell the exact shade of brick that made up its exterior walls. Carney was probably afraid to have the place cleaned for fear it might crumble without the filth to hold those walls together. I pressed the doorbell and waited for a voice over the old call box, but the door just buzzed and clicked open. I thought about taking the old-style freight elevator up and reconsidered when I saw the ratty shape it was in. At least the stairs were solid. I found Declan Carney on the top floor in a studio that looked like part sci-fi movie set, part photo lab, part artist's loft, and it seemed about as well organized as a bowl of spaghetti. Once I saw the man himself, I quickly forgot about the disorganization and remembered Rusk's warning about the man's idiosyncrasies.

Dressed in a blue, red, and yellow Hawaiian shirt, red tartan kilt, white tube socks, and Earth Shoes, his weird looks didn't stop with his attire. He had a bleached platinum Mohawk hairdo, brown and gray Hasidic sidecurls, a soul patch that grew five inches past his chin, and a Fu Manchu mustache that was braided at the tips. Then I realized there wasn't a tattoo or piercing on him. I guess he saw the question in my eyes, or maybe I asked it. I don't really remember.

"Tattoos go against all of my culture's beliefs and I am afraid of pointed objects. I grow faint at the thought of an injection. You do not think I would permit some untrained technician to drill me with a machine that your Thomas Edison invented to make print copies."

"Huh?"

"You did not know that the mechanism used for tattooing was a retrofitted Thomas Edison invention? Some fellow just added an ink reservoir, sharpened the point, and adjusted the cycling of the machine and, as some of your kind say, voila!"

"Sounds barbaric."

"I will not disagree."

I wanted him to speak a little more because he had a peculiar accent that wasn't, as his name suggested, Irish. Actually, I'm not sure I had ever heard any English speaker with an accent like it. And then there was his oddly referencing things like "*your* Thomas Edison" and "some of *your* kind."

"Where are you from?"

"Skajit," pronounced ska-JEET, "a planet four hundred million light years away from earth in the galaxy we call Plasnor."

He answered with a disconcerting nonchalance and a straight face. It was as if I'd asked him the time and he said three o'clock. Before I could utter another sound, he pointed to the bubble-wrapped paintings at my side. Paintings which, once I'd beheld Declan Carney, I'd nearly forgotten.

"Those are the artworks you wish me to authenticate?"

"They are."

"Sashi Bluntstone's, correct, Mr. Prager?"

"How did you—"

"Wallace Rusk telecommunicated with me about the possibility of your arrival. Please leave the paintings."

"How about a receipt?"

I thought Carney was going to break into tears. He was not only insulted, but wounded by my request. Apparently honor was meaningful to the people of Skajit.

"I meant no disrespect," I said, playing along. "It is customary to ask because the paintings aren't mine."

That seemed to make him feel better. "I will do as you ask."

He rummaged around for a piece of paper and found one under a can of turpentine. He scribbled on the paper with a pencil and handed it to me. It wasn't much, but it was something and I sensed it was all I was apt to get. I accepted it gracefully.

"Thank you for understanding. How long do you think it will take?" I asked, pointing at the three paintings.

"At least several days, depending on the tests, but by the Holy Doctrine of Thalmador, my conclusions will be beyond reproach."

"Wallace Rusk said you were good."

"A strange man, Wallace Rusk."

Talk about the pot calling the kettle black.

"Well, thank you, Declan."

I offered my hand and he shook it. As he did, he stared unflinchingly into my eyes so intently that it ached. Still I did not, could not turn away. He wasn't so much looking through me as into me. Then he broke eye contact.

"You do not think the child is still living," Carney said.

"No, I'm afraid I don't."

"Yet you continue the search?"

"It's my job."

"It is more than a job for you, Mr. Prager, is it not?"

"It's always more than a job for me, even when I don't want it to be."

"Yes, it is your future and your past."

"In a way."

"You would be much honored on my world."

I ignored that. "For whatever reason Sashi was taken, there's a beast out there somewhere."

"There are monsters everywhere," he said. "We are all monsters in our way. But on Skajit we say that it is the innocent monster we have most to fear."

"The innocent monster?"

"I do not think you need it explained. We have all known such creatures." He finally let go of my hand. "Beware the innocent monster, Mr. Prager, for it need not hide itself and lives closely among us. In your Nazi Germany there were many monsters, but not enough real monsters to make a Holocaust. No, it was the innocent monsters that made the Holocaust."

I handed him a card. "Thanks for the warning. Call me when you have an answer."

"Good day to you. Please, let yourself out."

He gathered up the paintings and disappeared into another room. I did as he asked and let myself out.

SIXTEEN

David Thompson, the ex-cop doorman, was there in the lobby in all his empty glory, standing guard over his piece of turf. Although I've crossed paths with many powerful and influential people in my life, I don't think I will ever fully understand the appeal of power. Little men, small-minded men like Thompson, thrived on it even if their kingdoms were so tiny they could fit three-fold inside a paper cup and the subjects over whom they held sway were barely human themselves. It was enough that they not be at the bottom of the totem pole. But that was just it; in the scheme of things, no matter how much power you wield or think you wield, you're always near the bottom of the pole.

"Looks who's back," he chortled when I walked in. "Is that your tail between your legs or are you just happy to see me? Martyr told me you tried to play hardball with him. Looks to me like you're the one who took it up the ass, pal."

"You seem pretty familiar with that look. You must see it in the mirror a lot?"

"Yeah, you keep talking like that and see where it gets you."

"You and Martyr seem awfully cozy. Strange pair, the two of you: the artiste and the doorman."

"Security, pal, I'm no doorman."

"And I'm the Emperor of Ice Cream."

"Huh? You fuckin' with me now? You don't wanna do that."

"Whatever. Forget it. In any case, Martyr seems to tell you all sorts of stuff."

"He trusts me," Thompson said, thrusting out his chest proudly.

"Either that or he must talk in his sleep."

"Fuck you, shitbird. Go ahead, say one more thing."

"He trusts you, okay, I get it."

"Yeah, he trusts me. His world ain't like when we was on the job. His world is full of hangers-on and liars."

"And you're straight with him?"

"Dead straight."

"That's why he trusts you?"

"I guess. All I know is he takes good care of me."

"Good enough care for you to lie for him?"

"That's it, motherfucka! That's it!" Thompson turned, flicked a switch on the desk, then, with amazing dexterity, reached under his blazer and snapped out an ASP, all in one motion. The twenty-one inch long, telescoping steel baton may not have looked like much, but I knew that in skilled hands it could break bones with a single blow or knock your senses halfway back to the birth canal. Although my .38 was less than a foot away from my hand, I wouldn't have gotten near it before he broke my fingers. "I just shut the lobby camera off, so it's my word against yours. I'm gonna t'row you a beatin' like you never had before."

"No, you're not, you dickless piece of shit," Jimmy Palumbo said, holding a 9mm Sig Sauer aimed squarely at Thompson's chest. The pistol looked like a toy in his huge hand, but it was no toy.

"Get the fuck outta here, you wouldn't dare shoot an ex-cop." Thompson sounded less than convincing.

"You wanna bet? Now there's two of us and one of you. It'll be our word against yours and you'll be dead."

Thompson was an asshole, but not a stupid one. He dropped the baton and it bounced off the terrazzo floor with a sharp clink. He then about-faced and made to quickly turn the lobby camera back on. Too late. Jimmy had already holstered his 9mm. To the camera we would look like three guys talking football or exchanging recipes. Sashi Blunt-stone's last painting rested against Palumbo's big leg.

"I'll borrow this," I said, scooping up the ASP. I pressed its tip against the floor and it folded up into itself. I placed it in my pocket. "I'll mail it back to you. Now ring your boyfriend and tell him we're coming up. And do me a favor."

"What?"

"Just let it alone. This is about a missing kid. I got no beef with you. I want to do my business and get out of here."

He said fine, but I knew he was lying. I'd made an enemy. Everybody makes enemies, most of the time without really trying. Most of the time circumstance has more to do with it than anything else. Still, I knew better than to ignore the enemies I made. I'd done that once and it got Katy murdered.

In the elevator, I finally exhaled.

"Thanks, Jimmy. One swing with that thing and he could've broken my femur. Good thing I had you along."

"Come on, that was fun."

"Yeah, for you maybe. You had the gun in your hand."

"Good point. You okay, Moe?"

"I'm good," I lied. It wasn't so much what had just happened with Thompson that was bothering me. It was just that I couldn't get my head around my visit with Carney. Specifically, I could not let go of what he'd said to me. He was, as Wallace Rusk had warned, idiosyncratic, but so movingly eloquent on the subject of monsters. When this was all over, I thought, I'd have to see what I could find out about him. One thing was for sure, he was going to get an invite to the grand opening of the new store in Bridgehampton. The Hamptons could always use a little shaking up and it would be worth having Carney there just to see the look on my brother's face.

Then, when I saw Nathan Martyr waiting for us out in the hall, the saliva practically spilling out the corners of his mouth at the thought of possessing Sashi Bluntstone's last painting, Carney's words came back to me once again. There were indeed monsters all around us. Martyr was so grotesque in the role that he was nearly amusing. Nearly. But there was nothing innocent about him and, I thought, if there was proof of original sin, he was it.

"Come on in, gentlemen."

Martyr's loft was a beautiful abyss. That's the only way to describe it. There were paintings and sculpture everywhere: some of it stunning, some of it crap, but all of it probably worth a fortune. The refinished broad plank oak floors left over from the building's former life were themselves works of art and the huge arched windows provided breathtaking views of the Brooklyn Bridge, the river, and Manhattan beyond. Yet it was as much a junkie's hovel as an artist's paradise. The place smelled like a high school locker room where the toilets had backed up. There were empty coffee cups, piles of old newspapers, and dirty, sweat-soaked clothing everywhere. Used cotton balls, alcohol wipes, and empty cellophane syringe packets littered the floor. The sink and kitchen counter were full of dirty dishes and open food containers. I didn't want to think about the feast the roaches must have had every time the lights went out. But when I looked over at Jimmy, he didn't seem half as disgusted by the condition of the loft as I did.

"The painting," Martyr said and actually had the *chutzpah* to snap his fingers at me.

"Jimmy," I said, "do me a favor and show Nathan what you showed the doorman down in the lobby."

Palumbo pulled his 9mm and aimed it at Martyr.

"Listen to me, you scumbag. Don't you ever snap your fucking fingers at me again. I got you your painting and you're gonna give me that list of names and that's that. Try and remember that when we're done here and whether I get Sashi back or not, I know where you live and I know how to get to you. You won't last five minutes in Rikers and I can pretty much guarantee you a free, all-expense paid trip. So let's get this over with. Do we understand one another?"

Martyr gulped and said, "Uh huh, I get it."

"It's okay, Jimmy, please put that away."

I handed the painting to Martyr as Jimmy Palumbo put his Sig back in its holster. Martyr treated the painting with great care, carefully slitting the tape and removing the bubble wrap. He held the canvas up before him, his eyes focusing on different aspects of the textured black- and red-speckled painting.

"She was growing up," he said, grudging admiration in his voice.

"You like it?"

"No, but you can see that she was actually thinking her way through it. This wasn't just about blue swirls and bright orange sunshine looking pretty for the eye of a little girl. There's depth in this. Too bad, really."

"What is?" I wanted to know.

"That the little bitch is dead."

Jimmy Palumbo, bad knees or not, pounced on Martyr and had a hand almost all the way around his scrawny neck before I could react. If you watch sports on TV, you can't really appreciate just how profound the difference is between a weekend warrior and a professional athlete, even a retired one. Pros are so much quicker, so much stronger, so much more instinctive that it's incredible. And Jimmy just reminded me of that difference. I guessed Martyr was learning that lesson for the first time.

"Okay, Jimmy, enough! Enough! Get off him. Let him go."

But Jimmy wasn't letting go and Martyr's face was turning twenty-three shades of red. I didn't know how much of this the junkie's body could take. My first instinct was to jump on the big man. Scratch that. Even at the height of my strength and athletic prowess, such as it was, I would have been no match for Jimmy Palumbo. I moved to reach around for my .38. I scratched that move also. I wasn't going to shoot the guy and I wasn't sure he was rational enough to heed a threat. The ASP snapped out as smoothly for me as it had for Thompson and I less than gently laid it across the back of Jimmy's left hamstring. That did the trick.

"Fuck!"

All the piss went out of Jimmy Palumbo. He let go of Martyr and rolled off the bastard. He rubbed furiously at the back of his leg, trying to work the pain out as if it were a cramp. For his part, Martyr was coughing up a lung and massaging his neck.

"Are you crazy?" Martyr choked out.

"Fuck you."

"All right, boys, that's it. Go to your corners and keep your mouths shut." I helped them both to their feet and they both did as they were told. Sashi's painting had miraculously survived the scrum intact.

I turned to Martyr. "Now you've got your painting. Where's the list?"

Chastened by Jimmy's neck squeezing, Nathan Martyr scrambled to find the list he had printed out. He handed the pages to me as quickly as possible. I think the list was probably the only thing he could have found in the chaos that was his apartment without a week's worth of searching. Well, that, a spoon, and a fresh syringe.

"I highlighted some names for you," he said. "See, in green marker, like there and there. Those are the real crazies. I also included some of their home addresses, the ones I knew, anyway."

"Thanks, but remember, if this turns out to be just some junkie scam bullshit, we'll be back and I won't stop him from wringing your neck. In fact, he may have to stop me from doing it myself."

"That's the list, Scout's honor."

"Okay. Come on, Jimmy, let's go."

Palumbo, still rubbing the back of his leg, followed me out of the loft and to the elevator.

"Shit," he said when we stepped inside the car, "did you have to hit me so hard?"

"Honestly, Jimmy, yeah. I thought you were gonna kill him."

"I guess maybe I would have."

"You working tomorrow?"

"I get off at three, why?"

I waved the list at him. "We got some people to visit. You up for it?"

"Does the pope wear red shoes?"

"I don't know. The angels stole Elvis Costello's."

"What?"

"Forget it. New Wave humor went out with skinny ties and electric drums."

"I'll take your word for it."

"Okay," I said, "but you've got to promise me no repeat performances of that little neck stretching thing you did with Martyr. The guys we're going to see tomorrow are apt to be even bigger assholes than he is. In fact, I can pretty much guarantee it. So—"

"I swear. I just lost my mind in there a little bit. Man, that guy is a piece of shit."

"Forget him. It's these guys we have to think about now," I said, waving the list at him.

"You're right."

"Just let me ask you ... that Sig you're carrying around with you, is it—"

"Registered? Yup. Totally legal. I got licensed when I was playing ball. You know, crazy fans and shit," he said. "The cops understand that you can get harassed by some pretty wacky people. Then when I got into security, it helped that I already had a carry permit."

"Cool. Just checking."

When we got back down to the lobby I could see that Thompson was still stewing over what had happened earlier. Men don't like getting their toys taken away from them, especially on their own turf. Freud would have said it was a castration thing. With a guy like Thompson, he would have been right. Thompson wasn't the type of guy to just let things go. I placed the ASP up on the security desk. It wasn't much, but it was the most conciliatory gesture I could manage on short notice. Needless to say, no thank you was forthcoming. He grabbed the folded baton and stuck it back under his blazer. As Jimmy and I left, I could feel the doorman's eyes burning a target on the back of my head. He would come for me some day when Jimmy Palumbo wasn't around for backup. It knew it wasn't a matter of if, but when.

SEVENTEEN

When I got home I faxed the list Martyr had given me over to Brian Doyle with a note asking him and Devo to get me as much on these guys as possible: addresses, contact info, bios, arrest records, whatever was readily available. I also made sure to say that this was a paying job and I needed the stuff stat. Sure, I could have relied on their loyalty to me since Carmella and I were the first people to hire them and teach them the ropes, but I'd already cashed in my goodwill marker and goodwill favors go only so far. No matter what people say, money talks and bullshit walks and those are the facts of life … Brooklyn style, anyway.

On the ride home from dropping Jimmy back at his car, the echoes of Declan Carney's eloquence were replaced by doubts: doubts about my next steps and how much risk was too much risk. The risk, after all, wasn't mine. I mean, I was taking the risk, yet it was Sashi Bluntstone who would pay if I fucked up. Had I been doing things by the book, I would have driven straight from Martyr's building over to Detective McKenna's office and handed him the list, but I couldn't do it. I worried that the pressure on McKenna to make something happen was too great and he might put on a full court press. The way I figured it was that if Sashi was already dead, it didn't matter what I did. The thing I worried about was McKenna bulling ahead and setting off alarm bells. If Sashi were still alive and that happened, the man who had her might panic and kill her in a rush to destroy evidence of any connection between him and the case. I wasn't about to be the cause of that. The kid's life was worth more than being second-guessed.

Just as I was pouring out a few fingers of Dewars, the call box buzzed.

"Hey, stranger." It was Mary Lambert and I'd be lying if I said I wasn't thrilled to hear her voice.

"Come up."

She wasn't decked out this evening. She wore a white sweater, jeans, and boots with a black leather motorcycle jacket. Damned if it didn't make her look even sexier than she had the last time. I'd forgotten what it was like to be smitten, to see a woman through foggy eyes. I think she could have worn a housedress and slippers and I would have thought her the sexiest woman alive.

"Scotch okay or would you prefer wine?"

"Scotch is fine. A little water in mine, please."

I handed Mary her glass. "I'm glad you're here, but to what do I owe the pleasure?"

"If you can't figure that out, I think you might need some remedial romance classes. I like you, Moe. I like you a lot. You're a gentleman."

Somehow I doubt her assessment would have been the same had she heard the way I spoke to Thompson and Martyr earlier that evening. Still, I wasn't about to argue the point.

"Thank you. I like you a lot too."

"And frankly," she said, picking up the photo of Larry Mac, Rico Tripoli, and me, "I'm pretty fascinated by the story of you three. Let me take you to dinner and you can finish the telling."

"Sorry, I've already eaten."

Her face fell. I'd disappointed her. I didn't like disappointing her.

"That's okay," she lied, and not very well.

"How 'bout I whip you up something to eat and I'll open up some wine and tell you all about the misadventures of the Six-O precinct's Three Stooges?"

That was more like it. Her face brightened. "An omelet?"

"I can manage that. How about cheddar, chorizo, and sweet peppers?"

"Perfect."

"And a bottle of Chianti Classico."

"Better yet."

It wasn't until Mary had made quick work of the omelet and we were both on our third glasses of wine that she brought up the Three Stooges. I gave it to her straight, the bad with the good, and the truth was there was a lot more bad than good. For the first time I said it all aloud. I put it all out there: Larry Mac's wheeling and dealing, his threats, his blackmail, his insatiable ambition, Rico's using me to destroy my future father-in-law's political career, Rico's selling protection to drug gangs, his time in prison.

"In the end," I said, "I guess I didn't know them at all. They were both on the pad while we worked together and involved in the execution of a local drug kingpin named Dexter 'D Rex' Mayweather. Larry killed himself before it all came out, but Rico tried to set me up to be killed and then ran."

"How awful, but there's something in your eyes when you talk about Rico that's different than when you talk about Larry."

"Anger?"

"No, Moe, it's way more than that. There's anger, yes, but ... I don't know. I can't put my finger on it."

"That's because no matter what shit he pulled, I think I still love him. Even now, after all of it, his betrayal of the badge and of me, of the loan he never paid back, of the shit he put me through, I can't say

I don't love him or miss him. A man makes and sheds a lot of friends in his life, but there are a few that leave holes when they're gone. Like I told you, he was once like a brother to me, and you don't stop loving a brother."

"I don't know about that."

"Maybe it's just me. Part of it is that I guess I feel a little responsible for how he turned out."

"Responsible? He was a grown man."

"He had a good first marriage and I sort of helped him blow that apart. I was single then and introduced him to the woman who—you get the picture."

"But you didn't make him unfaithful."

"No, you're right. It's just that Rico was like the kid on the block who never knew what he wanted, so he wanted what everyone wanted or had. It was hard to watch sometimes because he could never quite figure out how to get things. Unlike Larry, Rico had no patience. And the one thing he ever really wanted for himself that he asked for, I denied him."

"What was that?"

"When I got hurt and forced to retire, Rico begged me to be a third partner in our first wine store. I'm not exaggerating, he begged me. And at the time, my brother and I were short and Rico had the extra money we needed, but we turned him down. I always told him that it was Aaron who didn't want him to be a part of it, that the business was going to be dedicated to our dad who was a complete failure in business."

"Is that true?"

"Yes and no. The part about my dad is true, but it wasn't only Aaron who didn't want Rico as a partner. I hid behind my brother to shield myself from the truth that I didn't want Rico involved either.

There's been a lot of times over the years I've thought that things would have been very different if I'd been willing to take a chance on Rico or if I only fought a little harder for him."

"And maybe not." Mary stood up, put her glass down, folded me into her arms, and laid my head on her shoulder. She stroked the back of my neck. "People are responsible for their own lives, Moe."

"I guess, but if it wasn't for Rico, I wouldn't have met Katy and I wouldn't have Sarah."

"Speaking of having someone …"

"Huh?"

"Don't make me pay for those remedial classes," she said, then kissed me softly on the mouth. She took me by the hand. "Show me to the bedroom."

I did, but I couldn't help but look over my shoulder at the picture of Larry, Rico, and me still propped up on the coffee table. Even now, I missed those guys. I didn't suppose that was ever going to change.

EIGHTEEN

When I rolled over in bed, the first hints of sunshine coming through the bedroom window, Mary Lambert was still there. On the other side of the bed, but still there. As long as she hadn't crept silently away in the middle of the night, I would have been okay with her sleeping on the floor. I love how in movies couples manage to sleep in perfect symmetry like synchronized swimmers and wake up folded neatly in each other's arms. *Yeah, right!* Mostly, I liked the way the room still smelled vaguely of sex. The sex itself wasn't atomic. It wasn't disappointing. It was good. It was good because we liked each other. We didn't like each other because the sex was good. Those things are worlds apart. It was what sex between two slightly drunk, slightly nervous adults who didn't really know one another is like. There was a kind of innocence about it that I hadn't felt in a very long time. Of course the real test would come when she got up and the only opinion in the room wouldn't be mine.

I slid over to her side of the bed and wrapped her up in my arms. She didn't say anything, but smiled and pressed herself against me. Five minutes later, I was inside her again. The innocence was still there, but this time the sex was a notch closer to atomic. We were both wet with sweat when she reared back, tensed, and rolled off me. A little while later, she got out of bed without a word and walked slowly towards the bathroom. I enjoyed watching her as she walked. Her back and legs were well-muscled and her ass was a revelation. When I heard the shower, I got up to join her.

We came out of the shower and moved back into the bedroom, still playfully drying each other off, occasionally stopping for a hug and kiss. Then Mary looked away and the spell was broken.

"Your machine's blinking," she said. "You've got a message."

I wanted to believe it was disappointment I saw in Mary's eyes when she noticed the red light flashing on the phone machine. I wanted to believe she wanted the day to last and last the way I wanted it to. But that wasn't what I saw in her eyes. What I saw in her eyes looked like guilt and that wasn't lost on me. It was as if the unexpected red light had caught her off guard and she let her defenses down and beneath them was guilt. Guilt about what, I wondered? Was she married? Committed to someone else? Did I care? When I looked back, the guilt was gone and she was kissing my chest. Still, I wondered. That stopped when the phone rang.

"I better get this," I said, stroking her damp hair.

"Of course, I'll go make myself human." Mary grabbed her bag and disappeared back into the bathroom.

"Hello."

"Dad, where were you? I called about fifteen minutes ago."

"Hey, kiddo. I was in the shower. What's up? Did something happen to—"

"I need to talk to you."

"Is it about Sashi?"

"In a way."

"Go ahead, I'm listening."

"No, Dad, in person."

"Come on over."

"How about New Carmens in a half hour?"

"Okay. A half hour. If you get there before me, get us a booth."

"I love you."

"I've waited a long time to hear you say that again, Sarah."

The line went silent. I put the phone back in its cradle. I guess I was still sitting there looking at the phone when Mary came back out of the bathroom, a towel wrapped tightly around her, another covering her hair, and her face made up.

"Is everything all right?" she asked.

"It's my daughter. She wants to talk to me. Would you like to meet her?"

There it was again, that thing in her eyes. "Someday, but I've got to get back to my apartment and get to an appointment in the city. I've got a presentation to prepare as well."

Maybe that's what I was seeing, guilt over blowing off her responsibilities.

"I hope last night and this morning were worth a little rushing around," I said.

"Oh, it was worth a lot more than that." She leaned up, cupped my chin, and kissed me ever so gently on the lips. Then, with the swipe of her thumb, she brushed the lipstick residue off my mouth. "It was worth a lot."

"I have to get ready to meet her."

"Go ahead. I'll get dressed in the living room and let myself out."

"Call me."

"I will." She waved, winked, and turned to the living room.

●　.　　●

Sarah was waiting at a small corner banquette, a cup of coffee in front of her. She was nervously flicking her index finger against the thick white porcelain cup and watching the small ripples spread out along the surface of the steaming coffee. I had seen her like this only a few times in her life, always when she had something to confess. There was the time in second grade when she had shut the lights out in the gym, but her friend Megan got blamed for it. I found her that day after school, sitting at the kitchen table lost in thought, tapping her milk glass much as she was tapping the coffee cup now.

"What is it, kiddo?"

"I did a bad thing, Daddy."

We went to the principal's office together the next morning.

Then there was the time she was fifteen and had the drinking and pot party at the house when Katy and I were on a cruise. A few of the guys had gotten their teenage beer muscles on and got into a brawl and the neighbors called the cops. That time, like this time, she brought me to New Carmens to tell me what had happened. But the worst time was in her senior year in high school and her period was late and she wrongly, but understandably, thought she was pregnant by a boy she'd broken up with weeks before. Again, she'd told me here.

"I got a funny feeling you're not gonna tell me that you got Megan Costello in trouble for shutting out the gym lights."

She fought it, but couldn't stop herself from smiling. "You remember that?"

"I remember everything about you, Sarah. You're the most important thing in my life. You always have been. So what is it? What's up?"

"It's about what happened to Sashi."

"That much I figured out."

"Max and Candy lied to the police."

"About what?"

"Candy made me promise not to say anything, Dad. I owed so much to her. She was like the big sister I always wanted. I couldn't, you know … And Sashi is her kid, so I had to give my word."

"Come on, Sarah, tell me. If I can keep it quiet, I will."

"You can't. It's too big to keep quiet anymore. That's why I came to you because you'll know how to fix it."

"I won't know if I can until you tell me."

She bowed her head and looked away. I could see Sarah wanted to say something; her lips moved, but she couldn't seem to find the words. I figured I'd try to help.

"Did Max and Candy fake this whole thing?"

Sarah stared at me as if I were speaking Chinese. "No, Dad, nothing like that."

"Do they know who did it?"

"No, but there *was* a ransom demand," Sarah said.

"What?"

"There was a—"

"I heard you. How much? When? Did they—"

"That night, the night Sashi was taken, right after Candy called the police. The call came in on Max's cell phone. The caller used one of those distortion boxes like in the movies, so they can't even be sure it was a man's voice."

"But they think it was a man?"

"They think so."

"What did he say?"

"I don't know exactly. All I know is that he wanted money or he would do things to Sashi, horrible things. Candy couldn't bring herself to tell me exactly what was said."

"Did they pay?"

"Some of it," she whispered.

"What does that mean?"

"He wanted two million dollars, but Max and Candy, they're—"

"—broke. I know. They have about ten thousand dollars in the bank."

"But how could you know that?" The look on my daughter's face was a mixture of surprise and disgust, of pride and anger.

"I had to know it," I said. "My interest in this is Sashi, not Max and Candy. Everybody lies, Sarah: clients, cops, PIs, everybody. And I guess I was right, Max and Candy have been lying from the start. I had to know what anyone involved possibly had to gain if Sashi went missing."

"Still …"

"Hey, kiddo, it was your idea to get me mixed up in this. You don't get to judge."

"I'm sorry, Dad."

"That's okay. Keep going."

"There's not much else to tell except that Candy dropped fifty thousand dollars off in a garbage can at Caumsett Park a few days after Sashi was taken."

"They don't have a pot to piss in. Where did they get fifty thous—"

"I gave them some of it," she said, looking rather sheepish. "I think Randy Junction gave them some, and someone else, but I don't know who or how much."

"Did you know Candy was sleeping with Junction?"

Sarah hesitated, then said, "I knew about it."

"We may have to discuss that soon, but for now, I've got to call Detective McKenna and figure out a way to tell him and keep your name out of it."

"Don't, Dad, just tell him the truth."

"And maybe fuck up your career and your life because you were trying to do the right thing? No. That's not gonna happen." I stood up and threw a twenty on the table. "Eat something and go about your business as if it was just another day."

"I don't know if I can do that."

"You're my kid. You're Katy Maloney's kid. You can do it. You have to do it. And if the cops come to you, don't say a word without me or a lawyer in the room. Promise me."

"I promise."

"You did the right thing by telling me, kiddo." I leaned over and kissed her forehead. "But why tell me now? What happened to make you come to me now?"

"It's almost four weeks, Dad. I may not have been a cop or a PI, but I can hear the clock ticking too."

"It's okay. I'll fix it."

Walking away, I didn't look back.

As I rushed to my car, I felt sick to my stomach. I felt sick because I had visited my sins upon my only child. She was a secret keeper too and I knew there was only grief at the end of that road.

NINETEEN

When I got back to my apartment, there were several sheets of paper sitting in the bin of my fax machine. Apparently the promise of cash money had motivated Devo and Brian Doyle to burn the midnight and pre-dawn oil. PIs are like actors. No matter how good times are, they don't tend to turn down paying jobs. I scanned the faxes, but put them aside to call McKenna. On the ride over, I figured out how to play it to keep Sarah's name out of it. My guess was that even if McKenna didn't totally buy it, he would be too busy to realize it or care.

"Almost four weeks," Sarah said, but time was fluid and its viscosity was dependent upon your point of view. To McKenna it was an eternity. To the kidnapper—that's what this was, a kidnapping—it might not seem that long. If the fifty grand wasn't enough, Sashi might still be alive. Her continued good health would be in his best interest. On the other hand, if he panicked or if he decided to quit while he was ahead, she was dead and all the machinations of all the other players were moot. If Sashi were still alive, I couldn't imagine what the month in captivity felt like.

When I got McKenna on the phone, he sounded upbeat. I thought he might somehow have gotten word of the ransom demand and pay-off. I was wrong. He had other morbidly good news.

"The teddy bear that was left in your car was hers, Sashi's," he said. "The parents IDed it. The kid's beagle had chewed its leg up a little bit when she was younger and the teeth marks were there. We're running DNA tests now to confirm it."

"They didn't notice the teddy bear was gone all this time?"

"Guess not."

"I got something for you too."

"What?"

"It's a guess, but I think I know what they've been hiding from us."

"What's that?"

"My bet is there was a ransom demand."

"Get the fuck out of here! The kid was swiped, they paid ransom money, and what, it slipped their minds?"

"I think they were scared, McKenna. What if they'd already called you when they got the demand? It doesn't take much to figure out why they'd keep this between them."

"Bullshit."

"Go talk to them and see if I'm not right. I feel it in my *kishkas*."

"Are you kidding me? If I acted on every gut feeling I had, I'd still be riding around in a fucking patrol car or giving out speeding tickets on the LIE."

"I'm an investigator too, remember? I got a feeling and it couldn't hurt to confront them with it like you already know it's true."

"You got a point, Prager. Even if you're wrong, it might shake 'em up a little and get them to give up what they've really been hiding. Maybe between that and the shit we get from the bear and your car, we can finally make some progress."

"At this point, it's worth a try, right?"

"Okay, all right. I'll let you know how it goes."

"Thanks."

That crap I fed him about this all being one big hunch might not insulate Sarah forever, but I hoped it would work long enough so that it wouldn't matter in the end. I was doing a lot of hoping lately and that was always a dangerous thing.

When I got off the phone with the detective, I made myself some coffee and started looking through the pages Doyle had faxed me. These new developments—the teddy bear, the ransom demand and payment—would help me fly even further under the radar than I had been flying and I just needed to work out who I was going to see and when. It was difficult to know how to do a threat assessment with cowards who hid their identities with screen names, people who slammed the work of a little girl and the girl herself, but who were too frightened to stand up behind the venom they spewed. I figured I would see the people Martyr suggested first, the ones whose names he underlined, and then I'd take a look at the personal data of the rest and go from there. That's how I figured to do it until I saw a name and an address I recognized. Now I had my first stop. I had a funny feeling the rest of it wasn't going to be that easy.

● . ●

The house was pretty fucking impressive all right: big, brick, and showy with a semi-circular cobblestone drive and white columns reaching only halfway to heaven. The low-slung hedges were perfectly trimmed and the dormant, carpet-like lawn was dotted with just enough leftover leaves to make it look as if they were placed there by the hired help to lend it an air of nature but without the mess. It was just the kind of lawn that screamed to someone from Brooklyn, "Piss on me." And believe me, in the mood I was in, I was sorely tempted. I parked my gray rental at an awkward angle so it would discourage anyone else from coming up the drive. Like I said, I was in that kind of mood. Call me petty. I'd been called worse, much worse.

The front door chimes weren't quite as loud as the Vatican's on Easter Sunday, but they were close. The pope didn't come to the door. Apparently, I didn't even rate a parish priest. A chubby, rather pleasant-faced black woman in her forties in a nurse's get-up came to the door instead.

"How can I help you?" Her voice lilted with the song of Haiti.

"Mrs. Barrows-Willingham, please."

"Who is calling?"

"Just give her this, okay?" I handed the nurse a folded piece of paper and a business card. "She'll understand."

"*D'accord*, okay. *Ne quittez pas*, just a moment, please."

She disappeared, closing the door behind her and locking it. Nothing so welcoming as a closing door and a deadbolt clicking shut in your face. I wasn't fretting over it. The lady of the house would be coming to fetch me soon enough. The deadbolt clicked open and the mighty glass and wood door pulled back once again. Standing there in all her pinched glory was Mrs. Sonia Barrows-Willingham, only she hadn't come to fetch me. No, instead, she stepped out of the house, pulling the door closed behind her. She smelled of cigarettes and decay. I guess I half expected her to look scared at being found out. Wrong again. She looked positively thrilled … well, as much as a dour-faced woman could look thrilled.

"Oh, I've been a naughty girl, haven't I, Mr. Prager? Have you come to spank me, to threaten me, or blackmail me? Whichever it is, please get to it, I've got a husband up on the third floor who insists upon dying by the inch and he's in a particular amount of distress today."

She was good, Mrs. Barrows-Willingham, very good. She was prodding me, probing to see just what kind of manipulation I was susceptible to. I wasn't going to make it easy for her. This clenched fist of a woman who had the largest collection of Sashi Bluntstone's works used her spare time to go online and rip Sashi apart. Her blog was called Sushi Cuntstone Cooks and offered recipes, the ingredients of which included raw bits of Sashi Bluntstone's anatomy. And the dishes were served on trays and in Bento boxes inspired by Sashi's paintings.

"Sushi Cuntstone, very cute, Mrs. Barrows-Willingham. I particularly like your recipes for Sashi-me."

She laughed or made a little barking noise, which I supposed passed for laughter, and looked at me I was like a main course. "Candy told me about you, that she was thinking of hiring you. You know, Mr. Prager, I get the impression that she has a father fixation on you, but one with a rather disturbing sexual element to it."

"We weren't talking about Candy." I made sure to stay calm. "We were discussing your twisted hobby."

"Oh, do grow up, Mr. Prager. Welcome to the new millennium. Sashi Bluntstone as an entity is as much my creation as any of her paintings are hers. You might ask sweet Candy about that when next you two speak. I arranged for Sashi's first showings. I bought her first paintings. I created a market for her work. Me, not that buffoon Max, not Candy, not that fool Randolph Junction. Me! And in this new age, there is no market without controversy. Yes, Mr. Prager, I even helped create that. Who was it, do you suppose, who whispered in the ears of people like Nathan Martyr, a man who in spite of his legendary shortcomings and lack of talent as an artist, worked and studied very hard to achieve whatever success he managed? Can you even imagine how painful it is for the many worthy artists in the world who toil in poverty and rejection to swallow the success of the Sashi Bluntstones and Thomas Kinkades of the world?"

"I think I can." I wasn't lying. I remembered the bitter taste in my mouth when guys who couldn't find their own dicks without a road map made detective. No one said life was fair and the job was even less fair than the rest of life. So I had to swallow it as the parade of gold shields passed me by. Yeah, I knew exactly how those other artists felt.

"Well, then you must understand the need and inevitability of blogs like Sushi Cuntstone Cooks and all the others. Resentment, jealousy, envy are in endless supply and they help drive the market. It's part of an investment strategy, nothing more."

"Okay, I get that. I also get that Sashi's paintings have plummeted in value over the last years and I look around and I see who has the most to gain from her disappearance. That would be you, Mrs. Barrows-Willingham."

"Indeed. An astute assessment on your part. My collection is now valued almost as highly as it was before the disappearance. In fact, I've recently added to it."

"I know," I said, "Forty grand worth."

That caught her by surprise. "How could you know that? Did that ass Junction—"

"No, I was standing right there in the gallery, a few feet from you as the two of you bargained. I agree with you, that painting you bought is no 'Red Waves.'"

"I underestimated you, Mr. Prager. Maybe Candy was right to seek your help. You seem a resourceful man. Try not to be big-headed about it, though. My husband was once a most resourceful man. Now he defecates into a bag and has a catheter shoved into his bladder through his penis."

"Fair enough, so let me just ask. Did you—"

"No, I had nothing to do with Sashi's disappearance. Once she was a delightful little girl. She has, however, become a rather dreadful and morbid child. I confess to feeling that about her, but I have no wish for harm to come to her, however much I might profit from it."

"Oh, so you have your limits?"

"Some, yes. As much as I would profit, the money is almost beside the point. The ground under the garage on this property is worth more than all of Sashi's paintings at their highest value. My husband is quite wealthy and I didn't exactly enter the marriage as a pauper. So, no, Mr. Prager, I do so hate to disappoint you, but I had nothing to do with Sashi's going missing."

"Did you know that she was kidnapped, that there was a ransom demand?"

Again, she seemed caught off guard, as if she were looking for a left jab and I landed flush with a straight right to her liver. "I've heard nothing about that."

"You will. My guess is the story will break later today. Even so," I said, "it means she may not be dead and all the value that got built back up will vanish." She didn't like that and I piled it on. "What's the matter, Sonia, I thought it wasn't about the money?"

"Please excuse me, I have to get back inside."

"One more thing."

"If you must."

"If Candy came to you for ransom money, would you help her?"

A crooked line appeared where Barrows-Willingham's mouth used to be. "We will just have to see about that, won't we. Good day to you, Mr. Prager."

I stood stone still and watched her retreat back into her house. I actually reached around and touched the butt of my .38. I thought about shooting her through the door, but realized that as much sawdust would come out of her when the bullet passed through as would come out of the door.

TWENTY

Jimmy Palumbo was waiting out front of his house at four so we could head into the city without wasting time. While his place was a bit worse for wear with several mismatched cedar shakes on the front facade, a missing downspout on the garage gutter, the lawn ragged, and the bushes untidy and overgrown, it wouldn't take much to get it back into nice shape. And though it wasn't in the same class as the Barrows-Willinghams' massive Gold Coast manor, Jimmy's house was on a fairly secluded, lovely street south of Montauk Highway in Babylon. It was also appealing because all the lots down here had docks in their back-yards on West Babylon Creek that led out past Santapogue Point and into the Great South Bay, Fire Island, and the Atlantic beyond. I knew the area pretty well because one of our biggest wine customers belonged to a nearby yacht club and had taken Aaron and me out on his boat a few times.

"Nice location," I said.

"Needs a lotta work, but since the divorce …" He didn't explain further and he didn't really have to.

"Got a boat?"

His face, somewhat sour when discussing the house, broke into a big smile.

"Only reason I still live down here."

"Tell me about her."

"A Chris-Craft forty-two-foot Continental that I bought with part of my signing bonus. Three hundred and twenty horsepower twin engines. She's a beaut. She needs some work too, but not as much as the house. The house and the boat were the only things I got in the divorce. My wife pretty much took everything else. She even turned the girls against me. They never call or write and when I make plans to visit, they're always away."

"Why not sell the house? Even with the downturn in the market, you could get big money for it."

"What would I do with my boat? You know how much it would cost me to keep her somewheres else?"

I dropped it and turned on news radio. I could see the conversation was upsetting him and I needed him to be on his game. On the other hand, a bit of surliness probably wouldn't hurt since I had no intention of making nice to the people on Martyr's list. If we needed to twist arms, we weren't going to do it metaphorically. I told Jimmy as much. He didn't blink.

The radio filled the car with the usual background noise. Retailers were hoping for a big holiday shopping season. *There was that phrase again.* There was a war in Iraq. *No kidding?* Another one in Afghanistan. *Gee, I almost forgot.* John Lennon was dead for twenty-six years. I paid attention to that story. Lennon used to shop at City On The Vine when he wanted to buy gifts of fancy wine for friends. I remembered the time he came into the store near closing and playfully ripped Paul McCartney's songwriting skills. I keep the picture of John and me on the wall in my office. I hadn't looked at it for a very long time. I needed to look to remind myself that time passes and we leave things behind, even some things we shouldn't. Then, I thought, that wasn't really true, not for me. That's what other people did. I never really leave anything behind, ever. On more than one occasion, I wished I could.

What I didn't hear on the radio was anything new about Sashi Bluntstone. I knew Sarah hadn't lied to me, but I wondered if *she* had been lied to. It was pretty clear to me that Max and Candy weren't exactly reliable and were fairly desperate. Generally speaking, that's not a good combination. Was it possible they were so hard up for money that they concocted the ransom demand just to squeeze cash out of their friends? Everyone else seemed willing to use Sashi's disappearance to their own ends, why not her parents? In my life I had seen the best in people, but I'd seen plenty more of the worst. If Max and Candy *had* manufactured the ransom demand, it would set an all-time low and would go a long way in convincing me that the bottom is much deeper than the top is high.

Then my cell phone rang and McKenna saved me from myself.

"Yeah."

"Your hunch was right on, Prager. They paid fifty grand. Dropped it in a garbage can up in a state park in Huntington."

"Why aren't I hearing about it on the news?"

"We're going big with it tomorrow: a 1:00 PM press conference, new AMBER Alerts, whole nine yards. You wanna be there?"

"Nah. I've been a part of those circuses before and it always comes back to bite me."

"I figured I'd ask."

"And I appreciate that. Aren't you even a little worried that this may force the guy's hand? He may panic and—"

"Wasn't really my decision. The brass took it upon themselves to make the rest of the world think we're doing something besides chasing our own tails. Anyway, my bet is the kid's dead and no matter what we do or don't do, it won't matter, but maybe this way we can at least flush the bastard out of hiding."

I said, "You may be right."

"But what if I'm not?"

"That's the big question, isn't it? If it's any comfort to you, McKenna, I know what that particular purgatory is like."

"I'll let you know if it helps. By the way," he said before I could click off my Bluetooth, "if you think I believe in hunches, look under your pillow tonight and maybe you'll find five dollars."

"What's that supposed to mean?"

"It means you should thank your daughter for standing up and you have my word I'll keep her name out of this."

He hung up.

"What's going on?" Jimmy wanted to know.

"I guess I might as well tell you since the story's gonna hit tomorrow."

"What story?"

"Sashi Bluntstone's disappearance was a kidnapping after all. There was a ransom demand and a partial payoff that the parents didn't bother telling the cops about. We better get lucky tonight, because things are about to change. The cops are gonna try and flush the kidnapper out."

Jimmy fell silent. He understood what I understood. This might be our last best chance to make things happen before all hell broke loose.

●　.　●

Well, so much for brick manor houses and nice suburban homes on secluded streets. John Tierney's place gave shitboxes a bad name. Way at the ass end of Gerritsen Beach, the water lapping at the back deck, the deep color of the siding more a product of black mold than of dark paint, the rickety old house looked to be a single snapped nail away from total collapse. Jimmy took one look at the state of the house, the aluminum foil covering the upstairs windows and the plywood covering what should have been the downstairs windows and doors, and said: "Abandoned?"

"Seems that way," I agreed, but shook my head no, pointing up at the nearest utility pole. It didn't take an electrician to see that somebody had hacked into the local electrical supply and cable service. "Come on, let's go," I said loud enough for anyone in the house to hear.

We got in the car, drove down the block, and turned the corner. We parked.

"Doesn't make sense," Jimmy said. "If this is the guy's address, why's he living like a squatter?"

"Good question. Let's go get some answers."

Two minutes later, Jimmy Palumbo and I were working our way back down the street on foot, using parked cars and light poles for cover. When I reached the corner of the vacant lot abutting Tierney's shithole, I cut towards the water and crept along the shore towards the back deck. From there, I moved to the side porch. I hadn't grown up very far from here. In fact, I didn't live more than ten minutes from where I now stood, but Gerritsen Beach had always been a bit of a mystery to me, kind of like Breezy Point in Rockaway. My dad used to call Breezy Point the Irish Riviera because it was a tight-knit enclave of cops and firemen on the water at the western end of Rockaway. It was a different world. This part of Gerritsen Beach had been blue collar Irish when I was a kid. And not unlike Jimmy Palumbo's house, the places around here had access to the water and the Atlantic was just on the other side of the Belt Parkway.

The plan was for me to get into the house and either grab Tierney or flush him out into Jimmy Palumbo's welcoming arms. Too bad Tierney had different ideas. When I was about two steps up on the stairs to the side porch, a human tornado bowled me over, sending my .38 flying and my head bouncing off the railing.

"Fuck!"

Then there was a splash. I turned and saw someone swimming furiously in the dark water. With my brain rattled and night having fallen, keeping track of the swimmer wasn't easy. Jimmy tore past me, dropping his Sig by me as he went. Christ, I thought, he must have been tremendously fast for a big man when his knees actually worked. There was another splash, a louder one, and he too disappeared into the darkness. I got up, brushed myself off, collected the guns, and tried to get my head back on straight. I was too old for this shit. I had a nice lump under my hair, just above my right ear. Less than a minute later, Jimmy emerged from the water, dragging the exhausted John Tierney by the scruff of his neck.

"Come on, bring him inside."

The interior of Tierney's place was a time capsule, an eerie cross between a crypt and cathedral. It reeked of mold and mildew and it was cold enough so that we could see our own breath. The furniture was turn-of-the-century stuff, but in immaculate shape. The seat cushions were protected by heavy duty plastic slipcovers that had yellowed with the years. There were delicate lace curtains hanging on the inside of the boarded windows, dusty fringed lampshades, and white lace doilies under porcelain knickknacks. And there were crucifixes … everywhere. Jesus Christ suffered a lot in here. His passion was the central design theme. Every available inch of wall space was covered in paintings of haloed saints, all with appropriately beatific smiles and prayerful hands. Only these saints all bled from the ears and their eyes were solid black. John Tierney's handiwork, I imagined. We dragged Tierney upstairs, but he was getting some of his strength back and struggled a bit. One smack in the back of the head from Jimmy calmed him right down. Tierney babbled incoherently and crossed himself constantly. The babbling was a jumble of Latin prayers sprinkled with a few recognizable words, names, and phrases. He seemed rather fond of the CIA, FBI, Hamas, Satan, and, incredibly, the name Sashi. That stopped us in our tracks.

We sat Tierney down in a chair in a bedroom that had an electric heater going full blast against the chill. I told Jimmy to go stand by the heater and dry off as best he could. There was a flat screen TV. The TV was on but aimed so that the screen faced the aluminum-foiled windows. There was a shortwave radio, an old police scanner, and a laptop computer, but only a computer. There was no printer, no fax, no phone. The walls, ceiling, and floor were flat black and on each surface Tierney had painted a huge, bloody-faced Jesus, his eyes as black as the saints. I'd be lying to you if I said the Jesus heads didn't creep me out.

You didn't need a PhD in clinical psychology to figure out that John Tierney was schizophrenic and that, if he had meds, he hadn't taken them recently. The house, his mad ramblings, all went a long way in explaining the wild, meandering comments Tierney posted following Nathan Martyr's blog entries. Tierney's posts often alluded to the ritual mutilation of Sashi Bluntstone and the use of her blood like that of a Passover lamb to ward off the angel of death. His psychosis didn't mean he didn't have Sashi or hadn't had her or hadn't killed her, but I doubted it. I could see that Jimmy's presence in particular was making Tierney want to crawl out of his own skin. The last thing I needed was for him to go apeshit and for any of us to get hurt.

"Jimmy, why don't you go take a look around, okay? John and I have to talk about some stuff that you can't hear."

"You sure?"

"Yeah, and close the door behind you."

That calmed Tierney down a little bit, but once Jimmy left, he seemed only vaguely aware of my presence. He was in a very different place than me and his odd affect gave new meaning to the phrase *you can't get there from here*. I tried reaching him anyway.

"John," I said, "you've written some pretty awful things about Sashi Bluntstone."

"Satan."

That was promising.

"Is Sashi Satan?"

"Hamas is coming through the printers. Can't you see them?"

So much for promising.

"Does Sashi have anything to do with the printers? If you killed Sashi, would her blood stop Hamas from coming through the printers?"

"St. Peter. St. Peter. St. Peter," Tierney said, making the sign of the cross at me. Then he mumbled something I couldn't make out at all. He got off the chair and kissed the floor at my feet. "St. Peter. St. Peter. St. Peter."

We kept going round and round like that for another twenty minutes or so, but it got me nothing but a few more blessings and foot kisses. I found myself feeling nothing but sorry for John Tierney. Jimmy knocked.

"Come in," I said.

"It's pretty dark in the house, but I didn't find anything but more crucifixes and paintings."

"Okay, let's go."

I nodded for Jimmy to go first.

"Sorry to bother you, John," I said. "I hope you find some peace or whatever it is you're looking for. I just have to find Sashi."

He didn't move a muscle, his eyes still in that other place, but when I got to his bedroom door, he called to me.

"I didn't take her," he said in a calm coherent voice. "Her blood remains in the vessel of her body."

I made sure not to turn back around and then just let myself out.

Back in my car, I was quiet. Jimmy wasn't.

"Do me a favor and take me home. You don't gotta pay me, but I'm freezing my balls off and I got work tomorrow."

"Sure, no problem. I'm shot for the night anyway," I said. "And don't worry about the cash. You earned it. You up for this tomorrow night?"

"No problem, except maybe I'll bring a Speedo and some extra clothes."

Neither one of us said much after that.

TWENTY-ONE

The drive back from Babylon was the most hopeless hour I'd spent in a very very long time and it served as a cruel reminder of why I got out of the business of poking around in other people's lives. Lives, even the ones that looked so orderly and beautiful from the outside, were messy, complicated things, often very ugly and painful things. And then there was the miraculous and the magical. Most people never experience either one. I'd had my brush with the miraculous on an April day over thirty years ago when I looked up and saw a rooftop water tank and thought, *That's where she is! That's where Marina Conseco will be! In one of those.* I was right that one time, but there wasn't going to be a water tank miracle this go-round. I saw the futility of what I was trying to do reflected in the hopelessly lost eyes of John Tierney. What the hell was I doing looking for Sashi Bluntstone in such a place as that? She was dead. McKenna knew it. Even Max and Candy seemed to know. Was I the only one who refused to see the obvious?

When I dragged myself out of my car, my head throbbing from where it banged against the side porch railing, I was ready to pack it all in. So I had come to my senses and realized, what, that I wasn't going to set the world right with some singularly miraculous redemptive act? Who was I kidding? What did I have to go back to? What was ahead of me, endless and endlessly boring days of hiding myself in my office? Days of planning new grand openings? Days of arguing with municipalities over the size of our store signage? Shopkeeping, is that really what I longed to return to? I was old and I was as lost in my way as poor John Tierney. At least he had enemies, real or imagined. My enemy was me. Then I heard Mary Lambert's voice and all the self-pity receded.

"God, Moe, what happened to you?"

"Come on upstairs and I'll tell you all about it."

Except I didn't, not at first. First I let Mary hold me in her arms and tell me everything was going to be all right. I was so smitten, I think I almost believed her. Then, when I cleaned myself up and put some ice to my head and had a drink, I told her about the case. I told her about who I was, who I really was.

"You see, Mary, the thing is, I've been selfish my whole life. I wanted life to be exciting. I wanted it to be about more than making money and settling down. I talked to you about Larry and Rico, but I didn't talk much about me. I didn't tell you about how I got my first wife killed or how I lost my daughter and a son that never had a chance to know me."

"Now you're just beating yourself up."

"Maybe you're right. Maybe I am."

"Sure you are," she said. "You're frustrated. You think there's a dead girl out there somewhere that needed saving and you couldn't save her."

"I don't know where I would have been tonight if you didn't show up at my door."

She stepped very close to me and put her hand over my mouth. "Let's not talk anymore, not now. Can't we just be happy I'm here?"

I shook my head yes, but as she turned to the bedroom I saw that thing in her eyes again and this time I was sure it was guilt. Then I fell so deeply into her that I didn't question it.

In the morning, the sheets were cold on her side of the bed. Mary Lambert was gone. And though I couldn't possibly explain how I knew she would be, I knew she would be. The sex wasn't any less satisfying. On the contrary, there was a depth and complexity to it that we hadn't achieved during the previous night's awkward unfamiliarity. Yet it was the sort of depth and complexity that only comes from pain. I knew something about that. It was a major feature of sex with Carmella. She made physical art of her pain and anguish and it was intoxicating. Even now, seven years removed from her touch, I found myself craving her, but what made her so addictive in bed also made her impossible to live with in the light of day. I didn't know Mary Lambert well enough to make that judgment about her. Now I felt I never would. There was an air of permanence in her leaving. What there wasn't was a note. I was at least thankful for that. It gave me hope, fragile and torturous as it was.

I showered and got dressed and decided that I needed to keep myself busy. Jews don't generally buy into those rather puritanical adages about idle hands and the devil. I certainly didn't, but today was an exception. I knew I had to keep moving or I wouldn't be able to keep it all from crashing in on me. I needed to push away the feel of Mary Lambert's kisses, the easy lock-and-key way I slid inside her, her scent. I needed to run away from John Tierney's eyes. John Donne wrote that no man is an island. John Donne never met John Tierney. And the only way I knew to keep busy, to keep myself moving, was to work the case. I certainly wasn't going to sit in my office and stare at old pictures of dead rock stars.

TWENTY-TWO

Jeff Fisher was more like it. He wasn't schizophrenic. He wasn't lost. He was just an asshole. And he insisted upon proving it with nearly every word that came out of his mouth. Fisher was an adjunct professor in figure drawing and art history at Pratt who had a website that made Nathan Martyr's seem like a Sashi Bluntstone fan site. He was exactly the type of frustrated, resentful scumbag Sonia Barrows-Willingham had described. A man who had envisioned himself as the next great thing to come down the pike, but who wound up teaching the next generation of resentful bastards instead. The problem was, Fisher was nearly as big as Jimmy Palumbo and not nearly as friendly.

"Get the fuck away from me, dickhead," he said, when I asked if I could step inside his basement apartment in Greenpoint.

"What's the problem, your mommy and daddy don't let you have visitors?"

"Fuck you."

"That's quite a vocabulary you got there, Professor Fisher. You pick that up at the Rhode Island School of Design?"

Knowing where he went to school got his attention, but not so that he was going to let me in to talk.

"Big deal. You could get that info off the school website. Now get the fuck outta here or I'll have to make you."

"You think so, huh?"

His answer was a stiff arm to my chest that knocked me back to the steps. My response was to show him my .38.

"You wanna try that again?" I asked.

He eyes looked scared, but the rest of him remained pretty calm. "No, I think I'll just call the cops."

"Do that. I used to be a cop and trust me, they'll take my word over yours."

"Gee, I'm just shaking in my shoes."

"You're not wearing shoes, Mr. Fisher."

He actually looked down, then put his hand on the door. "Get outta here."

"I wouldn't do that. Shut the door, I mean. Because if you do, I think I might have to let your dean at Pratt and your neighbors know about your record."

His hand stopped. His face went from angry to blank to scared, very scared. Now I had his attention.

"I think this is where you invite me in. Or maybe I should start screaming about what a bad boy you used to be at the top of my lungs. What do you think? She was what, thirteen years old?"

"I was thirteen too, goddammit!" he growled. "We were just exploring and kissing. It was a mutual thing. Don't tell me you didn't feel any girls up before you were eighteen."

"We aren't talking about me."

"Besides, how the fuck did you—"

"In or out, Professor Fisher?"

He opened the door and retreated into the apartment. It wasn't a bad place: a mix of modern and Scandinavian furniture, bare wood floors, a drawing table in the center of the living room, art supplies scattered all around it, walls covered in art that wasn't all that different from Sashi's.

"Those records are supposed to be sealed," he said, lighting up a cigarette.

"Sealed, not expunged, Professor. Ain't technology grand?"

"What do you want?"

"Where's Sashi Bluntstone?"

He choked with laughter, little puffs of smoke giving form to his amusement. "You're kidding me, right? Look around. Where do you think I'm keeping her, in my fucking pocket? This place consists of this room, a bedroom, and a bathroom. I got people upstairs who never leave. I don't have a car. Go, take a look around while I finish my cigarette."

I looked. Nothing.

"You happy now?"

"No," I said, and introduced his testicles to my right foot. "Now I'm happy, asshole. Take that website down or I'll create one of my own about you. Understand?" He shook his head yes. "Today!"

I waited around until he started breathing again, then I left.

The next two stops involved less violence, but got me to the same place. Nowhere. I hated to admit it, Sonia Barrows-Willingham was right. The antipathy for Sashi was founded on the study, hard work, and sacrifice her detractors had invested in careers that barely put food in their mouths or paid the rent.

My fourth stop of the day was my last stop. It was at a tenth-floor pigsty in a big faceless apartment house in Alphabet City on the lower East Side of Manhattan. The person who lived here used the screen name Leonardo when posting comments on Martyr's blog, but the information Devo got me showed the name on the lease was Delia Parker. Whoever lived here, Delia, Leonardo, or Michelangelo, he or she didn't have much love for Sashi Bluntstone. There didn't seem to be a whole lot of love for her anywhere in this world.

I pushed the black, rectangular doorbell just below the peephole on the metal door to the apartment. No one stirred, but I sensed someone was home. Muted music drifted under the door riding piggyback on the stink of cigarette smoke and dirty diapers. I put my knuckles to the door and the rapping echoed along the hallway. Feet shuffled on the other side of the door and I felt an eye on me. I showed it my old badge.

"Open it, now!" I wasn't in the mood for coaxing and cajoling.

Locks clicked. The door pulled back.

"Delia Parker?"

"Yeah, yeah, what is it, Officer?" she twitched more than asked between nervous puffs on her cigarette. "I got a sick baby to take care of here."

Nearly six feet tall and weighing no more than ninety pounds, Delia Parker was a human scarecrow. Her blond hair was dull and lifeless, uncleaned and unbrushed. Her skin was red and blotchy and her gums had so receded that her smoke-yellowed teeth looked enormous in her hollow head. She was dressed in dirty, loose jeans and a t-shirt. She didn't even try to hide the raw track marks running up and down both her arms. Delia Parker was a tweaker, a crystal meth addict and, by the look of her, she wasn't going to be one for very much longer. She smelled like death and the next person who showed up at her door holding official credentials was apt to be from the medical examiner. At that moment, I couldn't have known just how horribly right I was going to be. I put my badge away.

"May I come in? I'm not here to bust your chops about the crank."

She almost seemed disappointed by that. I think she knew she was beyond helping herself and wanted desperately to be rescued. But we all want that, don't we? What must it have been like, I wondered, to watch yourself drowning? Delia stepped back and shut the door when I stepped in.

"What then?"

"Sashi Bluntstone."

She began laughing wildly, her whole body shaking. The laugh became a cough and the cough became vomit. The vomit was mostly yellowy-green mucus and blood. She fell to her knees. I found a towel, the least dirty one in the bathroom, and wiped her up. I put her down on her side to rest. Then I realized that that much noise would have woken up almost any baby. I left Delia where she laid and ran through the apartment looking for the baby. I found it in a filthy crib in the corner of the bedroom. The baby boy, blue and unbreathing, cold to the touch, was dead. His mother wasn't the only soul in this place beyond help. I dialed 911, then sat down on the bed and waited, too numb to cry.

TWENTY-THREE

I didn't listen to the press conference. I guess I couldn't have even if I wanted to or had the strength to listen. I was too busy explaining myself to the long list of New York City officials who drifted in and out of the tenth-floor apartment. First there were the two uniforms, then the EMTs, then the detectives, then the ME's man, then the housing rep, then it was the detectives again and again and again. That I was a retired cop and a lapsed-license PI helped, but not so much. The days of a badge getting you a pass were over. The necessity and art of ass covering had always been part of the job, but now with intense media scrutiny, cell phone cameras, and *Gotcha!* blogs, a smart cop didn't give too many breaks to anyone just because he was once on the job. Maybe a little courtesy, but no breaks. That was probably a good thing, but it sure as shit didn't feel like it to me.

Delia Parker's story wasn't much different than the rest of the Sashi haters. She was a promising artist who had come to New York after 9/11 to find out if she could make it on the main stage. She was an MICA graduate. I'd found her diploma on the floor next to her bed under some used condoms. It wasn't tough to figure out what she'd been doing for drug money and, by the wasted look of her, she'd been doing a lot of it and not for very much a pop. Beneath the diploma I found photographs of the pre-meth Delia and her family. She was pretty once. She had been someone's daughter and sister. She looked like her mom. Her sister looked more like her dad. I wondered about them. What did they think had become of their girl? Did they even know about the baby? They would know soon enough.

It's a stretch to say that on the day you find a neglected, malnourished, and dead child in its filthy crib that things could get worse. A stretch, but not impossible. Because when I got back home to Sheepshead Bay, there was an envelope wedged between the jamb and my front door just above the knob. This was the note that had been missing this morning in the wake of Mary Lambert's leaving.

> Dear Moe,
> I came to tell you last night that I had been promoted and called back to the home office, but when I saw the shape you were in, I couldn't bring myself to say the words. These last few days together have been some of the best of my life, certainly the best in the last ten years. You are a wonderful, trusting, and tender man, Moe Prager, and I know I will regret not chasing our relationship where it would have gone. But there are things about me you didn't know. Things, that if you knew them, would have stopped us in our tracks. So please think of me with a smile and not anger. I will always think of you that way and I will always think of you. Please don't come looking for me. It will ruin what we had and hurt us both. Goodbye.
>
> With Love,
> Mary

I didn't have it in me to tear up the note or act the jilted lover. I put the note on my kitchen table and took a long shower that must have used up all the hot water for the entire building. When I got out of the shower, I wrapped a towel around me, poured myself a scotch, and watched the news. McKenna wasn't kidding around. They had gone big, all right. And Sonia Barrows-Willingham had given me a pleasant and unexpected *Go Fuck Yourself, Prager!* in the form of offering a $100,000 reward for information leading to Sashi Bluntstone's safe return or to the whereabouts of her abductors. I raised my Dewars to the screen when the nasty piece of work finished making her announcement. Then I made three calls, two of them the hardest phone calls I'd ever had to make.

This time I got to New Carmens first and was seated in the same banquette that we had occupied the day before. The world had turned upside down in the brief eternity since then. Twenty-four hours ago I had Mary Lambert in my life and the feel of her still fresh in my memory. There was a baby boy still alive in an apartment in Alphabet City, his mother not yet a full-fledged monster. Sarah was about to breathe life into a moribund case and I still had hope.

Sarah snuck up on me, wrapping her arms around my shoulders. It was all I could do not to weep. My troubles were not lost on my daughter.

"Dad, Dad, what's wrong?"

"A lot of things."

"Sashi?" She sounded frightened. "Is it—"

"No, kiddo, it's not Sashi."

"Did you see the press conference?"

"I couldn't, but I watched highlights on the news. Very impressive."

The waiter came over and we ordered coffee and pumpkin pie with whipped cream. When he left, Sarah asked, "Do you think the reward money will help?"

"It will do something, but I'm not sure it will help."

"What do you mean?"

"It will create a lot of activity. Reward money always does. The cops'll get a million calls with tons of leads, but …" I shrugged my shoulders. "When your Uncle Patrick was missing, we had a reward hotline for him that was active for twenty years. Your mom forgot to shut it down even after we found out what had happened to him all those years ago. The hotline was still getting fresh calls on the day your mom finally closed it down and that was a month after the whole story had appeared in the papers and on TV. Not one of those leads was worth a damn thing."

She bowed her head. "I see."

"On the other hand, these things do sometimes pay off. That's why they do them. At this point, kiddo, the cops need material to work with because they've exhausted everything else."

"What about the stuff you're working on?"

"That's what I wanted to talk to you about."

"Yeah."

The waiter came over and delivered our coffees and pies. We each grabbed our forks, but it seemed neither one of us had much of an appetite.

"I can't do this anymore, Sarah. I found a baby dead in its crib today. His mother was a meth addict and hadn't fed him for days. It was more important that she feed her habit than her own kid. I didn't sign on for this. Last night I was prepared to beat information out of a total schizophrenic. He was as lost as Sashi in his way. This is not who I am. The only reason I agreed to do this in the first place was because I wanted you back in my life again. I still want that more than anything, but not at this price."

"I'm sorry, Dad."

I reached across the table and stroked her face. "I can't apologize anymore about what happened to your mom. I can't take any of it back, kiddo, and I can't make up for it either. I've tried. You're going to have to forgive me because you forgive me, but I can't earn it. Do you understand?"

"It's okay. I understand."

"By the way, the detective in charge of Sashi's case has promised me to keep your name out of things. I tried to give you deniability, but he saw through it. Anyway, you're safe. I gotta go now." I stood.

"Wait, Dad." She took my hand. "I'll walk out with you."

I looked behind us at the coffee and untouched pies. I smiled, but I wasn't sure why.

● . ●

Detective McKenna met me at a bar in Elmont so I wouldn't have to schlep all the way out to him. Besides, I think he wanted a break after the pressure of the press conference and the calls that had already started pouring in. I had the list Nathan Martyr had supplied me with, the info Doyle and Devo had gotten for me, and a little write-up on the visits I'd made to Tierney, Jeff Fisher, Delia Parker, and the two others. He was sitting at the bar when I came in, staring past his drink into the abyss. He knew today was his last chance to get anywhere with the case and I imagined he was thinking again about whether going so public about the ransom demand had been the right thing to do.

"It wasn't your decision," I said, putting a hand on his shoulder, "so stop worrying about it for a few hours. If you fucked up, you'll have all the time in the world to regret it."

"Thanks, Prager. You're a cheery motherfucker."

I flagged down the barman and ordered a Dewars rocks. "If you think you had a bad day, McKenna, believe me, mine was worse."

"What happened to you?"

"I'll tell you about it some other time. Here." I put the folder on the bar and slid it over to him as the bartender put my drink down. "Cheers."

"You trying to be funny?"

"Ironic," I said. "I'm in no kind of shape to do funny today. Anyway, that folder's got some information on possible suspects. I talked to a few of them. I don't like any of them for it, but it couldn't hurt to double check."

McKenna then asked the one question I dreaded him asking. "How long you have you had these names?"

"A couple of days. Trust me, you wouldn't have approved of what I did to get them and you would've had a tough time legally obtaining some of the info in there. Go ahead, take it. I hope you have better luck with it than I did."

His face was undecided about what expression to wear. I could almost hear him working out his reaction. Bottom line was, I'd broken the deal we made at the start. I'd held stuff back. I lied to him. On the flip side, I'd done some of his legwork for him and gotten some information he probably would have only been able to gather forensically. And he knew the way of the world: PIs lied. It was never a matter of if, but of when and how much.

"Okay." He opted for neutrality and took the file. He flipped through some of the pages. "I'll have this stuff checked out."

We sat there silently sipping our drinks, him slipping back into the land of What-might-be and me into the land of What-was.

TWENTY-FOUR

The next morning I slept in. I'd removed myself from the case, but I had no intention of telling my brother about it and running back to my office at Bordeaux In Brooklyn. I figured I had another week or two to avoid the rest of my working life, until either Sashi was found or the story and the trail went cold again. I did, however, owe it to Candy and Max, despite their lies, to tell them in person. I also wanted to thank Jimmy Palumbo and give him some bonus cash for doing quality work. He was a good guy and good company and I guess I kind of felt sorry for him. I knew firsthand what divorce could do to people, how it could blow up their lives in an instant. A lawyer once told me that the saddest reading in the world was a divorced person's credit report.

"It's like reading a dying man's EKG, Moe. The heart's beating fine and then … boom! You'll look at the credit report and everything is perfect for thirty years: no late payments, no judgments, no liens, no repos, not a single blemish. Then somebody cheats or is bored with their spouse or for whatever reason someone wants to end the marriage. But there's more to a marriage than the kids and the pets. There are joint accounts, joint credit cards, car payments, loan payments, the mortgage. Cards get maxed out, loans don't get paid and for what, to punish the other party? The finances go to shit and their lives follow in short order."

Those words rang in my head as I turned onto the Bluntstones' street in Sea Cliff and their Victorian loomed up before me. I wondered what would become of Max and Candy when this all came to a conclusion. If Sashi never came home, would there be anything left to hold them together or would the shared loss bind them to each other in a way that love never could? As appealing and romantic as the latter notion might be, my experience taught me that the former was much more likely. That with Sashi gone, their nuclear bonds broken, Max and Candy would go spinning off into the void like random particles.

One thing was for sure, the circus was back in town. The press conference, as expected, had relit the fire and the block was a Noah's Ark of news vans, inconvenienced neighbors, cop cars, the curious, and, worst of all, the tragedy pimps. There were just some people addicted to the scent and spectacle of tragedy. Drawn like swarming flies to a fresh corpse, it was easy to spot their faces in the crowd. They were the lean and hungry onlookers, the ones waiting to feed off the bad news. They were the ones with the vacant lives whose condolences were more for their own empty selves than the families of the lost. They were the eager wreath-layers.

A uniform stopped me when I approached the house. I explained who I was; then he explained, "They're not here."

"Is Detective McKenna around?"

"He's the one that took them outta here. Look at this place. It's a freakin' circus."

"It is that," I said, smiling at his confirmation, and retreated to my car.

The museum was abuzz with its usual emptiness when I showed up in Cold Spring Harbor about twenty minutes after leaving Sea Cliff. Jimmy Palumbo still looked a little worse for wear from the other night. I imagine a dip in freezing water in December is probably not the best thing for your health, especially if you're going to stay in your wet clothes for another two hours. Still, he seemed glad to see me and even more glad when I slipped him the envelope with his bonus cash. He didn't make a show of pretending to not want or need it. Instead, he thanked me and tucked the envelope away in the inside pocket of his blazer.

"Listen," I said, "just so you know, I had to turn over the shit we got from Martyr to the detective in charge of the case."

Jimmy was suddenly much less happy to see me. "Fuck!" summed up his feelings nicely, but his sick expression was much more eloquent.

"Don't worry about it. I didn't mention you at all. As far as he knows, I did all of this on my own. You're fine."

"Great. Thanks. I didn't mind helping you, but you gotta leave my name out of all this. Because all I would need is for my ex to find out I was earning cash off the books. Her lawyer's already straining my nuts for extra pennies. And if I got in any legal trouble, she could keep the kids away from me forever."

"Believe me, I understand. I got you covered."

He looked relieved. "I appreciate it."

"Rusk in?"

"Always."

"Can you phone him and see if he's got a few minutes for me?"

"Go ahead downstairs, I'll make sure he got time for you."

Wallace Rusk was waiting for me at the elevator door as he had on my first visit. He was also dressed in identical clothing. The expression he was wearing was rather more perturbed than on my first visit, though he did offer me his hand in greeting.

"I suppose I have you to thank for that visit from the local con-stabulary," he said, gesturing towards his office door.

Now I understood the look on his face. McKenna had been to see him and had no doubt been a little less polite about it than me. As evidenced by Rusk's demeanor and Jimmy's before him, people have a distinct distaste for dealing with the police. I forget that sometimes, although given my own experiences with the police, I shouldn't.

"I'm sorry about that. I mentioned your name in passing and Detective McKenna seized on it."

"I suppose I can't hold that against you," he said, motioning to a chair opposite his desk. "Would you like a drink, Mr. Prager?"

"Yeah, actually I would. Thank you."

"Sherry, cognac, or scotch? I'm having a sherry myself."

"Sherry would be nice. Thank you."

He left the room, but returned with two small, delicate crystal glasses. He offered one to me. I stood when I took it. We raised glasses. Sherry isn't a glass-clinking and *sláinte* kind of drink. Rusk smiled as he sipped.

"Very fine sherry," I said.

"A discerning palate."

"I own several wine stores with my older brother. He's the real expert, but I know the fine taste of things." As I said the words, Mary Lambert's flavor filled up my senses.

"You are a man full of surprises, aren't you, Mr. Prager?"

"Fewer than you'd think."

We sipped some more.

"When I was at school, one of my professors taught our class a little rhyme about sherry. I think it goes, 'I must have one glass of sherry at eleven/'Tis something that must be done/For if I don't have one glass at eleven/I will have eleven at one.' I shall never forget that." He took his place at his desk, a wistful look in his eyes. "It is strange, is it not, what a man remembers?"

"It's funny you should mention that. I wanted to ask you about a rather strange man."

"So you availed yourself of Declan Carney's services."

"I did."

"And you're curious?"

"I am, but who wouldn't be? Between the fake name and outfit, the hair and the rest, he suggests a thousand questions."

"Of course, what I know of his history I don't know directly from the man himself. I don't even know his given name. I imagine some of what has been related to me is more myth and exaggeration than fact, possibly most of it, but it makes a fascinating story. Though I somehow doubt he feels that way about it."

"About what?"

"The story goes that he finished near the top of his class at West Point and he was being groomed for some important position within the intelligence community. But when Iraq invaded Kuwait, he was yanked out of whatever training program or graduate school he was in and pressed into combat. Then during Desert Storm, after there was nothing left for the air forces to bomb, his unit was ordered to oversee what I believe is euphemistically referred to as mop-up duty. Only in Desert Storm, this form of mop-up duty entailed bulldozing millions of tons of sand over panicked Iraqi troops and burying them alive in what would become their tomb."

"Nice."

"Rather monstrous, I think."

"That's what I meant by nice, monstrous."

"Oh, I see."

"So he flipped out?"

"Not initially, no. He returned home and resumed his education. Then, after several months had passed, he was given an honorable discharge. He resurfaced years later as Declan Carney."

"A man who studies the authenticity of beautiful things."

Rusk shook his head in agreement and finished his sherry. "Yes, I suppose that is one way to see it."

"Beware the innocent monster," I whispered barely loud enough for me to hear.

"Excuse me?"

"Nothing," I said, standing up and placing my empty glass on the desk. "I appreciate the time and the sherry. Thank you, Mr. Rusk."

"You're quite welcome, Mr. Prager. Please feel free to visit whenever you wish. I enjoy our little chats."

"Me too. Be well."

On the way home, I drove to Max and Candy's house, but it was even more of a circus than when I'd been by earlier. I had no stomach for it and went home to lick my wounds in peace.

TWENTY-FIVE

Two days later, the world wobbled on its axis and roused me from sleep. The wobble came in the form of a phone call and its voice asked, "You remember John Tierney's address?"

"Yeah."

"Then get over here. Now!"

I threw on a sweat suit and an old pair of sneakers, and brushed my teeth. Even as I drove, the earth shook beneath the wheels of my car. The wobbling, apparently, had only just begun.

My estimate was spot on. It took me about ten minutes to get from my condo to John Tierney's ass-end retreat in Gerritsen Beach. Only this time a cold, mocking sun was rising overhead and the street was lit up like a Christmas tree from all the spinning, whirling roof lights atop cop cruisers, crime scene vans, ambulances, and other assorted vehicles. My stomach churned at the sight of Detective McKenna standing alone and ashen-faced just inside the band of yellow tape surrounding Tierney's house and property. He noticed me coming his way, but it wasn't anger I saw in his expression. I wasn't sure what it was, just what it wasn't.

"What was that call about?" I asked as if I didn't already know.

"He's dead. Come on." He held the tape up for me like a cornerman holding up the ropes for his boxer. As we walked, he handed me some latex gloves and Tyvek booties. "Put those on and be prepared. It stinks in there."

We walked upstairs, the paintings of the bloody-eared, black-eyed saints staring at me accusingly as we went. In spite of the stench of feces, urine, and decay, the bedroom was alive with activity. John Tierney, the centerpiece of all the fuss, was quite dead. He was seated facing the door, his head pitched forward, a chunk of his skull and scalp missing. A big old Webley revolver lay on the floor at the foot of the chair. The way it landed made it look like a tear leaking from the black eye of the Christ-head Tierney had painted on the floor. *Jesus wept.* There was dried blood splatter all over the foil-covered windows, some of the foil shredded by shards of his skull and brain tissue as they flew away from the shock wave and bullet. There was a larger hole in the foil where the bullet had exited the house after exiting Tierney.

"Okay," I whispered to McKenna, "he killed himself. How long ago?"

"A couple of days."

"Is there a note?"

"Uh huh."

"Where?"

McKenna pointed at the laptop, its screen also smeared and dotted with blood and tissue, but not overwhelmed by it.

"What's it say?"

He reached into his back pocket and pulled out a little note pad. "It all runs together on the screen, but when you put in spacing, it reads: 'My quest is over. My job done. I did it. I did it. I did it. Burned and scattered to the wind. Ashes to ashes. I did it. *Ave Maria, gratia plena, Dominus tecum.*'"

"Hail Mary, full of grace, the lord is with thee," I mumbled. "Blessed art thou amongst women. Blessed is the fruit of thy womb, Jesus …"

"I thought you were Jewish."

"I was married to an ex-Catholic for almost twenty years. And try and remember, Jesus's last supper was a Passover Seder."

He snorted and shook his head. "You're just full of surprises."

"Everybody seems to think so." Then I asked the million dollar question: "Do you think he really burned her body?"

"Let's go for a walk."

We went back down the stairs, turned around the staircase into the kitchen, but when we stepped into the kitchen, a young detective, NYPD shield hanging out of his jacket pocket, put his hand up and said to McKenna, "Wait a second. Who's this guy now?"

That set McKenna off. "This guy is the PI that gave me the lead that got us here. He's the one who tracked Tierney down in the first place."

"We'll wanna interview him when you're done." He continued to talk to McKenna directly as if I wasn't standing a foot away from him.

"That's fine," I said. "Now can I see what there is to see?"

The young detective jerked his head over his left shoulder. "Go ahead. I'll be outside when you're ready."

The kitchen, like the living room, was a museum piece. The floor was a sheet of yellow and green linoleum—the real stuff—and the appliances were from, as my mom used to say, the year of the flood. The wallpaper, a green floral print, had been around since WWII. The table was green Formica with a fluted aluminum border and the chairs were bent tubular aluminum with jade green plastic cushions. We turned right at the ancient fridge and then right again to an open door. The door led down three rough-hewn wooden steps to a small combination root cellar/pantry. In a house built so close to the water, this was the nearest thing you could get to a basement. The room was on the opposite side of the house from the porch, so I hadn't noticed it when I was here the first time. Windowless, it was dark in here even though the sun was peeking through the kitchen windows. There was a bare bulb overhead in an old ceramic ceiling fixture. McKenna pulled the beaded chain that hung down from the light.

There before us was a kind of makeshift altar and shrine. The altar, complete with a kneeling step for prayer, was covered in candles and old candle wax. Above the altar was a collage of images of Sashi Bluntstone. Most were cut out of newspapers and magazines and glued and lacquered to the wall. Not unexpectedly, Sashi's eyes had been blackened and blood poured from her ears. But there were other photographs that sat on top of the altar and leaned against the wall. They were of Sashi Bluntstone, her hands and legs bound behind her like the arms and legs of the stuffed bear left in my car. In the photos, she was propped against a blank wall and nude except for panties. She was limp and her eyes shut.

"See those panties?" McKenna whispered, pointing at the photos. "They were on the altar when we found this room. They were bloody, Moe. It was dried blood."

"Fuck!"

"It gets worse."

"How much worse?"

"Wrapped inside the panties we found some small charred bones. Human bones. One of the guys thinks they're from a finger, maybe a pinky, a child's pinky."

The world began wobbling so fiercely, it was all I could do not to throw up right there. I managed to make it outside to the water's edge before giving up whatever I had inside me. Then I plunged my head into the icy cold water. Now the what-ifs weren't McKenna's cross to bear. They were mine. And the cold water would have helped only if I'd managed to keep my head under.

TWENTY-SIX

I sat in Dr. Mehmet Ogologlu's waiting room, thumbing through the magazines and trying very hard to fight my own desire to leave. Nothing new in that, in fighting myself. I'd been doing it for the two very long weeks since I'd thrown my guts up at the water's edge behind Tierney's house. Christmas was at hand, the world had stopped wobbling, and everyone had seemed to move beyond Sashi Bluntstone's kidnapping and murder to the next petty, scandalous, or violent thing the media ran up the flagpole to distract us from what was actually important. Sometimes I think George Orwell got it right. He was just off by twenty years or so. Yes, people had moved on, but I hadn't. That's why I was here.

The first week was the roughest, although several days of it are lost to me forever. I spent nearly twenty-four hours at Brooklyn South Homicide on Mermaid Avenue in Coney Island following the discovery of John Tierney's body. There I was interviewed for hours on end by myriad detectives and representatives from the Brooklyn DA's office. What happened after that I've been forced to piece together. I remember I started drinking the moment I walked back into my condo. I don't know when I stopped or if I stopped, only that Sarah found me passed out and half-dressed on the bathroom floor three days later. She said I hadn't been answering my phone messages or my emails and that everyone was worried about me. What did that mean, everyone? Isn't everyone's everyone different? How many people did my everyone constitute? Three? Four? Two? What was the formula? Thinking about it just made me feel more wretched.

Then, for a few days after that, I sat alone in my apartment. I wasn't feeling much of anything. I was numb. I wasn't drinking. My body'd had quite enough of that, thank you very much. I played some old vinyl records without listening. I watched a lot of movies on cable, though I couldn't tell you which ones. I screened my calls, answering only Sarah's. She called every day. My daughter was back in my life, which was exactly what I'd hoped for when she begged me to get involved that morning at New Carmens. What I couldn't figure out was the value of hopes realized versus the price paid. I didn't know how to do that kind of calculus, but somewhere I heard the devil laughing, or maybe it was God.

I waited and waited for the cops to call me back in, but the call never came. It wasn't going to. That's what Detective McKenna told me when he showed up at my door, eight days of newspapers cradled in his arms. The first thing he said was, "Christ, Prager, you look like shit."

"That I do," I said, staring in the mirror and running my hand over the thicket of gray stubble covering my face. "What's going on?"

"We've dug up every inch of Tierney's property and taken his house apart, moldy stick by moldy stick."

"Find anything else?"

"A few things, yeah."

"Like what?"

"Like ten thousand dollars of the ransom money in a paper bag in one of the kitchen cabinets."

"How do you know it's from the ransom?"

"For starters, the parents identified the bag. It's from a supermarket in Glen Cove. Their fingerprints are all over the bag and the money," he said. "We also found a length of bloody gauze shoved under a mat in the backseat of his car. It's the kid's blood."

"Fuck! Anything else?"

"Like what, Prager, a map to the pit where he burned her body?"

"Like the rest of the money?"

"No more money. Who knows what that wacky fuck was thinking? Maybe he flung it into Jamaica Bay or ate it for lunch."

"Any more bones?"

"None of those either. We're never going to find her ourselves. You know how it's going to be. Ten years from now, some old fart will be walking his dog in a state park or along a parkway and he'll trip over something and he'll look back and see a bone sticking out of the ground. That's how she'll be found."

"I guess you're right."

"Sure I'm right."

"What about the way he was living?" I asked.

"Tierney? Oh, it was his house, all right. The mother died like two years ago and left it to him, but that's when he started going completely over the falls. Had all the utilities shut off because he told his shrink that he was worried Hamas could listen in on his thoughts through their special wires."

"What's the deal with Brooklyn South Homicide?" I asked. "They gonna keep me waiting until I start crawling on the ceiling before they call me back in?"

"That's why I'm here."

"Let me shower and shave before—"

"No. I'm here to tell you it's over. They're done with you. *I'm* done with you. Both the Nassau County PD and the NYPD have finished our investigations. We'll keep looking for the remains, but the case is pretty much over. It's all on Tierney, not on you. We figure the girl was already dead by the time you showed up and both departments agree that in his house at night in the dark, anyone could have missed the door to the pantry. The police get second-guessed all the time and we're not about to play Monday morning quarterback with you."

"But what if she wasn't already dead? What if I'd just come to you with the list when I got it? What if I hadn't been so fast to dismiss Tierney as a suspect?"

"Come on, Prager, we went over this a hundred times when you were at Brooklyn South. There's no way of knowing any of that. You want to beat yourself up over it, I can't stop you, but it's a waste of time. The fact is, you led us to Tierney. You found him, not us. Maybe if the parents had come to you sooner, we could have saved the kid. You think that doesn't eat at me? That me and a whole team of detectives were chasing our own tails around and you come in and in a few days … voila! None of this is on you. Whatever peace the parents have now is because of you."

We didn't talk much after that. He'd had his say, done his duty, and now he needed to move on. Goodbye was a simple handshake.

Somehow, none of what McKenna had to say made me feel better. Sure, I'd neglected to tell the cops that I hadn't checked the house, that it was Jimmy Palumbo who'd done it, that it was him and not me who failed to find the altar room. But that didn't get me off the hook. The fact is, I should've looked for myself. Maybe I would have found that room in the dark, maybe not. That's not the point. The answer to why I didn't have a look for myself was easy and it had nothing to do with believing Jimmy. It wasn't even about believing Tierney. Now, looking back I wondered why I was so quick to believe a crazy man's ten seconds of coherence.

"I didn't take her," John Tierney had said.

Those words were going to haunt me for the rest of my life; a lot about this case would. There was Delia Parker's dead baby boy, a baby whose name I still didn't know. And there was that other question, the bigger question, hanging over me like my own personal rain cloud. Why hadn't I turned Martyr's list over to McKenna the minute I got it? The thing is, the answer that I gave the cops was perfectly reasonable. It sounded so much like the truth I swear I almost believed it myself when it came out of my mouth.

I told them that it didn't make much sense to me to turn over reams of unvetted data, that I was afraid it might slow down their investigation and waste manpower by sending the cops off in a hundred different directions. I said I thought I was being responsible by paring down the list, by doing some of the initial legwork myself. And hadn't I turned the list over to McKenna the second I saw I wasn't up to the task?

Even now, repeating the words in my head, it sounded like the truth, but it wasn't. It was a rationalization. The real answer to both questions, to all the whys, was the same and much more simple than the answers I gave the cops. The answer was that I was a prideful son of a bitch. I always knew better. I always had too much faith in my own decisions, in my gut, in my ability to read people. So when Tierney said he didn't do it and it rang true to me, I accepted it like the gospel truth. Hence there was no need for me to double-check Jimmy and search the house for myself. I'd already declared John Tierney a non-suspect by reason of insanity. And the list ... I didn't turn it over because it was mine, because in my gut I felt that if Sashi could be found, I would find her, not the cops.

The irony in this was that I was already wearing the albatross necklace before I ever heard of Sashi Bluntstone. Her death wasn't a new lesson to me, but an old one, one I thought I had learned, but hadn't. I'd simply kept my pride locked safely away in my office with the rest of my life for the last seven years. The lesson was that people don't change, that I didn't change, that my promises were just lies in waiting. That my pride and faith in my gut persisted in the face of a mountain of evidence to the contrary. My two divorces and Katy's murder weren't enough to humble me. And for fuck's sake, my ability to read people was as much a myth as the exploding poodle in the microwave. Me, read people? The two closest friends I ever had turned out to be corrupt murderers. What did I really know about people?

Funny that that should be my last thought before John Tierney's psychiatrist opened the door to his office and asked, "Mr. Prager, would you like to step in?" What do any of us know about people?

TWENTY-SEVEN

Dr. Mehmet Ogologlu was a tall, olive-skinned man with a round face and thinning black hair. He had penetrating brown eyes, a very full mouth, and a beak-like nose. He was comfortably dressed in a burgundy sweater over a blue Oxford shirt and gray cords. His shoes were scruffy old Bass loafers. I guessed most people would feel pretty much at ease around him. He gestured at a brown leather chair that faced his desk and waited for me to sit before he sat himself. I didn't know if that was a function of good manners or of his training. I wasn't in a trusting frame of mind.

"Well, Mr. Prager, what motivated you to come see me today?" Although his accent was as Oxford as his shirt, there were still some traces of Turkey in his speech.

"Guilt," I said.

"We all live with guilt," he said dispassionately, lifting a notepad and pen off his desk.

"Not this kind of guilt."

"What kind of guilt would that be?"

"I think I might be responsible for someone's murder."

That put a crack in his wall of dispassion. The psychiatrist leaned forward and stopped writing. "Whose murder?"

"Sashi Bluntstone's."

Now the wall came tumbling down. He stood up. "Are you a reporter? I will not discuss this with the press."

"I'm not a reporter."

"Please leave."

"I swear, I'm not the press."

"Who are you?"

"Just who I said I was. My name is Moe Prager."

He studied me more carefully now. "I am still at a bit of a loss. If I accept you are who you say you are and I am to take you at your word, what is it that you believe I can do for you?"

"Can we sit?" I sat and he followed in kind.

"It's customary for the patient to volunteer information and for the doctor to listen."

"I was the private investigator who found John Tierney, Dr. Ogologlu."

"I was under the impression it was the authorities who discovered John."

"Through me. I developed the lead and tipped the police off to his activities. They followed up."

"Pardon me, Mr. Prager, however, I fail to see in what capacity I can be of any service to you. In any case, I feel duty bound to warn you that I am loath to discuss my patients, living or deceased, with anyone."

"I understand, but maybe if you hear me out …"

"Possibly. It might facilitate progress if I knew in what capacity you come here today: as a private investigator or as a potential patient?"

"Honestly?"

"That would be best, I think, don't you?"

"I don't know what I'm doing here," I confessed. "I just knew I had to speak to you."

"Why is that, do you suppose?"

"Two days before the police went to Tierney's house, I paid him a visit. He just seemed so detached from the world the rest of us operate in and so lost in his own, that I was convinced he couldn't have had anything to do with Sashi Bluntstone's kidnapping. Without a second thought, I disqualified him as a suspect. I was so sure of myself that I didn't bother searching his house. I even considered not telling the police about him at all. That's how sure I was. Then, just as I was leaving, he came right out and said he didn't do it. He was coherent long enough to tell me that."

"Oh, I see. You *are* feeling guilty and responsible."

"Wouldn't you, in my shoes?"

"It need not be that academic a question, Mr. Prager. I feel quite responsible enough in my own."

"Then maybe we can help each other."

"Yes, maybe we can. But if we can, this is not the proper venue. Come."

For as long as I could remember, this part of Atlantic Avenue, from Court Street down to the BQE, was the main drag of a thriving area for Near and Middle Eastern businesses of all kinds. With Bordeaux In Brooklyn only a five-minute walk away, I sometimes came to the area for lunch or dinner. The Constantinople Café, a short stroll from Dr. Ogologlu's office across from Long Island College Hospital, was a tiny coffeehouse with four small tables, a few decorative water pipes, rugs hung on the walls along with travel posters of ruins and mosques. That's where the atmosphere stopped and reality set in as a local news radio channel filled the air instead of strains of exotic music. The café was shouldered on one side by a large Syrian-owned food shop and on the other by a Pan-Arab bookstore.

"Have you ever had Turkish coffee, Mr. Prager?"

"No."

That elicited a big smile from Ogologlu. He clapped his hands together and held up two fingers to the counterman. Then, as he pointed at some pastries in a glass case, he and the barista had a brief conversation in their native tongue. When he came back to the table, he was still wearing the smile.

"This city is a remarkable place," he said. "I only wish we appreciated that fact."

"How do you mean?"

"Here we are in a Turkish café surrounded by Arab businesses in a city with perhaps the largest Jewish population in the world. I live in Ditmas Park or, as some call it, Little Pakistan. Little Pakistan abuts Midwood, which is dominated by Hasidic Jews. History would say none of this should be possible. And let us not even discuss Queens, where there are over one hundred and thirty languages spoken each day."

"I've lived here my whole life, Doc. The melting pot is a crock of shit."

"I am not naïve, Mr. Prager, but I have lived in other places, places where the people are victims of their histories. Here, in this place, people rebuke the yokes of their histories. Not always, but on most days."

"Nice speech. Maybe you should run for mayor."

"I am afraid I would make a most dreadful politician. And I realize that the things I so admire about this place make it a target as much as anything else."

The barista brought over two espresso-sized cups on saucers and a larger plate with a selection of crusty and syrupy pastries. Some were sprinkled with chopped pistachio nuts, others covered in a kind of shredded wheat. All seemed to feature gobs of honey. Ogologlu thanked him and watched him retreat back around the counter.

"I know it looks like espresso, but I would advise against drinking it so. The grinds are at the bottom of the cup. The pastries ... for them, I will leave you to your own devices. Enjoy."

I took a sip of the coffee, which the psychiatrist watched with delight. "Amazing," I said, "strong and sweet. I've never had anything quite like it."

For the next ten minutes we sat there making small talk, sipping our coffees, sampling the pastries.

"You were talking about people being prisoners of their histories, Doc. Was John Tierney a prisoner of his?"

The smile ran away from Ogologlu's face. "As complex as we like to believe human history is, schizophrenia is a far more difficult a proposition. It defies the kind of analysis and deconstruction we feel comfortable with. Oh, we can describe it well enough, list its various manifestations, symptoms, drug therapies, and the rest, but ..." He didn't finish his thought. He didn't need to.

"He suffered from paranoid schizophrenia, right?"

"Broadly speaking. And before you ask, most people with this diagnosis tend not to be violent. Sometimes, however, they turn on people, even those closest to them."

"How long had you been treating him?"

"Since he was about nineteen. He was a sophomore at the Rhode Island School of Design, a fine arts major, I believe. Apparently, he had been displaying some symptoms since his mid-teens, but his mother and teachers dismissed his unusual behavior as the eccentricities of a talented and precocious child. When he was forced to withdraw from college, his mother was referred to me."

"Did the cops tell you about the paintings of the saints on his walls, the Christ-heads, the altar?"

"They did. It was not a surprise to me. From the beginning, John, like many schizophrenics, had incorporated a strong religious element into his organizational scheme. Schizophrenia is an amazing disease, Mr. Prager, in that its manifestations can be very similar from patient to patient. The aluminum foil on the windows, the conviction that someone or some group is trying to read and influence thoughts, these are common things."

"Did he ever talk about Sashi Bluntstone?"

Ogologlu swallowed hard. "He had, but more with a kind of religious reverence. He had mentioned a hundred people this way. What is it you are really asking me?"

"You're a smart man," I said. "There's lots of questions, but the one I guess I want answered is, could anyone have seen this coming?"

"I don't know if anyone could have seen it coming. I can only say that I did not."

"So there was no indication that he could turn violent."

"I did not say that. Maybe there were a thousand indications that he was capable of such heinous acts and I failed to see them. Maybe there were none. As I said, John's disease defies easy answers. I *can* say that there were no overt and obvious signs that John was a danger to himself or others. On the other hand, I hadn't seen him for several months before this happened. Therefore, I cannot say with any degree of certainty that his psychosis hadn't deepened or evolved into something different and dangerous."

"There's a lot you cannot say."

"There is one thing I can say, though. It seems to me that you are searching for some kind of absolution. Looking to me for that will only lead to disappointment. Absolution does not fall within my purview, I'm afraid. And frankly, in this kind of situation, I'm not certain there is anyone who can grant it to you. I can also say that I treated John and was myself shocked to hear the news about what he had done. Therefore, I would not be so fast to judge myself as harshly as you have judged yourself. You spent a few minutes with him and made an error. I spent years with him. If there is guilt and culpability here, there is plenty to go around. So you see, there is no hope of absolution for me either. Now, if you'll excuse me," he said as he stood. "I think I would like to go home and see my family."

I stood and shook his hand. "Thanks, Doc. If I have any other questions, would you mind if I called?"

He shrugged, not looking thrilled at the prospect of rehashing the subject of John Tierney. Yet, he said, "If I can be of assistance, certainly feel free to contact me."

When he left, I ordered another coffee and sat, listening mostly to the traffic noise on Atlantic and my even noisier thoughts. No matter what Dr. Ogologlu had said, I was choking on guilt. I'd been through this kind of thing before, in the wake of Katy's murder and, all things considered, I'd take a lungful of cancer over guilt. You can cut cancer out, burn it out, starve it, poison it. And if none of that works, the worst thing it can do is kill you. Cancer has a spot, a place, a name, even a face, but guilt is more insidious. It doesn't spread because it's everywhere to begin with, and it has a voice. It sings to you, but it won't kill you. No, that's on you. Guilt is the cab that drives you to the airport, but you have to crash the plane yourself.

Then, above the traffic noise and the din of my guilt, a news story came over the café speakers that just made my day complete.

… for that we go to our Long Island bureau chief, Marsha Farmer …

"We're here at the Junction Gallery in Sea Cliff where, only minutes ago, patron of the arts Sonia Barrows-Willingham announced that the hundred thousand dollar reward she offered for information leading to a break in the Sashi Bluntstone case, has been awarded to Moses Prager. Prager, a Brooklyn native, is a private investigator and retired NYPD officer. A friend of the Bluntstone family, he was brought into the case three

weeks after the young artist was kidnapped from this scenic North Shore village. Within a week, Mr. Prager had gotten a line on a possible connection between Sashi Bluntstone and John Tierney. Following the lead developed by Prager, the NYPD and detectives from the Nassau County Police went to Tierney's Gerritsen Beach, Brooklyn home ..."

I left ten dollars on the table and my second cup of coffee untouched.

TWENTY-EIGHT

That first night was worst of all. My phone machine was already full by the time I got home and I shut off my cell after taking calls from Aaron and Sarah. Both were politic enough and knew me well enough not to ask if I was happy about getting the money. There was nothing happy in any of this. Well, maybe Sonia Barrows-Willingham caught a buzz. Her extensive collection of Sashi's art had probably just gone up several fold in value and the thought of dipping me in a hundred thousand dollars worth of blood money probably made her wet. I wondered, did a woman like her ever get wet?

It didn't take me long to figure out what I would do with the reward. I knew I wasn't going to keep any of the money for myself, but I'd grown up too poor to make some grandiose gesture with it. Money came too hard to most people at too high a cost for me to simply hand it over to a charity. With money comes responsibility and I wasn't going to cede mine, not to a board or committee. If I thought it might've unhinged the albatross from around my neck or calmed the guilt, I would've considered it. I knew better. Didn't I always know better? Sarah, because of our estrangement, had insisted on paying for vet school on her own and had only reluctantly let me help her buy into her practice. I thought maybe now that we had come to terms of forgiveness about Katy's murder, that Sarah would be more amenable to letting me help. I hoped she'd take some of it, if only the money she'd fronted Max and Candy for the ransom, and I thought Jimmy Palumbo had done as much to earn the reward as I had. He sure as hell needed it more than I did and I didn't suppose he was the type to be too proud not to take it. In his shoes, I'd take it.

I heard a lot of noise coming from Emmons Avenue and peeked through the window. The inevitable frontal assault had begun. Three news vans were parked out there and a crowd was forming around them. I threw two changes of clothing and my shaving kit into a gym bag and locked the door behind me. I didn't figure this story had much staying power. One day, two at most. I could hide for that long. I'd pretty much hidden for the last seven years. Outside in the hall, I went straight to the stairs and took the extra half flight down that led to the parking lot. The reporters hadn't found their way back there yet and I got into my car. It smelled almost new, having just been returned from the body shop after the cops released it. Still, on such a day as this, I would have been better served by the generic rental I'd been driving for the past few weeks. I made a quick right out of the lot and sped towards the Belt Parkway service road. I didn't know where I was headed, but that wasn't exactly a new experience in my life. I figured to stumble into something.

I drove around aimlessly for about an hour, listening to Steely Dan CDs, singing along, trying to blot out the noise in my head. And it worked for a while too. When I snapped out of my personal fog, I found I was parked next to Nathan's Famous in Coney Island. I wished I had parked anywhere else. In all the tumult of the last several weeks, I really hadn't given much thought to Mary Lambert. Now, remembering our dinner here, the walk along the boardwalk, our nights together, she filled every corner of my head. I thought about how romantic it would have been to escape to her Greenpoint sublet. How

I would have coaxed her into ditching work so we could spend a few days together in her bed, fucking our brains out like a couple of teenagers. Much like a teenager, I found myself fantasizing that the story of the reward money would make it up to Boston, and hearing it, Mary would get back in touch with me. Like I said, everybody wants to get rescued. Of course, that wasn't going to happen. I would never hear from her again.

Christ, it was freezing cold on the boardwalk, but after a few minutes I barely noticed. I just kept moving. That seemed to be my plan: just keep moving. There was barely enough light left to see down the boardwalk towards Sea Gate. There was something achingly beautiful about this nearly deserted and decrepit stretch of beach that had once been the world's playground. The truth of it was best seen in the dying light. In the summer, crowded with people, with the rumble of rides, the shrieks and screams, the barkers' crooked come-ons, cotton candy, the pops and whistles, the siren's song of french fries and hot dogs, Coney Island still had enough magic to fool you, to make promises it couldn't keep, promises that it had probably never really kept. But now under the falling curtain of night, I could see it for what it wasn't, for the lie I had let it tell me my entire life. There are lies to hate and lies to adore. Even now, seeing it clearly maybe for the very first time, Coney Island was a lie I adored. Coney Island was a lover who never kept her promises, but somehow it didn't matter. Maybe it was no accident that I wound up here, that Mary Lambert was on my mind.

TWENTY-NINE

I was right this time. The reward story had no legs, no legs at all. The news vans and crowds were gone by the next evening. I spent my one night in self-exile at a faceless New Jersey motel out on Route 9. Although it lacked the romance of my Mary Lambert fantasy, it felt almost like a vacation. There can be great joy in anonymity. The story had no legs because Sashi was now just a collection of charred bones on the cold pyre of the twenty-four hour news cycle. She was no longer destiny's child, now only a child of mind. I imagine that if Max and Candy had been willing to do the morning shows and Larry King and Oprah, they could have kept the machine churning by stirring the ashes and feeding the beast, but, to their credit, they had refused to play the game. The one thing in the world that bound them together was gone forever and I guess they were too busy staring into the abyss to worry about staring into the camera.

I listened to my phone messages to make certain that I didn't delete anything important. Most, as I suspected, were from the media requesting comment on the reward and the case. There was one from the code enforcement officer in Bridgehampton. Apparently, my moment in the sun had had an impact on the folks out east and they had magically approved all the permit requests, including the one for external signage, for our new store. Then there was the chilling message from Sonia Barrows-Willingham about the reward itself. It seemed a certified check was on its way to me via FedEx. There was this creepy sort of delight in her cool, bloodless voice.

"Oh, and by the way, Mr. Prager, I wanted to let you know that we're having a little memorial service for Sashi at my house on January second. Max and Candy have requested you be in attendance. Your daughter has already accepted the invitation. Do come." Said the spider to the fly.

I guessed I would go. The thought of Sarah alone around that woman brought out my fatherly protective instincts. Besides, I had some stuff I needed to say to Max and Candy that I hadn't had the chance to say in person.

With all the messages erased, emails answered or deleted, and the good news about the new store passed on to my big brother, I took a tour around my condo and realized it looked like a war zone. During my two weeks in brooding isolation, I hadn't done much house cleaning or laundry or much of anything. I got to it. And though the hard edges of the guilt had softened a bit over the last few days and its voice was no longer operatic, I didn't need to play music as I cleaned.

• . •

I woke up, the pillow wet on my cheek from drool. The downstairs buzzer was ringing, but I didn't jump out of bed to get it. I had dreamed and I didn't want to lose it. I sat up, closed my eyes, and tried to get the dream straight in my head. When I thought I had it, I went to the intercom.

"Who's there?"

"FedEx."

"Come on up."

I must've been too quick for him because the buzzer rang again. I depressed the button again and, this time, held down for many seconds.

Less than a minute later there was a rap at my door. The FedEx guy had that end-of-a-long-day look on his face and it was only then that I noticed it was completely dark outside. After tidying up, I'd had a Dewars, my first since my lost weekend, and laid down on my bed just to rest my eyes for a few minutes. I guess I rested more than my eyes and for more than a few minutes.

"Sign this, please," he said, passing over a handheld device with an electronic signing pad. When I was done, he handed me an envelope.

"Busy, huh?"

"Christmas." His expression went from bored exhaustion to worry. He had slipped and used the C-word, Christmas.

"That's right. I almost forgot. Merry Christmas."

"Happy Holiday Season to you, sir," he said too emphatically.

"Don't worry, I won't report you to the Thought Police."

His face went from concern to confusion, but neither one of us had the energy nor the inclination to discuss it. I shut the door and ripped open the shipping envelope. Inside, along with the check, was a folded prepaid shipping envelope and some waivers to sign. I didn't figure it was going to be simple. Nothing is simple anymore, especially not money.

Before I could step away from the door, there was another knock. I thought it was the FedEx guy coming back for some reason beyond my reasoning. Maybe my signature hadn't taken in his handheld. I didn't suppose the day was far off when they'd just want to scan your fingerprints or your retina or take a drop of blood. When I pulled back the door, it wasn't the FedEx man at all. In the end, however, it was about blood, not my blood, but blood nonetheless.

I swallowed hard at the sight of the man standing before me because I immediately recognized his face. Not him, his face. I realize that doesn't make much sense, but there it is. He must've been around

Sarah's age, I thought, about my height, slender, yet well put together under his open cashmere overcoat and dark gray Italian suit. His black hair was thick and as well-groomed as hair that wavy and thick could be. He was a dead ringer for the young Tony Bennett and his mouth smiled at me out of the past. His eyes were a lighter shade of brown and shaped a little differently from the face I recognized. Still, in spite of what I knew in my heart and in my marrow, I said, "Sorry, I'm not talking to the media."

"I'm not from the media. I'm from Vermont." He laughed at his own joke.

"I don't care if you're from Verona. Who are you?" I asked, my voice breaking up.

"My name is Paul Stern, but that's only part of who I am. And if I'm reading your expression and voice correctly, I think you've figured out the rest."

"But Rico didn't have kids," I heard myself say.

"None that he knew of, no. May I come in?"

What could I do? I waved him in and closed the door behind him.

Five minutes later, Paul Stern was sitting on my couch, holding the picture of Larry McDonald, Rico Tripoli, and me in his hand. It was the same picture Mary Lambert had held in her hand only a few weeks before and, as it happened, that was no accident. It was uncanny just how much he resembled Rico. Even some of his movements and gestures were reminiscent of my old precinct buddy. He took a long sip of the red wine I'd poured for him, then held the picture up to me, his thumb under Rico Tripoli's chin.

"This was my father?"

"You tell me."

He put his face up close to the photo. "You tell me."

"Sure, you look a lot like Rico Tripoli," I said. "But I've trusted my eyes in the past and things couldn't have turned out worse."

"How so?"

"It got my ex-wife murdered."

"I'm sorry."

"Yeah, me too. So you're gonna have to do better than looking like that photo."

"I understand."

"Whenever you're ready," I said.

"I was adopted."

"I figured you might say that."

He growled, "Look, Mr. Prager, are you going to let me do this or what?"

That response, like his laughing at his own joke, should have been proof enough. It was so fucking Rico.

"I'm sorry. Go on."

"I was adopted and raised in Vermont by …"

When he said Vermont again, I got a sick feeling in the pit of my stomach. I recalled that Brian Doyle had mentioned a female PI from Vermont calling him several weeks back and asking about Larry Mac, Rico Tripoli, and me. Because of that I only half listened to the rest of what Paul Stern had to say about how his parents never pretended that he was theirs. About how they were well-to-do, but never spoiled him. About how his adoptive parents had done everything they could to support him when, a year ago, he decided to track down his birth parents. About how his mother had been a waitress up at a hotel in the Catskills. About how an NYPD fraternal organization used to sponsor annual golf and ski weekends at that same hotel. How he had the documentation to prove all of it if I needed further convincing.

"You hired an investigator!" I blurted out. "You hired a private investigator named Mary Lambert, didn't you?"

"What? Yes … no. What I mean to say is that yes, I hired a private investigator to come down here and look into my biological parents' pasts, but no, her name's not Mary Lambert."

"Fifty years old, but looks forty-ish. Blue eyes. Black hair with some gray in it. Just this side of beautiful with high cheekbones, plush lips, and a perfect nose. Not too much makeup, but classy. Okay, she may not have used the name Mary Lambert, but that's her, right?"

"I don't see the point in this."

"But I do. And if you want me to talk about Rico, I suggest you—"

"Yes, that's her. You seem upset and I don't understand," he said. "You're a private investigator, aren't you?"

"Sort of, yeah."

"In my place, given the things in the public record about my biological father, wouldn't you have hired someone to check into them?"

"Probably."

"Then I really don't understand why you're upset."

"You don't have to understand. Look, Paul, you seem like a good guy, but I'm not in much of a talking mood tonight. I've had a rough few weeks."

"I heard," he said. "I've been following the story. It's terrible, but at least you found out what happened to that poor little girl. That's something, isn't it?"

"In the scheme of things, it's very little."

"I'm sorry."

"What are you doing tomorrow night?" I asked.

He seemed confused. "It's Christmas Eve."

"Yeah, and I'm a Jew, not much of one by most standards, but still, it's not my holiday. Since I've been single again, I do a traditional Jewish Christmas: Chinese food and a movie."

He laughed, that charming smile returning to his face. "At home we did a variation on the theme. For us it was usually Indian or Thai and a movie."

"You're Jewish?"

"You want to see my bar mitzvah certificate *and* my adoption papers?"

"Your father—I mean, Rico—is probably spinning in his grave, but laughing too. He used to call me a heathen fucking Jew all the time and that was when he was being nice."

"You were close. That's what I heard."

"Rico broke my heart. Only someone very close can do that to you."

He bowed his head. "I know our talking will dredge up bad things, but—"

"Don't sweat it, kid. Be here at eight tomorrow night and for god-sake, don't bring wine. We'll figure something out."

He shook my hand, but couldn't look me in the eye. "Thank you, Mr. Prager."

"Moe."

"Thank you, Moe."

"One thing before you leave," I said. "I have to know why you came to me?"

"Because of all the people left from his world, it seems you knew Rico Tripoli better than anyone."

"Sometimes I think I didn't know him at all."

"Then that makes two of us."

For a long time after Paul Stern left, I stood staring out my front window at the ambient streetlight dancing on the water of Sheepshead Bay. The kid was going to bring papers with him to prove who he was, but it would be a waste of time. He was Rico's kid. I knew it from the second I saw him and once my brain filtered the New England out of his voice, it dawned on me that he even sounded a lot like Rico. If I was the type of person who believed in prayer, I would have said one right then and there. Paul Stern seemed like a good man, and I would have prayed for him to avoid the demons that had eaten his father alive.

THIRTY

Between the shock of Rico Tripoli's newfound son showing up at my doorstep and the trauma over the realization that Mary Lambert had played me for a love-hungry dope, I had forgotten the dream I tried so hard to remember. Then, when I finally got back to sleep, it came to me again, but only in fragments and shards. In it, I was a dreamer once removed, like I was watching someone else's dream and taking notes. There were flashes of John Tierney's house and the altar room. This time the candles were lit and the panties were on the altar, but somehow the dreamer knew her bones weren't there. The dreamer kept staring from the collage on the wall to the other photos on the altar, but then we were on the staircase to the bedroom. Black tear stains marked the faces of the saints, their moist, blackened eyes reflecting candlelight. The dreamer turned. I turned. The altar was there below us. On the wall, only a solitary photo of Sashi Bluntstone, eyes shut, her arms and legs bound behind her, her face almost beatific in death. Then nothing.

●　.　●

I called Sarah and for the first time in as long as I could remember, she sounded really pleased to hear from me.

"Hey, Dad."

"Hey, kiddo. Where are you?"

"The office."

"It's Christmas Eve."

"Pets get into all sorts of mischief at the holidays. Think about it: big trees, loose pine needles, lit candles, tiny glass bulbs, chocolate everywhere. Besides, Dad, when did Christmas Eve matter to you?"

"In a way it does. I think about Katy. When your mom and I were first married, I wanted to get a tree, but she wouldn't hear of it. Converts are the worst."

"Yeah, she was pretty strict about that stuff."

"She was a better Jew than I ever was."

"That's not what Grandpa Izzy used to say."

"You remember Mr. Roth? You were so young when he died."

"I was almost ten. He told me you were a good Jew because you did good for people."

"Then it was good he died when he did, before he could see the mess I made of things."

"It wasn't all your mess, Dad."

"Thanks, kiddo."

"You doing the usual tonight?"

I hesitated before answering. I wasn't sure I wanted to try and explain Paul Stern to her. Shit, I wasn't sure I could explain him to me.

"Yeah, the usual," is what I said.

"Are you going to the memorial for Sashi? Max and Candy want you there. They want to thank you."

"I'm coming, but I—"

"Hold on a second." Sarah covered the mouthpiece. "Dad, I've got to go. I've got a beagle in here named Olivia who decided to eat a pound of chocolate Hanukah gelt."

"Go."

"Love you, Dad. Bye."

Hearing her say those words, the way she said them, so naturally, so unencumbered by the last seven years, made me think the guilt was worth bearing. They say there's nothing like the love of a child. True. What I'd found out was that there was also nothing quite like the loss of that love. And hearing her mention Mr. Roth brought him back to me. Israel Roth, the father I had chosen. And me, the son he had chosen. I thought again about how pleased Mr. Roth would have been to know his real son had finally found his way in the world and that his son and I had been together when we scattered his ashes on the grounds of Auschwitz. Auschwitz, a hell Mr. Roth had survived, but a place from which he had never been fully liberated.

I went online and started researching the best Chinese, Thai, and Indian restaurants in the New York area. As I did, thoughts of Sarah, of Israel Roth, of Carmella's son, who was named for Mr. Roth, of Paul Stern, and of Sashi Bluntstone swirled around in my head. The dream flashed back to me and was out of my head as quickly as it came. Then I found myself laughing at the thought of a beagle feasting on a pound of chocolate. My reverie was interrupted by the phone.

"Yeah."

"Happy Holidays." It was Detective McKenna.

"Merry Christmas."

"How you doing?"

"Feeling pretty guilty, but it's not all bad, I guess. My kid's talking to me again."

"That's good."

"Not for nothing, McKenna, but why the call?"

"Well, I heard about the reward."

"I just bet you did," I said. "I guess I have you to thank for that."

"You deserved it even if you don't think so."

"Christmas is tomorrow, so we won't argue about it. Why the call?"

"You were in terrible shape the last time I saw you and I was worried."

"Thanks, but I'm okay. I've dealt with this shit before."

"You going to the memorial?"

"You're the second person to ask me that today. Yeah, I'm going, but I'll keep my distance from the hostess. She's a real piece of work."

"That's a kind way to put it. Just so you know, we're calling off the search and wrapping stuff up."

"Can I look at the evidence?" I heard myself say.

"What? I thought you said you were—"

"I am okay. I swear. It's not that. Look, I talked to Tierney's shrink."

"Ogologlu?"

"Him, yeah. It helped me deal with the guilt. I just want to see if there was something I missed, something I should have seen. That's all. I've started dreaming about Tierney's house, for chrissakes."

"I guess it's okay. This case got to me too. Come around the day after Christmas. I'll meet you in my office, but it stops after that."

"Deal."

"Sure. That's what you said the last time. Merry Christmas."

He hung up and managed not to apologize for wishing me Merry Christmas. Things were looking up.

THIRTY-ONE

Paul Stern showed up at eight sharp with a bottle of scotch, but it wasn't any kind of scotch I'd ever seen.

"You've heard of single malt scotch, right, Moe?"

"Don't be a wiseass, kid. I'm sure your PI told you how I earn a living."

"Sorry. Yeah, she told me you own wine stores."

"Well, we've been known to sell a bottle or three of Glenfiddich, Laphroaig, and Macallan."

"This is single barrel scotch. A friend of mine belongs to a club that buys single barrels of fine unblended scotch and the club members get equal shares. Sometimes they have the barrel shipped over here and they have a party. Sometimes, like with this one, they have it bottled."

"Just when you thought the idle rich had run out of ideas on how to waste money …"

"You resent money?"

"No. Just what people do with it," I said, getting two rocks glasses from the shelf. "It's just that when you grow up without money, you have a different kind of respect for it. That's all. Your dad—shit! I mean Rico. He understood. He grew up like me."

"It's okay. You can call him my dad. I know who you mean and it will stop you from correcting yourself every thirty seconds."

"Fair enough."

"My friend gave the scotch to me as a gift a few years ago and I've never found the right occasion to drink it. I brought it down to New York with me because I hoped you'd talk to me about my biological father."

"Call him Rico or we'll be tripping over each other all night," I said, pouring a finger's worth of the honey-colored scotch in each glass. "So you think this is the right occasion, huh? You know some of the stuff I'm gonna tell you about your dad isn't apt to make you very proud to be carrying around his DNA."

"That's okay, Moe. I'm a lawyer and did a little research on my own before I hired ... before I had someone else look into things. I know all the stuff about his trial and prison time. I know he sold information and protection to drug dealers, so I get that he was no saint."

"Another lawyer, just what the world needed." I winked at him. "Listen, kid, if that was the worst of it ... Maybe we better drink some of this."

We raised glasses, neither of us making a toast, and sipped. I could taste the difference immediately. It was like the purity of a single sustained note coming out of John Coltrane's sax. Of course, even a single note is a thousand different things. Maybe it was the same note a million other sax players might have hit, but it was just slightly different when he played it. But that was the thing about the scotch, as unique as it was, it was still scotch and inevitably disappointing. Single sustained notes played even by a genius aren't *that* much different. It was like the first time I smoked a real Cuban cigar. It was great and sorely disappointing all at the same time.

"Good stuff, Paul. Thanks."

"Tastes like scotch," he said.

"Yeah, pretty much."

"I want you to tell me the truth about Rico, and not like you told me the truth about the scotch."

"Okay, sure." I recapped the scotch and broke out some red wine.

It was ten o'clock by the time we noticed we hadn't eaten. And by then I'd gotten past the hard stories about how Rico sold me out, how he was on a drug dealer's pad even when we were first on the job, and how he let me walk into an ambush once at an old Mafia Don's house in Mill Basin. I knew the PI had told him some of these stories, but he wanted to hear them from my mouth. I guess I understood that. We had since moved on to the funny stories, like the one about how Rico walked off post on the Fourth of July to sleep with a nurse in the back of a city ambulance and how the sergeant caught him with his pants around his ankles.

"Your dad and women … man, he was like a magnet. Women loved him and he looked so cool in his uniform. I remember those weekends up in the Catskills. Rico and I used to go sometimes. It was wall- to-wall drinking and fucking around."

"I'm living proof of that," he said.

"I didn't mean to be insensitive, sorry. What about your birth mother?"

"Her name was Alice Weathers. She died about five years ago, but I talked to her sister. She said Alice fell in love with Rico that weekend, that he was the most gentle lover she ever had, but knew he barely even remembered her when he woke the next morning. When she had me, she wrote that the father was unknown on the birth certificate."

"Then how—"

"Her sister. She told her sister Rico's name."

"Amazing. So, you wanna go eat, kid?"

"Sure."

Just as we opened the lobby door, Sarah came strolling into the building carrying a tiny, fake Christmas tree in one hand and a bag full of gift-wrapped boxes in the other.

"Hey, Dad." She kissed me on the cheek. "I thought you'd be out at the movies. I wanted to surprise you."

"You did. I thought you were working."

"I got off at eight. I think we have something to celebrate this year and figured now that Mom's not around, we could have a tree."

"How's the beagle?"

"She gives a whole new meaning to sick as a dog, but she'll live."

"Oh, I'm sorry. Paul Stern, I'd like you to meet my daughter Sarah."

He made to shake her hand and gave up. "Why don't you come to dinner with us?" he said.

"I wouldn't want to impose."

"Don't be silly, kiddo. C'mon with us. I've been talking about my past all night and I think I might want to let Paul do some talking for a change."

"I've got the keys, just let me drop this stuff off upstairs. You guys wait for me."

Paul Stern grabbed the bag. "Let me help."

I waited downstairs in contemplation of the smile on my daughter's face and letting go of the emptiness that had haunted me for the last seven years.

THIRTY-TWO

The day after Christmas I met Jimmy Palumbo for breakfast at a diner on Sunrise Highway. He told me he'd spent the holiday with family and that it was an okay time. He barely ate his eggs, mostly pushing them around his plate. Nor was he in a particularly talkative mood. I could tell there was something on his mind and it didn't take a genius to figure out what it was. I didn't imagine the stultifying life at the museum was the future he had envisioned for himself when he was pancaking linebackers in the NFL. But now that the extracurricular work I had for him had dried up, the museum was all he had ahead of him. At least, Jimmy said, he didn't have to go back to work until the second week in January. I considered offering him something at one of our stores, then thought better of it. It would have been a lateral move: trading in one life-draining job for another.

And, I suspected, there was something else eating at him. Didn't take a genius to figure that one out either. He had no doubt heard the stories about the reward money. I could see him trying to work out how to broach the subject without pissing me off. He even made an abortive attempt at talking his way around to it.

"I guess I didn't do a very good job when I searched that fucking lunatic's house. If we'd brought a flashlight, it might have ended different."

"That wasn't your fault," I said. "No matter what, I should've taken a look for myself. I told you that already. The cops said they would probably have missed seeing that room too in bad light. They also think Sashi was probably already dead by then."

Jimmy got silent again. He understood as I did that the space between what the cops thought and what they knew for sure was the place where the gnawing questions lived. If only we could have known for certain that Sashi was already dead by the time we got to Tierney's house. If … if … if … The sad refrain of so many lives. The silence and unspoken questions continued for another couple of minutes, when, mercifully, the waitress brought the check. I snatched it away from Jimmy, threw a five-buck tip on the table, and made to stand up.

"Shit! I almost forgot," I said, handing Jimmy an envelope. "Merry Christmas."

I slid back into the booth and watched him open it up.

"Holy shit, Moe!" His hands shook as he held the check. "This is—"

"—a lot of money. Yeah, Jimmy, but you earned it as much as I did and you sure as shit need it. Maybe it'll give you time to find a new job or maybe you can fix up the house or work on the boat. Whatever you want. I wish I could've given it to you in cash."

"No, that's all right. Thanks, man. I don't know what to say."

"You already said it."

This time I stood in earnest. Jimmy was still staring at the check when I left.

•   .   •

Detective Jordan McKenna looked as beat-up as I felt.

Sure, Christmas Eve and Christmas Day had gone great for me. Dinner with Paul and Sarah at a little Indian place in Park Slope was amazing. Park Slope, that's the part of Brooklyn where people who aren't from Brooklyn live in Brooklyn while pretending they live in Manhattan. We walked into the place just before they closed the kitchen and so the owner/chef, who felt as awkward about Christmas Eve as any Jew, fired up his Tandoor and baked up an array of breads and meat dishes the likes of which I had never seen or tasted. He gave us a round of Taj Mahal beers on the house. And when we got back to my condo, Sarah and Paul decorated the tiny Christmas tree and placed it on top of the stack of gifts my daughter had bought me. I drank a little bit more of the fancy scotch and decided it was pretty fucking good after all. The next morning, Sarah came back and we celebrated the guilty pleasure of our first Christmas by opening the presents and staring at photo albums for hours on end. That said, the questions about the costs of having Sarah back still remained. One child lost for one child found, could that ever be balanced out?

McKenna, on the other hand, had been forced to deal with the same sorts of questions without any of the benefits. The case had been his from day one; Sashi had been killed on his watch. At least I'd gotten close. He didn't get close. He didn't get a daughter back. He didn't get reward money. I knew what he got.

"The brass is breaking your balls, huh?"

"Pretty much. Looks like I'm going to get reassigned."

"But you didn't do anything wrong."

"But I didn't do anything particularly right either, Moe. Let's face it, you come on the scene and within a week you track the guy down. I had the case for three weeks."

"We both know that's not how it works."

"Doesn't matter how it works," he said. "It's how it looks that matters to the bosses."

"So what are they going to do to you?"

"You know the drill. They're going to give me a bump up and stick me in an office somewhere. I'll be a supervisor consulting on supervising on consulting or I'll be like a community relations guy ... some bullshit like that."

"Sorry."

"Yeah, me too. So you wanna have a look-see at the evidence?"

"I do."

"Come on with me."

I followed McKenna down a hallway into what I supposed was a lunch room. There on the table were several cardboard evidence boxes.

"I don't know what you hope to find," he said, "but you're welcome to it."

"Like I said to you the other day, I don't know what I hope to find. Some solace, maybe. I don't know."

"There may be solace someplace in this fucking world, but not in those boxes. Only more misery in there."

"Maybe."

"I have to stay in the room. It's the rules."

"No problem."

I began sorting and sifting through the evidence and files. Most of the evidence came from John Tierney's house. The early stuff with the files was what you'd expect, written reports, interviews, a lot of pictures of Sashi at different ages. Through all of this, I realized, it had been a long time since I'd looked at Sashi Bluntstone. I mean, really looked at her and thought of her as a person. She had been many things to me throughout these last weeks: a means to an end, an artist, an object, a goal, someone else's kid. But I'd only really ever thought about her as a child, a pretty sad one at that, early on in the process. Now I stared at her, Cara the beagle snuggling next to her. Even with that goofy kid's smile on her face and the dog she loved more than anything next to her, her eyes looked ancient and tired. No kid, I thought, should look like that.

McKenna was right, there was no solace to be had in those boxes. There was something in them—not misery exactly, regret maybe—but certainly not peace of mind. If anything, I had more questions now than when I left my condo that morning. And as I drove back to Brooklyn from McKenna's office, I felt an itch. My mind was working on something, but on what I could not say. It didn't really matter, for even if I solved all the riddles the universe laid at my feet, Sashi Bluntstone would still be dead. Even I understood that all this rooting around in Jordan McKenna's files and my conversation with Dr. Ogologlu were ways to come to terms with that one simple fact.

THIRTY-THREE

I trolled the aisles of my local big box pharmacy. This was how I did it. I'd wait till I needed nearly everything and then do a massive shop. Running out to pick up this or that just wasn't my style. Besides, men of my generation are kind of lost about a lot of things. Oh, if I needed a suit, I was aces. I knew what I liked, what looked good on me, and how to get it. But when it came to things like socks and underwear, I was hopeless. So there I was, rummaging through shelves of briefs when that itch flared up again. Then, when I was standing there with a three-pack of white Hanes briefs in my hand, it hit me. I dug my cell phone out of my pocket and dialed McKenna.

"Moe Prager, Christ, what now? Didn't I just see you yesterday?"

"Her panties!" I shouted into the phone. A young woman in the aisle next to me abruptly about-faced.

"Sashi Bluntstone's?"

"Yeah."

"What about them?"

"They're different," I said.

"Different than what?"

"Than the ones she was wearing when she was taken. The ones she was wearing in the pictures on the altar, the ones you found with the bones in them. Read your report."

"I read the reports a hundred times. I know they're different. So what?"

"So what? Come on, McKenna."

"So Tierney either was prepared to hold on to her for a long time and bought some underwear for her before he grabbed her or he bought new stuff for her after he had her. I repeat, so what?"

"John Tierney strike you as the kind of guy to go on little shopping excursions?"

"I don't know. You tell me. He was dead when we met."

"Well, he wasn't dead when I met him. In fact, I'm standing in the middle of one of those big pharmacies right now. It's brightly lit, full of people and security cameras. I can't picture John Tierney strolling down the aisles here whistling a happy tune."

"So he went to a Pathmark or Stop & Shop at four in the morning or asked a neighbor or one of his freakazoid soul mates on the internet to do it. There's a hundred ways he could have done it."

I took a deep breath. Fact is, Detective McKenna was right. Still, I wasn't buying it. "Maybe you've got a point."

"You don't sound convinced."

"I'm not," I said.

"Doesn't change a goddamned thing, Prager. Stop looking at the edges of the thing and look at the big picture. The kid's dead and Tierney killed her. Nothing's going to change that, so stop it."

"You're right. Sorry to have bugged you."

He didn't say goodbye.

When I got back to my condo, I made another call.

* . *

The house was a white Victorian on Westminster between Beverly Road and Cortelyou Road. Though certainly a big house by Brooklyn standards, it was nothing like the size of Max and Candy's fussy Victorian on the hill in Sea Cliff. The lot was tiny by any but New York City standards, yet because nearly all the houses in the area were about this size and of the same era and built on exactly the same-sized lots, it worked somehow. Finding a legal parking spot on the street was something else again. After a few trips around the block, I pulled into the narrow driveway behind the blue Lexus SUV with the MD plates.

Mehmet Ogologlu didn't seem especially pleased to see me coming up his front steps, though he had invited me over. During our rather terse conversation on the phone the doctor had reinforced his lack of enthusiasm for my curiosity and his continued reluctance to discuss John Tierney. Still, he was a man of his word and kept his promises. I couldn't say that about many people these days. Maybe I was being naïve and people in the past were just more skilled at camouflaging their insincerity. These days it seemed people wore dishonor like a badge. God, I was sounding more crotchety by the minute and even I found my incremental slide towards citizenship in Curmudgeonville annoying.

At the threshold, I removed my shoes and though Dr. Ogologlu didn't burst out in a song of praise, he did at least seem pleased by my gesture of respect. He offered me his hand and asked me to follow him into a comfortably messy parlor.

"We may speak freely here. Would you care for a soft drink, some juice perhaps?" he called to me as he left the room.

"Water's fine."

I sat myself down on the beat-up brown leather sofa.

"Here's your water." He handed me a tall glass and positioned himself on the arm of a recliner.

"Where's the family?"

"Visiting my wife's family."

"In Turkey?"

"Amsterdam, actually." It was only then I noticed a family portrait on the wall. Dr. Ogologlu half sat on an invisible stool, his wife, a lovely Asian woman, at his side, and they were flanked by their two boys, one in his mid-teens, one about ten. New American Gothic.

"They're lovely."

He turned his head to look. "I think so."

"Your wife is Indonesian?"

"From the Netherlands, but yes, her family is Indonesian. That's very astute, Moe. How did you—"

"It seems like I'm always reminding people that I'm like a detective and that I used to be a cop. I'm good at figuring things out. But when you said that the family was in Amsterdam, I figured."

"Most Americans are not very good at remembering colonies and colonial powers. I think that is probably a good thing."

"It's a double-edged sword, that. Americans are better at making history than learning from it."

"Yes, well, I am properly impressed by your broad knowledge and powers of deduction, but that is not why you've come. Now I realize you must want to discuss John Tierney, yet you were most vague on the phone."

"Yesterday, the detective in charge of Sashi Bluntstone's case let me look at all the evidence: case file, interviews, pictures … all of it."

"Still searching for absolution?"

"Answers."

"For you, in this instance, they appear to be synonymous. If you can get answers to the questions, you will be relieved of your guilt."

"You're good, Doc."

He laughed, but with little joy. "Moe, a student in freshman psychology could make that leap."

"But you feel the guilt too. Don't you want answers?"

"We all want answers to big questions, but the essential struggle of being human is to grapple with questions for which there are no easy answers: Where do I come from? Where do I belong? Where am I going? What does it all mean? Religion and philosophy, literature, even science, are human reactions to our ability to ask these fundamental questions. Knowing this doesn't make me feel any the less guilty about the child's murder, but I accept as an occupational hazard that I am not omnipotent and cannot predict how my patients will react under any and all circumstances."

"Sounds like a rationalization."

"It is," he confessed, "but a useful one. So now that we have discussed my own personal house of cards, let us move on to what you wish to discuss?"

"When I was reviewing the formal statements, I noticed that Candy, Sashi's mom, in describing her daughter's clothing, said Sashi liked colorfully patterned bikini-style panties. The detective who searched Sashi's room confirmed this, but in the pictures of her that the cops found on Tierney's altar, she was wearing full-cut, plain white panties. It occurred to me that John—"

"—would have to have planned to have the child for a period of time and would have had to go into a store to purchase this item of clothing."

"Exactly."

Ogologlu's calm and professional demeanor took a sudden turn. He stood up from the arm of the chair and paced the floor, brushing the back of his hand against his face.

"I'm no shrink, Doc, but given Tierney's problems, I can't see him in that environment at all. I mean, this is a guy so nuts he had aluminum foil on his windows, his TV screen facing out away from him, and who was so dead certain he was being monitored and his thoughts were being infiltrated that he had the utilities turned off. But I'm supposed to believe he strolled happily into a Kmart or CVS—well-lit places full of people, security guards, and cameras—and bought a package of little girls' underwear? C'mon."

"No, in my estimation that is a very unlikely scenario. Possibly, if he were still under my care, medicated, and we had gone over a strategy to make such a purchase, he might have, and I strongly emphasize might have, been able to perform such a task. Yet when those conditions were in place, John found it too anxiety-provoking to perform those sorts of errands. Shopping for his most basic needs was beyond him. He could no longer purchase his own clothes. After his mother died, he continued wearing the same few outfits. Even his meals were delivered to his home by a charitable organization."

"Detective McKenna says that maybe he did it at four in the morning when the store was almost empty or that maybe one of his internet friends—"

"He had no friends, Moe. His level of distrust sabotaged any old friendships or family ties and his pathology was such that forming new social bonds was not possible. And I think I have made it clear that it would not have mattered what time he went to the store."

"Yet the new panties are an undeniable fact," I said.

"So it is also a fact that John committed suicide, that the child was murdered, and that John was responsible. That is the your central problem, Moe. It is the problem of bees."

"What?"

"For a very long time it was believed that the laws of physics and aerodynamics indicated that bees could not fly. But bees do fly. We know it. We see them fly. It is an undeniable fact. Just because some answers escape us does not mean there are no answers."

"Well, try this one on for size, Doc. Days before I found John Tierney, someone vandalized my car and left Sashi's teddy bear with its legs and arms bound exactly like her legs and arms were bound in the pictures. Explain how John managed that one."

"But I do not have to explain it because it changes none of the essential truths. Bees fly. John Tierney kidnapped and murdered Sashi Bluntstone."

"You're quite the philosopher, Dr. Ogologlu. Thanks for your time and the water." I stood and walked in the direction of the front door.

"If you were my patient, Moe, I would suggest a certain course of treatment for you because I believe you are on the threshold of a very dark place."

"But I'm not your patient."

"Precisely. And because you are not my patient, I urge you to follow your questions wherever they may lead."

"You're telling me this as a psychiatrist?"

"No, not as a psychiatrist, but as a man who understands that regardless of what I suggest, you will not heed my advice." He laughed that joyless laugh again. "I am being a realist. I can see that you are determined to do this thing. In all frankness, I hope that you succeed, for I have as much to gain by that success as you. The facts, though, will remain unchanged. My fear, however, is that you will not."

"So long, then."

"And to you," he said.

I slipped back into my running shoes and as I knelt to tie the laces, I thought about bees and about the dark places I'd already been.

THIRTY-FOUR

This time it is her eyes, Sashi's eyes. They are on me and in the realm of pinned and wriggling, Prufrock is a distant second. Her lids are closed, not squeezed shut, just closed and transparent, a clear reptilian membrane through which her green eyes accuse. She stares down from Tierney's mildewed walls, the black-eyed saints all gone. I hold the hog-tied teddy bear in my arms. I am frozen, unable to move, to look away. Then, a gunshot. A window breaking. My legs working, I run up the stairs. John Tierney, nude but for little girl's white panties, is dead in his chair. His head impossibly intact, his eyes blackened. I stand in the doorway, pinned again. I unfreeze, step into the room and slip on the blood. I fall through the floor into an ocean of blackness. My eyes won't close. Above me, I somehow see the headless teddy bear floating just out of reach. I extend my arm. I grope for it and the ocean is gone. Now I am falling through air, endless black air, the wind rushing in my ears. I am falling and falling and falling and …

When you're twenty and wake up in a sweat, you've had too much to drink. At my age, it's probably lymphoma. Not this time. It hit me as soon as I woke up from my endless fall: there was more wrong with the accepted version of Sashi's kidnapping and murder than the panties and the vandalism to my car. In his psychosis, John Tierney had blackened the eyes in every photograph and painting and drawing in his house. Tierney had even done it to paintings in portfolios and photo albums stored in boxes in his attic. Why did he do it? Maybe he did it for the same reason he turned the TV to the wall and cut off the utilities. Maybe it had some quasi-religious significance that only he understood. The reason was beside the point. What he hadn't done was to blacken the eyes in the pictures of Sashi that were found on top of the altar. Why do it to the paintings and drawings and photos of Sashi that were in the collage on the wall behind the altar, but not to those on the altar?

If I hadn't already burned both bridges, I would have been on the phone to McKenna and Dr. Ogologlu. Unfortunately, I had burned those bridges. There weren't going to be any second looks at the evidence nor would there be any more polite philosophical conversations with the doctor. Both of them, McKenna and Ogologlu, were right about me, but they were wrong, too. I wasn't *going* to a dark place. I was already there and I was there alone. I wasn't sure I believed in undeniable facts, bumblebees notwithstanding. I was less and less convinced that John Tierney had anything to do with Sashi Bluntstone's murder, no matter what all the hard evidence indicated. That was ice-cold comfort because there was the part of me that distrusted my own motives for believing in John Tierney. Because if Tierney *was* guilty, he really wasn't. That's what'd gotten lost in all of this heartache. Tierney wasn't responsible for the chemical imbalance in his brain or for the genetic flaw in his DNA. If he killed Sashi, he was an innocent monster. And if he was, the only guilt left on the table would be my own.

Then, as if on cue, Declan Carney called and asked me to come get the paintings and the test results.

● . ͜

Dressed in carpenter pants, a paint-smeared Hunter College sweatshirt, and work boots, Declan Carney wasn't quite as fancifully decked out as when we first met. Gone were the Hawaiian shirt, kilt, tube socks, and Birkenstocks. He'd also shaved his head of the Mohawk, side curls, Fu Manchu, and soul patch. But I found out soon enough that his newfound Bohemian look did not mean he had abandoned his idiosyncrasies. When I made to shake his hand, he backed away.

"Take no offense," he said, "but on Skajit it is our holy month and physical contact with other sentient beings is forbidden."

"No offense taken."

Outside, on the street in front of his building, they were tearing up the pavement. And though the noise was far from unbearable, it was enough to get your attention. It certainly had Carney's attention. He could not seem to stop himself from staring over his shoulder at the filthy windows that would have looked down on the work below.

"Mr. Carney, can I have the results, please?" He didn't react immediately, apparently still distracted by the work noise. "Please," I repeated.

"Yes, the results."

Continuing to look over his shoulder, he walked over to a workbench and grabbed a bound report about an inch thick. "These are my findings. There is a detailed analysis of the tests I ran, the methods I used …" His voice drifted off as he handed me the file. He made sure our hands didn't touch.

I flipped through the report. It seemed incredibly thorough, but frankly, I didn't give a shit about anything other than his conclusions.

"So, what's the verdict?"

"Excuse me," he said, his attention elsewhere.

"What are your conclusions?"

"The results are there in the—"

"Look, Carney, no offense, but I'd like a few minutes of your time. I realize we didn't agree on a price, but by the appearance of this report, it's not gonna be cheap."

"What?"

I repeated myself.

"I will send you the invoice. The paintings are there." He pointed to a crate at the side of his workbench. You've got to love someone who returns things in better packaging than the packaging you delivered the goods in. "Please, just leave."

"Will you go look out the goddamned window already so we can talk."

He relented. "All right. What is it you want to know?"

"Did Sashi Bluntstone do those paintings?"

"Yes and no."

"Well, that just clears everything up, doesn't it? Did she or didn't she?"

"The first painting shows a consistency of brush stroke, material—"

I was beginning to lose it. "For fuck's sake, Carney, just give it to me in English, clear, concise English for idiots."

"She did the first painting entirely on her own. The second painting she had some help with. The third painting was done almost entirely by the person who helped her do the second painting. Now that you have your answer, please leave."

"The last time I was here, you warned me about monsters."

"Yes."

"Innocent monsters in particular."

"Yes." I seemed finally to have drawn his attention.

"I found one, you know?"

"I know, the man who murdered Sashi Bluntstone."

"Him, yeah."

"I was saddened to hear of the child's death, but it is what you anticipated."

"Yes and no," I said, tweaking him a bit.

He smiled briefly. "But you expected she would already be dead, so what is the matter?"

"I did, but I was shocked—I am shocked by who they say did it."

"You do not believe this man Tierney killed her?"

"I don't want to believe it."

He smiled again, but this time it looked like a gunshot wound. "It would seem you are his second victim, then."

"You know I did a little checking up on you."

"To what end?"

"I don't know," I said. "I guess I was a little curious and I felt sorry for you."

"Your sorrow was misguided. Sorrow often is."

"So are guilt and blame, Carney."

"Oh, do you really think so, Mr. Prager? I think the guilty know exactly who they are. Goodbye."

When I got downstairs with the paintings, a workman stopped me from going to my car as a yellow front-end loader scooped up huge bucketfuls of chopped-up asphalt and dropped them into the box of a Mack dump truck. I turned and looked up and saw an open third-floor window. Declan Carney was staring down intently at the commotion in the street, but I was fairly certain he was seeing and hearing very different things than was I. I tried to imagine what he was seeing and hearing, yet no matter how hard I tried to hear the screams of the Iraqi soldiers Carney had suffocated beneath the chuff and grunts of the bulldozer and desert sands, I could not hear them. I noticed Carney wiping his cheeks. I could not see his tears.

THIRTY-FIVE

I was never much of a New Year's Eve kind of guy. I guess I'm not much on holidays all the way around. I never liked being told how to feel or when to feel it. Besides, holidays, all of them, not only Christmas, seemed either too commercial or artificial or both. I liked Passover. I liked everything about it because, even if you were in the most fucked-up mood imaginable, there's no two ways to feel about being freed from slavery. Then again, if I was destined to like a holiday, Passover was going to be the one. My name *is* Moses.

Oddly enough, I found myself on the couch half watching football, drinking some more of Paul Stern's single snob whiskey and missing the hell out of Mary Lambert. I started out mad, but by my third sip it was all just melting away into missing her. She lied to me. PIs are liars. I was a liar. I made a mental list of who I hadn't lied to over the last few weeks. Very short list, that. But Mary and I had chemistry. I felt it. That couldn't have been a lie. It just couldn't. Can women fake orgasms? The answer's pretty obviously yes and I didn't even like thinking about who might have acted her part in my bed. What pissed me off about the concept of faking it is that women assume we're so fucking fragile that we need to feel the roof rafters shudder when they come. Well, no, that's not what pissed me off. What pissed me off was that they were right. We are that fragile. There are things, however, that can't be faked. That's what got to me, her walking away from a rare kind of connection that no one should ever walk away from. But what did I know? Maybe I had been played for a love-hungry idiot. Maybe there wasn't anything in the world that couldn't be faked.

It wasn't that I couldn't live without someone to come home to, someone to need, and love. I functioned pretty well on my own the whole time I was on the job and I managed to dress and feed myself for the last seven years without someone packing my lunch and laying my clothes out on the bed—but I didn't want to just manage or function anymore. My life always had more meaning when I was with Katy as it did during my brief time with Carmella. I didn't want to die alone in a wheelchair-accessible apartment that Sarah and her husband-to-be-named-later set up for me in their house. Sixty might be the new forty, but there was no such thing as the new dead. Same as it ever was. There was no denying that I was closer to the end, a lot closer, than the beginning.

By my second glass of scotch, it dawned on me that I'd only felt the kind of connection and chemistry I had with Mary Lambert twice in my life. Now both those women were gone. That's why I cursed Mary Lambert or whatever the hell her name was for walking away from it. You don't just walk away from such a rare gift. That's why people want to live forever, you know. Not to go through the daily grind and pain and bullshit, but for the hope of those few things that make your heart race. What's the rest of it worth, really? And somehow, even with my Scrooge-ian take on holidays, I just knew Mary would have been the perfect woman to spend New Year's Eve with. She would have made it fun. I saw in her someone to make the other stuff worth it.

I suppose I was in an especially grumpy mood because I'd hoped Sarah might go to dinner with me, but she said she'd already made plans. Then she rubbed salt in the wound by telling me she couldn't come to Sashi's memorial with me either. I didn't press her for details. We were still making a comeback. We weren't quite there yet. Even my newfound friend and scotch supplier, Paul Stern, turned me down. After I hung up the phone with him, I started grumbling to myself about him being just like Rico, and that was before I had anything to drink. Aaron invited me to spend the night with him and Cindy, but regardless of my love for them, I politely said no. For the last thirty years they'd gotten together with the same group of friends and played board games and watched the ball drop. It was tradition. Theirs, not mine. I would rather have gone to the dentist.

I actually did call Jimmy Palumbo and offered to meet him in the City or somewhere out on the Island and buy him a New Year's steak dinner. He turned me down flat, but in the nicest possible way and it had nothing to do with his latest financial gains. Well, maybe it did, sort of.

"Sorry, man, I just can't. I'd really like too, but I gotta say no." In the background, I heard a young dog yapping for attention. "Excuse me for a second, Moe." Then to the dog, "Okay, you, calm down. Atta girl, calm down. Good girl."

"New puppy?"

"Had her a couple a weeks."

"What about tonight?" I asked. "A family party or something?"

"Nah, I'm packing up and gettin' outta here. There's nothing for me here anymore except bad memories. I gave my notice to the museum yesterday and the house goes on the market later this week. I need a new start."

"Where?"

"I don't know yet. I'm puttin' some stuff in storage, gettin' on the boat with the pup, and going. I guess I'll head south first with the shitty weather here and all. Then, who knows."

"When you leaving?"

"Maybe tomorrow."

"New year, new start," I said. "Nice symmetry."

"Maybe, but probably I'll leave the day after tomorrow. Loose ends and shit. You know?"

"I know. Well, good luck, brother. I hope things work out for you."

"Me too, but I got a good feeling about it. Things are different now. Thanks for everything, man."

I'd thought about offering up some tired platitudes about there being no escape from yourself and that wherever a man goes, he takes his woes with him. No need to inflict my rotten mood on him, I thought, and just said goodbye.

Another scotch later, I actually found myself wondering what Dr. Ogologlu was doing, if his family was still in Amsterdam. My stubborn refusal to buy into the facts about Tierney's role in Sashi Bluntstone's death had finally begun to fade. I think it was when Declan Carney implied that my desperately clinging to belief in Tierney's innocence had made me yet another victim that I began to wake up as if from a fitful sleep. On my ride back from Long Island City, I'd gone over all the possible scenarios and the only one that made any sense involved John Tierney and Sashi. I could manage to implicate Randy Junction, Sonia Barrows-Willingham, Max, and even Candy in some of those scenarios, but I couldn't see it ending up the way it had. I was tempted to call both McKenna and the doctor and swear that I'd finally seen the light. *Hallelujah! Praise the Lord!* But what would they have cared? Besides, I was going to see McKenna soon enough.

When I woke up on the couch, the ball had dropped, the new year had come in without my notice, and the world had moved on. It always does.

THIRTY-SIX

There was a rather bizarre carnival-like atmosphere to the whole thing. Mrs. Sonia Barrows-Willingham had hired a valet parking service to handle the cars of the memorial attendees. And by the look of the makeshift parking lot, there were going to be more people here than at an April Mets game at Shea during the mid-'70s. I arrived at about the same time as Detective McKenna and he was in a fairly pissy mood to begin with. Maybe a little drunk too.

"Can you believe this shit?" he asked, pointing at all the cars already parked in neat rows on the east lawn. "So much for that intimate little memorial service, huh?"

"Let's hang out here and maybe the MetLife blimp will show up for overhead coverage."

"Too cloudy for that. Snow's in the air."

I looked up. "Yeah, you're right."

"Here are your claim checks, gentlemen," a very polite, dark-skinned East Asian kid said, handing us our receipts.

The claim tags were playing card–size renderings of Sashi Bluntstone paintings. Just amazing. Inside, they probably had life-size Jell-O molds of Sashi's paintings.

"You see these guys parking the cars, Prager? All freakin' Indians and Chinks. What'd she do, hire the high school chess and math teams?

Un-fuckin'-believable."

I didn't bother saying anything to him about his not so subtle racism. Some guys bring their racism to the job. Sometimes the job brings the racism to them. And no matter which way you were infected, alcohol made things worse.

"You think this thing's catered?" he asked.

"Given that there's valet parking, I'd say the chances are pretty good."

"I hope they have those little hot dogs. It's not a party without the little hot dogs."

"It's not a party," I reminded him.

"You think?"

"Come on, let's get inside before it starts snowing."

I put my hand on McKenna's shoulder and urged him forward. Closer to him now, I could smell the alcohol strong on his breath. He wasn't staggering, but he was tight. Apparently I hadn't been the only one struggling with his part in this whole ordeal.

A very large, head-shaven, well-dressed black man stood guard at the door. He kept his hands at his side and wore a practiced expression that walked the line between dispassion and threat. His suit jacket was cut loosely enough to hide the sidearm he was no doubt carrying beneath it, but given the circus atmosphere, I wasn't sure whether he was here to keep the press in or out. McKenna took one look at the guy, blew air loudly through his lips, and shook his head in disdain. He did it specifically so the security man would notice. If he had noticed, he didn't show it.

"What the fuck, Prager? They think a fight's gonna break out here or what?"

"I think it's just a precaution. Rich people can get pretty weird about security, especially if paparazzi are involved."

"Who even gives a shit anymore?" he said. "The kid's old news. You have any idea how many other little girls have been murdered over the last few weeks?"

It was a question that required no answer, but I answered anyway to try and move him off the subject: "Too many."

"One is too many."

"You'll get no argument from me."

"Gentlemen," the security man said, politely nodding his head and opening the door.

We stepped in.

"They're really gonna screw me, Moe."

"Who is?"

"The fucking bosses. My rabbi says they want to stick me in IA and there's nothing he can do to protect me. Me, in Internal Affairs! Jesus, I might as well put in my papers or eat my gun."

"Don't be an ass. Come on, let's see what's what."

It was apparent pretty quickly what was what. There were bars set up in the main hallway at the base of each of the two staircases. At one of the bars, I recognized the faces of some local female TV reporters, their heavy makeup looking ridiculous under normal lighting. What was a circus without clowns, right? I guess the news vans were parked around the rear of the house. At least I didn't see any cameras, but that didn't mean the cameramen weren't setting up in the room where the memorial was to be held. There was a small army of tuxedoed servers passing trays of hors d'oeuvres. None of the silver trays seemed to contain those little hot dogs. This didn't much please McKenna nor did the presence of the media.

"Fuck this! I'm getting a drink." He walked away. I didn't try to stop him. He was a man on a mission.

On the other hand, I had no intention of drinking. While I'd made a dent in the bottle of fancy scotch on New Year's Eve, I hadn't overdone it. I meant to keep it that way, but when I saw Sarah walking towards me, I changed my mind on the notion of temporary sobriety. She was holding someone's hand as she approached. That someone was Paul Stern. I was painfully aware of her taking note of the disapproval in my expression before I even realized exactly what it was I was feeling.

"Hi, Dad." She leaned over and kissed my cheek.

"Moe," Paul said, letting go of Sarah's hand to shake mine. I shook it. I wasn't happy, but I wasn't a complete idiot.

"We've been seeing each other since Christmas Eve," Sarah said. "Be happy about it, Dad."

"You don't need my approval to date."

"Yes, we do," Paul said. "You know we do."

"Well, I need a drink. I'll see you guys later."

I walked over to one of the bars where Randy Junction was milling about with a rather spectacular blond. She wasn't young, but the forty years or so she'd managed to live hadn't laid a glove on her. She had that perfect Morgan Fairchild nose and violet eyes that were impossible not to stare at. She saw me staring, but she was used to being stared at. Junction was used to men staring at her.

"Mr. Prager," he said, after I collected my scotch, "this is my wife, Jill. Jill, Moe Prager. He's the—"

"—man that found Sashi's killer, yes." Her voice was as husky as she was lean. "It's a pleasure to meet you." She offered me her hand. "Thank you for finding out what happened, though I wish things had turned out differently."

"Me too."

"A lost child of any kind is a tragedy," she said.

That cut deep. I remembered back to Katy's miscarriage, how it tore her up inside, how it caused the first subtle cracks in our marriage. I took a prodigious gulp of scotch. "It's awful for everyone."

"Except for my husband and the cunt throwing this strange little affair."

"Jill!" Junction snapped.

"Don't *Jill* me! You and that dried-up bitch will need your own private bank tellers now that Sashi's dead."

"Okay, that's quite enough from you." He grabbed his wife's arm, but she pulled away from him.

"Again, Mr. Prager, a pleasure to meet you." She sauntered off into the crowd.

"You'll have to excuse my wife. She's had a little too much to drink already."

"Seemed in control of her faculties to me."

"It's Sashi. You see, she can't have children," he said with blame in his voice. It wasn't that they couldn't have children. *She* couldn't have them.

"She can't have children and you can't keep your dick in your pants. I think I'll take her side in this."

"You don't understand. Sure, she's very beautiful, but—"

"Save the explanations for someone who gives a shit, okay? And by the way, I got some of the paintings back."

You've got to love human reflex because in spite of himself and his surroundings and his wife's commentary on his greed, Randy Junction's eyes got big and he smiled a big wet juicy smile. *Money makes the world go around, the world go around, the world go around …* The best part was watching him struggle to wipe his face clean of joy. He just couldn't do it and I guess he figured it wasn't worth the effort. I wasn't worth it.

"Try not to ejaculate right here, Randy," I said, waving my glass at the bartender for a refill. "A double." The bartender more than obliged.

Junction was gone before the words were out of my mouth. No doubt to hunt for Sonia Barrows-Willingham and tell her about the recovered paintings.

As I walked away from the bar, Candy looped her arm through mine and marched me into a library like the ones that I used to think existed only in movies. You know, shelf after walnut shelf of colorfully bound volumes with gilded titles on leatherbound spines. There was even a painting of a fox hunt and a big antique globe from when Ogologlu's home country was losing its grip on a nice chunk of the world. She closed the door behind us.

"I saw you talking to Randy and Jill."

"I saw Mommy kissing Santa Claus, so what?"

"Come on, Mr.—Moe. Did you tell—"

"Not for me to tell."

Candy exhaled for the first time since she found me. "She's beautiful, isn't she?"

"Jill? Mrs. Junction? Yes, very."

"Why would he want me when he could have her? I know that's what you're thinking."

"Not even close."

She seemed not to hear. "You don't know about their situation. You don't understand."

"Funny. That's what Randy tried to tell me."

"And …"

"I'm not judging you, Candy, but what are you doing?"

"I don't know."

"Exactly. Now's not the time to trust your decisions. You're grieving."

"I want my life back. I want a life where I can have some joy. Do you know what it's been like being a slave to my own daughter? To be an adjunct, a second thought, to have my needs be the last rung on the ladder? Everything I've done since the day Sashi first picked up a brush has been about her career."

"Well, you're free now."

"That's right," she said, stepping uncomfortably close to me. "I can do whatever I want." And before I could react, she kissed me on the mouth, and with intent.

"Stop that!" I pushed her away hard and wiped my mouth with the back of my hand.

Candy made to slap my face, but I grabbed her hand before she even came close. When she calmed down, she said, "Why did you do that, push me away like that? I've wanted to kiss you like that since I was fourteen."

"Well, you're not fourteen anymore, but you are acting like someone who wants to be punished. Try and remember that today is about Sashi. Let yourself feel the grief and the guilt if you have to, but don't look to me for answers. I don't have the ones you want."

She was sobbing now, quietly, into the palms of her hands. Grief does stupid things to people. I knew firsthand about that. I'd done my share of acting out too. If I'd made Candy take note of that, then good, I was glad. If I'd just hurt her feelings … Well, it was a day for hurt feelings.

"I've got three of the paintings back."

She looked up out of her hands, her makeup smeared, but the tears turned off.

"What? How? I don't under—"

"I did use one to bribe someone and that got me to Tierney," I said. "I had the other three tested by an expert for authenticity."

"But—"

"They're in the trunk of my car. I've already told Junction. You guys can get them when this thing, whatever this is, is over. Right now, I need another drink."

Actually, I felt more like I needed another shower, but a drink was the best I could do under the circumstances. I got a double on the rocks and went to find a quiet little corner for myself. Even with all the people in attendance, I thought, there were lots of quiet corners in a house that size. One of the things thwarting my quest was that there were an inordinate number of flat screens set up around the house showing endless videos of Sashi. Some of the images registered, but I mostly tried to avoid watching. Finally, I found a kind of nook on one of the staircase landings between the second and third floors. There was a small stained glass window that let in light and a pillow-covered oak bench built into the landing wall. I sat down and slowed down my drinking, trying to sip at this one. It was lovely up here and the noise from the main floor was only a quiet medley of shuffling feet and soft whispers.

"My husband used to love this spot." It was Sonia Barrows-Willingham in all her desiccated glory. "That's a Tiffany window there behind you."

"Nice place," I said, feeling the scotch.

"I understand you've managed to recoup certain assets, some of which are mine."

"News travels fast around here."

"It travels fast everywhere, Mr. Prager, or hadn't you noticed?"

"Nah, I'm a Pony Express kinda guy myself," I heard the scotch say.

She did that grotesque barking laugh of hers. "Where are my paintings?"

"In my car. The kids out front have my keys," I said, reaching into my pocket for my claim check. "Give this to them and they can get them out of the trunk."

She snatched the card out of my hand and headed back down the stairs. I waited to speak until she'd almost made it to the landing below.

"Oh, Mrs. Barrows-Willingham, I nearly forgot to mention …"

"And what would that be, Mr. Prager?"

"Next to the crate with the paintings is a copy of a report on the authenticity of the paintings that you might find a fascinating read. I'm certain the press will find it equally fascinating. It was convenient of you to invite them, by the way. Thanks. You saved me a lot of bother."

She didn't say a word, but about-faced and was standing back in front of me within seconds.

"That reward money was merely a token of my generosity, Moe."

"It's Moe now, is it?"

"If you like. As I was saying, that hundred thousand was only a tiny sampling of my generosity. I can be far far more giving. Unfortunately, I am not blessed with Candy or Jill Junction's looks, but I find that men are more easily swayed by money in any case. Money can get you all the Jills and Candys you could ever want."

"No sale, sorry. I don't want them or your money. I already gave the hundred grand away."

She didn't flinch. "Force is also very effective and much less expensive."

"You're threatening me now? I don't much like threats."

"No one does. I believe that's the whole point."

I put my scotch down and reached around for my .38. I unhinged the cylinder and spun it like a wheel of fortune. "Round and round she goes …" I snapped the cylinder back in place and pantomimed shooting her. "Pow, pow, pow."

She said nothing, but swallowed hard.

"Don't ever threaten me again, Mrs. Barrows-Willingham. I know some people who would make what John Tierney did to Sashi a pleasant alternative to what they would do to you. And if you think I'm fucking around, try me."

I picked up my scotch glass and left her standing there, shaking. I went downstairs to try and find a real human being. In a million years, I never thought I'd be happy to see Max, but grief and loss make for strange bedfellows. I found him in the butler's pantry, drinking bourbon straight out of the bottle and looking even more wrecked and wretched than when we last spoke. He wasn't crying, but he recently had been, a lot. Through all this, he was the only one who seemed fully in touch with what he'd lost. Love, even parental love, is a complicated thing, but Max's was pure. In the end, he was the only *mensch* amongst the monsters. *Mensch*, in Yiddish, means a real man. He handed me the bottle and I took a sip.

"Tough day," I said.

"Impossible."

Then there came an announcement over the intercom. The circus was about to begin.

Showtime.

THIRTY-SEVEN

I got the point of last rites and wakes, funerals, and spadefuls of dirt thrown on sunken caskets. I understood funeral pyres and scattering ashes on the wind. In my middle age, I'd even come to grips with the tradition of sitting *shiva*, but what the fuck was the point of a memorial service? It was like group masturbation, a communal circle jerk. That's what I kept thinking as speaker after speaker got up in front of the crowd and spewed polite niceties about Sashi Bluntstone. Talk about being damned with faint praise ... I hadn't known her and now I never would, but, Jesus Christ, didn't anyone like her? The only people who had genuinely heartfelt things to say about Sashi herself were Ming, the last real friend Sashi had had; Ming's mom, Dawn Parson; and old Ben Schare, who used to walk his dog along the beach with Sashi and Cara. All the rest of them could do was to fall over each other in praise of the kid's work, her artistic vision and talent. Neither Candy nor Max had it in them to speak, thank goodness. I'd already done a slug of bourbon, a single, and two big double Dewars. Listening to them make a public spectacle of their grief would have pushed me over the top. McKenna was already there.

He was buzzed when we walked into the house. Now he was absolutely legless, which he proved by loudly stumbling out of the cavernous room in which the service was being held.

"Where's the fucking bathroom in this mausoleum?" he shouted angrily at the security man who helped him to his feet and presumably the facilities.

As I stood there half listening to the moneychangers in sheep's clothing drone on about Sashi's brilliance, I felt like I was trapped in a made-for-TV Agatha Christie movie or a game of Clue. *Colonel Mustard in the library with a candlestick.* God knows, the setting was perfect: a country manor house. Shit, we even had the lead detective and private investigator on hand. The doubts I had about Tierney reasserted themselves and, with a push from my scotch consumption, my mind drifted off, meandering through all the scenarios I had tried to work through on my ride home from Declan Carney's.

Yet, none of those scenarios had made any sense at the time. That, or they all led to obstacles that could not overcome logic or the facts, but I hadn't entertained the thought that more than one or two of them—Sonia, Junction, Candy, maybe even Max—were working in concert. They all certainly had motives, whether it was greed or debt or a need for escape. It wasn't a big leap to see how they might've planned a fake kidnapping that had gone terribly wrong. My guess was that McKenna and the cops had had that very same thought early on in their investigations and had clung stubbornly to it until it was too late. But even if they had all been in it together, Sashi having been killed accidentally, there was still John Tierney, the photographs, and the bones. The only link there was me. Then, just as something flashed in the corner of my mind—a vague image from the videos showing all around the house—I was roused from my trance by a loud ovation. When my eyes looked outward again, I noticed that all the assembled were looking at me as they stood and applauded.

"Yes, it is Mr. Moses Prager to whom we owe a great debt of gratitude," said Sonia Barrows-Willingham, now at the podium. "It was through his efforts and his alone, that we learned of poor Sashi's fate. Without his efforts on her behalf, we would all have been left to suffer endless years of torment over what had become of her."

I don't think I ever felt more uncomfortable in my life. My skin crawled at the perversity of the spectacle and it was all I could do not to run. I bowed my head and walked quickly out of the room. I found the bar and McKenna found me.

"Two double Dewars," he said before I could breathe.

"Don't you think you've had enough, McKenna?"

"Enough! I've only just begun to fight."

"Somehow, I don't think scotch was what John Paul Jones had in mind."

"You like Led Zeppelin?"

"Not that John Paul Jones," I said.

"I know, you asshole." He slapped my back hard, a little too hard, as the barman put our drinks down and the memorial crowd began shuffling out of the big room. "So that was a nice round of applause there."

"Nice isn't the word I would use."

He either hadn't heard me or didn't agree. "You get a hundred grand and a standing fucking O and I get to become Detective Cheeseeater and rat. IA, here I come." He wasn't exactly whispering as he spoke. Heads turned our way.

"Try and keep it down, okay?"

He shrugged his shoulders and put his hand over his mouth. "Yeah, we wouldn't want people to stare."

I didn't think pushing back was the best strategy with McKenna in his current state. Push a drunk and he pushes back harder. This was the classic bar brawl setup: two drunks in shitty moods, one with a particularly nasty bug up his ass. Frankly, in a different setting, I might have been willing to go at it with him. I was pretty fed up with the whole situation too. I hadn't asked for any of it: the money or the applause. Over the last three or four weeks I'd found a dead baby in its crib and seen the ugly side of things I thought I'd left behind years ago. I found love or what I thought might be love and had it walk away from me, and to top it off, my daughter was dating the son of a guy who had sold me out and tried to get me killed. A fight was just what the doctor ordered, but instead of throwing punches, we clinked glasses.

"*Sláinte*," I said.

"*Póg mo thóin*, Prager." Kiss my ass.

We drank. I sipped, he guzzled, slamming his empty down on top of the bar like it was a shot glass.

"Again!"

"Yo, McKenna, there are other people on line. Let's slow down a little, okay, buddy."

"Buddy! I ain't your fuckin' buddy. Do you think you'd get a standing O if these pricks knew you withheld evidence?"

Now all heads were turned, everyone staring our way. You could almost hear the whir and whoosh of the machines keeping Barrows-Willingham's husband alive up on the third floor. The time for pushback had arrived, but I didn't want to do it on the main stage. There was only one way to manage it.

"All right, come on, let's go do this somewhere else."

McKenna wasn't expecting that. He was an aging cop, but I was just old, about twenty years his senior, and I don't think he expected me to bite. Unfortunately, he was a little too drunk to let reason enter into his decision. I had hoped he would take it as an offer to talk it out.

"Okay, fuckhead." Apparently, talking it out wasn't an option.

"Dad, don't do this!" Sarah screamed, pushing her way through the crowd with Paul's help.

"I'll be fine. I know what I'm doing."

"But you—"

"Let him go, Sarah," Paul said, looking me straight in the eye and pulling my daughter gently away from me. "Trust him."

I felt in a time warp, like Rico Tripoli was talking to me out of the past, telling me he had my back. Funny thing is, Rico never really had my back, but for some reason I knew his son did.

"Come on, McKenna, follow me," I said.

I had an idea of where I was going as I'd walked the house in my search for a quiet spot. I marched us towards a den that was full of soft and cushy furniture and not as many breakable objects d'art as in some other parts of the house. There was a giant, wall-mounted, flat screen TV in there too, but unless I missed a room with a boxing ring, this was the best I could do on short notice. To my dismay, the crowd seemed to be following us and at the head of the mob was our hostess.

"Come on, Prager," McKenna shouted behind me, "you trying to tire me out or what?"

"Just shut up. You'll get a piece of me soon enough."

Then we all seemed to spill into the den I was looking for. The TV was on, but even in my agitated state, that same vague image caught my eye once again. Before I could fully focus on the image, McKenna charged me, knocking me back onto the thick Berber carpeting. That was a good thing because my head thumped down pretty good. McKenna was on top of me and I could hear and feel that the fall had taken as much or more of a toll on him as on me. I chopped the side of my left fist down into his right kidney and the air rushed out of him with a sick groan. He went limp. With that, I bridged my neck and shoulders and rolled him off me. I stood. He staggered to his feet.

"Pretty good for an old fuck," he said, rubbing his kidney.

He swung a roundhouse right at me, but he was even drunker than

I thought and I easily ducked the punch, delivering a right to his liver. He went down on his knees and vomited all over the nice carpet. Everyone's attention was on him, but mine was on the screen. There it was again.

"What's this?" I shouted, pointing at the screen.

"A Panasonic," an unseen voice answered back.

"No. What's this playing? What am I watching?"

"These are videos I had of Sashi's shows," Sonia said, somewhat disappointed that the fight hadn't made it out of the first round. "I had a film editor put them together to run in a loop and had them transferred to a disc. Why do you ask?"

"I'm not sure, something caught my eye." I turned and watched some more.

People were attending to McKenna, who was on his knees, drinking bottled water as someone applied a cold cloth to the back of his neck. Staff had appeared out of nowhere and were busily blotting up the mess the detective had made on the rug in front of him.

"What is it, Dad? What do you see?" Sarah and Paul stood on either side of me.

"I don't know," I said, watching scenes of Sashi and Ming and Cara the dog racing about as adults ogled her paintings, sipping Chardonnay and acting as if they were in the presence of greatness. It was all so surreal. "I don't know. Something. There! Stop. There!" I shouted. "Go back. Somebody stop it!"

Sonia found the controller and flashed back in that odd, still frame-by-frame way digitized video does.

"There!"

"For goodness sakes, what is it?" Sonia was screaming now.

"Him!" I pointed to a large man in the background, his arms folded across his massive chest, his eyes focused on Sashi in the foreground.

"What's he doing there?"

"Security," Candy said as she stepped forward. "He worked for a security firm we hired to keep an eye on Sashi after she had gotten some weird fan letters."

I shoved my way towards McKenna and yanked him up onto his feet. "Come on, McKenna. Let's go."

"Where're we going?"

"To catch the real killer."

"What? Not that—"

"Somebody call the Suffolk County Police Marine Bureau and tell them to get a boat to Santapogue Point."

McKenna squinted at me. "Santapogue Point. Where the hell is that?"

"It's on the Great South Bay in Babylon. I'll explain on the way. Let's go!"

There had been another link between John Tierney and Sashi Bluntstone, only it hadn't dawned on me until that moment.

THIRTY-EIGHT

Fuck!

There was a three-inch blanket of white on the ground, the cars, the long driveway, and darkness had crept in under the cover of snow. Wind howled, icy flakes lashing our faces. I reached a gloveless hand into my pocket for my claim check and remembered that I'd given it to Sonia. No way I was going back inside.

"McKenna, give me your claim check."

"Huh?"

"Your car claim check, give it to me."

He was dazed, a little child just woken from sleep, patting his pockets down without rhyme or reason. The fight had braced him a bit and the vomiting had done him some good, but he was still drunk. Only time was going to make that better. Even fueled by my adrenaline rush, I wasn't exactly feeling like a prize rooster either. Finally, McKenna pulled the playing card–sized stub out of his coat pocket. Paul Stern rushed past, grabbed it, and handed it to the eager valet.

"Neither of you guys is in any shape to drive," Paul said, "and especially not in this weather."

"This is police business, Paul."

He flipped open a shield at me. "And I'm an assistant State's Attorney in Windham County, Vermont. I told you I was a lawyer, but you never asked what kind. You probably assumed I was an ambulance chaser?"

He was right. That's exactly what I'd assumed. "You're out of your jurisdiction," was all I managed to say.

"And you're a drunk sixty-year-old man who hasn't worn a badge in almost thirty years. Besides, I grew up in Vermont and was raised to drive in snow like this with my eyes closed. I've seen how downstate New Yorkers drive in this soup and it's not pretty."

McKenna opened his mouth to say something, but he either forgot what he had to say or thought better of it. Then the valet pulled up to the front entrance with the detective's car. Paul Stern handed the kid a fiver and went straight for the driver's seat.

"In or out, gentlemen? Come on."

We both got in, me up front with Paul Stern and McKenna in the back.

"Hang on," Paul shouted and hit the gas. The Crown Vic held a pretty steady line as we drove down the long drive and through the front gates. "Just tell me where I'm going and I'll get us there."

I gave him directions how to go south and east, but once we got off Chicken Valley Road and onto 107, it was a total slog.

After about five minutes and two hundred yards of torturous progress on 107, McKenna seemed to regain some brain function and lose all his patience. "Fuck this! Moe, hit that switch and that switch there," he said, leaning over the seat and pointing at the dash.

When I did as he asked, the wailing siren kicked on, lights embedded in the grill strobed ahead of us and a bar of like-colored lights mounted to the back window flashed behind us. Now we were cooking and Paul seemed to know exactly what he was doing at the wheel.

"A highway patrol unit?" I asked.

"It's what they gave me. Good thing too."

"Call the Suffolk cops," I said, turning back to McKenna, reciting Jimmy Palumbo's address to him. "Tell them to close off his block, but not to approach him. He's a big, strong motherfucker and he's got a carry permit. I know he carries a Sig 9mm and probably has other weapons too. No need to get anybody hurt here."

"Jimmy Palumbo, the guy who played for the Jets?" McKenna puzzled.

"Him. Just make the call and remind them to have their marine unit in West Babylon Creek at Santapogue Point. I just hope he hasn't split yet."

"What's that ex-jock got to do with this?"

"Everything," I said. "Everything."

I listened as McKenna made the call. Things were going fine until he said the part about them not approaching the house. Cops are more territorial than Siamese fighting fish and they don't want to hear a cop from a neighboring county telling them how to handle business inside their own bailiwick. Hell, when I was on the job, we didn't like guys from the next precinct over even setting foot on our turf. McKenna wasn't exactly in the best of shape to begin with and he was a bad drunk: one of those guys who had it all under control when they were dry, but who seemed to completely lose it after a few drinks. And at that moment he was fighting a losing battle with his Suffolk County counterpart on the other end of the phone. I waved to get his attention.

"Hold on a second," McKenna slurred, covering the phone with his palm. "What?"

"What's going on?"

"The police boat's in position, but they want to send in the freakin' troops. You know, in Suffolk they don't get to use the SWAT team too often except to break up loud summer parties in the Hamptons. What am I going to say to him? He's pissed off enough as it is."

I thought for a few seconds. "Tell him we think Sashi's still alive."

"What?"

"You heard me. Just tell him that. They're not gonna storm the Bastille if there's a chance she's alive."

"You don't think she really is, do you?"

"No," I said, "not for a second."

"*They're* not going to believe it either. They may be Suffolk County yahoos, but even they can read papers and watch TV."

"Tell him whatever the fuck you have to to convince him we've got new evidence that she's alive. Have your chief call their chief, whatever."

I needed to talk to Jimmy Palumbo and the only way to make sure the cops didn't go in guns blazing was to convince them he still had Sashi with him and that she was still alive. He was our only hope of finding her remains. The cruel irony of having to pretend she was alive to find her dead wasn't lost on any of us and we all bowed our heads there for a second. Then McKenna shrugged his shoulders and repeated what I said. After another few seconds, he got off the phone.

"Fuck me if it didn't work. That asshole captain changed his tune as soon as I said we think the kid might still be alive."

"No one wants to go in shooting if a little kid's around. Would you?"

"Well, we stalled them for now, but they won't wait forever."

"It won't be forever, just another couple of minutes."

• . •

I flicked off the siren and lights a block before we turned south off Montauk Highway. Without being told to, Paul slowed the car down. Unlike Main Street, the streets in this part of Babylon were really slick and had yet to be plowed, though the police cruisers that had preceded us left several sets of tire tracks cut into the otherwise pristine layer of snow. About three blocks before Palumbo's street, I told Paul to pull over.

"What are you planning on doing?"

"What if I told you I had to take a leak?"

"With all due respect, I'd say you were full of shit. Forget it."

"Yeah," McKenna agreed, "you're not going to get yourself killed on my watch."

"It's not your county and it's not your watch. I led Palumbo right to John Tierney and gave him more than enough money to get away. You said it yourself, McKenna, the cops won't wait forever. If they kill Palumbo, we'll never know what happened to Sashi's body. I'm not risking it. I think he'll talk to me."

"I don't like it."

Paul agreed with the detective even as he slowed to a ten-mile-an-hour crawl to take a left turn. I didn't put it up for further debate or a vote. I simply opened the door and rolled out of the Crown Vic into a drift. Ten miles an hour was about eight miles an hour too many. The snow cushioned my landing a little bit, a very little bit, and I banged down pretty good, the breath knocked out of my lungs as if a house had fallen on me. But the adrenaline kicked in again and I was up and running. Not very steadily or fast, my bad knee killing me, but running nonetheless. I didn't look back and I didn't think ahead. I just knew I had to get to Palumbo before the cops did.

The wind was more ferocious down here on the Great South Bay and it whipped the snow up so bad that it was hard to see more than half a block in front of me or hear anything more than the wind's angry howl or my own labored breathing. I cut a parallel path to Jimmy's street, but in the opposite direction. Up ahead of me and to my right, I could see the eerie soft glow of the cops' colored lights reflecting off the blowing snowflakes. Wisely, they had set up choke points on two of the three north-south roads leading away from this stubby thumb of land that jutted slightly into the Great South Bay. They were far enough away so that Jimmy wouldn't have been able to see their lights from his house, but if he tried to drive north from where his house was located to one of the main roads, he'd run smack into a wall of cops.

Now that I had moved far enough in the opposite direction, I changed my course from parallel to perpendicular. The cops hadn't bothered blocking off the most easterly of the three north-south roads because there was no way for Jimmy to access it by car or on foot. To reach this last road, he'd have to swim the narrow channel I was now standing in front of. And unless human evolution took a sudden, unexpected turn and I miraculously sprouted wings, swimming was exactly what *I* would have to do. Problem was, I wasn't much of a swimmer under the best conditions and these were pretty fucking far away from the best conditions. Like I said, I hadn't thought ahead. I knew the channel was here, that I'd have to get across it and another one like it to reach Jimmy's house. I guess I hoped I'd find a ladder or something so I wouldn't have to go in the water, but there was no ladder, no something, and I still had to get across. It looked like I was about to join the Polar Bear Club and I had begun untying my shoes when I heard a loud knocking, wood against wood.

I got down on hands and knees in the snow and looked along the length of the channel. There, to my right, fifty or sixty feet behind me, was a dinghy that had broken loose in the storm and drifted up this channel. I'd walked right past it. I got up, went back the way I'd come, and stood over where the dinghy had caught on a wood piling. She was rocking pretty hard in the water, but I climbed down into her without going over. Shit! One of her oars was missing, so there was no way I'd be able to row all the way over to Jimmy Palumbo's house. Given how choppy the water was and the size of the swales even in this narrow, sheltered channel, I probably wouldn't have made it anyway. I used the one remaining oar to push the dinghy off the piling, paddled across the thin strip of water, and pulled myself up on the opposite side. One down, one to go.

I was running again, heading for the short block that ran parallel to Jimmy's street. Other than the sounds of the ocean and the storm, it was strangely quiet. I slowed down, searching the street for a house with a backyard that faced across the channel at Jimmy's dock. There was only one candidate on the right side of the street. The house was totally dark and the driveway was empty of cars. When I threw a snowball at the front window, no dogs barked, no alarms sounded, no lights flashed. I crept up the driveway and went through the unlocked gate into the backyard. And there, across the second narrow channel, was Jimmy's dock. That's where my luck ran out. This house, like all the houses down here, had a backyard dock too, but it was empty. No boat. This time there would be no dinghy to get me across the water.

I thought about just letting the police do what they wanted to do in the first place, but no. Jimmy Palumbo had made me an accomplice to at least one murder and maybe two. He was mine. If there was only an ounce of redemption for me in finding out where Sashi was buried, I was going to get it. Besides, I noticed the lights were on in Jimmy's house, which was a good thing, but so too were the running lights on in his boat. That, and beneath the howl of the wind and the crash and slap of the surf, I could make out the low growl and purr of the boat's idling twin engines. Fuck me, but I was going in. I was still a little boozy and figured the water couldn't drown me any faster than my own raging guilt. Now I had three people's blood on my hands: Katy's, Sashi's, and Tierney's. I meant to wash some of it off or to die trying. I threw off my shoes and sports jacket, bundled up my parka for a makeshift flotation device, and dived into the black water.

It was worse than I ever thought it would be, much worse. The shock of the wet and the biting cold robbed me of my breath, my will, my ability to think. I flailed about, slapping at the water, but couldn't find my bundled coat. Panic was as near to me as the pounding of my own heart and I felt it about to pull me under. Then I thought I heard a splash behind me. The distraction saved me for a brief moment as my increasingly heavy arms and legs kicked and pushed the dense, unforgiving water. But I could feel myself failing, slowing down, falling under the soulless water's icy spell. There wasn't enough adrenaline in all of Suffolk County to keep me afloat any longer. Then something grabbed me and just like a drowning victim in a Learning To Swim video, I went bonkers. I swung my arms wildly, striking out into the blackness. Something, the back of a hand, a clenched fist, something, slammed into my face and stunned me. I was no longer flailing.

"Moe, relax! I've got you. Relax!" a voice screamed to me from beyond the fog in my head. "Come on, we can do this." It was Paul Stern. "Can you swim at all?"

"Yeah, I'm all right now."

"Okay."

He grabbed me by the belt and urged me forward. When I started stroking and kicking again, he let go and we made it to the opposite dock. He got out first and then helped me out of the frozen water. I was so cold, it burned. Now I knew what a steak forgotten at the back of the freezer felt like. Paul and I stood there shivering, teeth chattering. The surging water had pushed us a house or two north of Jimmy's. This house was dark and quiet as well.

"I'm going in," I said. "You stay here out of trouble."

Paul showed me a Glock. "Detective McKenna gave it to me and went to stall the cops for time. I hope the damned thing works wet." He looked down at his waterlogged watch. "We've got maybe ten more minutes."

"*We* don't have shit. You're staying here."

"We outgun him, don't we?" There was that we again.

"Maybe not and neither of us is in any kind of shape to go toe to toe with him. He's warm, dry, and gigantic. Plus, given the strain he's been under for over a month, he's probably about ready to explode."

"Then you need me and I'm helping whether you want me to or not."

I was in no position to argue and I needed to get out of the cold. "Okay."

"How are you going to deal with him if, like you say, he's ready to blow?"

"In his way, I think he's expecting me. But it really doesn't matter, does it? We're here and I'm going after him. Cover me until I get around the side of the house, then take care of the boat. Do whatever you have to do to it, but just make sure he can't use it to make a run."

As I worked my way to the side door, back against the clapboards, ducking below the windows, I tried figuring out a play that would get me inside the house without Jimmy knowing about it. Who was I kidding? Even if I wasn't soaked, frostbitten, and shoeless and hadn't consumed a third of a bottle of scotch or had a fight or been punched in the face, I don't think I could have figured out a reasonable plan. I wasn't a goddamned cat burglar, so I did the only thing that made any sense at all: I knocked. I put my arms in the air high above my head, my old .38 in my hand, butt end out, and waited. I didn't have to wait long.

Jimmy Palumbo almost smiled at me when he answered the door. He grabbed my .38 and tossed it into the darkness and drifting snow behind me. He had a big, nasty-looking revolver in his hand and it was pointed right at my belly.

"Come on inside," was all he said as he backed up into the house. "Close the door behind you."

As cold and scared as I was, I did as he said without hesitation. I guess I didn't care so much about getting killed as long as I could be warm when it happened.

"There's a comforter on the couch over there." He pointed with the gun. I went to the couch and had the comforter wrapped around my shoulders and the rest of me in a flash. "Sit," he said. I sat.

The interior of the place looked as I imagined it would, like a well-decorated house that had been rented out to a couple of irresponsible frat boys. Dirty floors, dirty dishes, half-empty food containers, a big TV. Except for the lack of used needles and cotton balls, it kind of reminded me of Nathan Martyr's place.

"No way to sell a house," I said, my teeth still chattering. "The place is a mess."

He ignored that, walking over to the front window and pushing the curtain aside with the muzzle of the revolver. "Fucking weather. I should have been long gone by now." Jimmy let the curtain fall back into place.

"Probably wouldn't've mattered."

"Maybe, maybe not. I thought you might figure out it was me eventually, but not so soon."

"You killed Tierney?"

"Hey, that's on you, Moe." Didn't I know it? "You led me straight to him and paid me for the honor. He was perfect. Fucking crazy as a bedbug. He didn't even put up too much of a fight. Who wasn't gonna believe he did it?"

"Me."

"Who else?" he asked.

"No one."

Jimmy gloated. "See what I mean?"

"So you *did* find the altar room when you searched the house. You went back to Martyr's house that night and planted those pictures of Sashi, her panties, the bones."

"How'd you figure it out?" He was curious too.

"A lot of little things," I said, happy he was willing to keep talking. More talk, less bullets. "I couldn't accept that Tierney had it in him to plot and plan and carry out such a complicated scheme. People kept telling me I was nuts and I almost started believing them too. I noticed she was wearing different underclothes in the pictures on the altar than the ones she was wearing when she was taken. Tierney just wasn't the type to shop for little girl's panties. Then I realized that Tierney had blackened out the eyes in every photo and painting in his house, but not the ones you planted. I just couldn't let it go. Then, tonight, I saw an old video of Sashi's art shows and there you were, standing guard over her."

"Shit!"

"It still all might have worked too if I hadn't seen that video. That was just dumb luck."

"Bad luck for me."

"You vandalized my car, but why? It didn't fit. That was another one of the things that really got in the way of me believing Tierney did it. Why didn't you just split after you got the initial fifty grand?"

"Look, it was like my lucky day when you walked into the museum and hired me. Until then, I was thinking that it was only a matter of time till the cops came knocking at my door. It would've looked pretty bad if I cut and run before they showed up. They'd know I was guilty, and I'd be fucked. But you saved my ass. You brought me close to things, close enough so's I could find a patsy and get away free and clear. No looking behind me, no waiting for a knock at my door. Besides, fifty grand wasn't enough for me to make any kind of new start. I thought the Bluntstones were worth millions. I mean, I used to work

Sashi's shows and see people spending hundreds of thousands of dollars at a clip on her stuff. How was I supposed to know her parents pissed all the money away and were broker than me?"

"But why fuck up my car and leave the bear?"

"It was a win-win for me. If it worked to scare you off, then great. If not, you'd keep paying me and keep me in the loop until I found the patsy. It worked, didn't it?"

"Yeah, but it ends here, Jimmy. There's a Suffolk Police boat waiting for you at Santapogue Point and they've got the roads out of here blocked off. That's why I'm wet and frozen. I had to swim across the channel to get here without the cops noticing. Believe it or not, I'm trying to save your worthless fucking life."

Oops! That was a mistake. We were pals up till then.

"Fuck you! You don't know about me, about who I am," he shouted, tightening the grip on the big revolver, a grip that, until a few seconds ago, had been steadily relaxing. "Well, if I gotta go, I ain't going alone."

"Calm down, Jimmy. You still have a bargaining chip."

He sneered. "You? Get out. Are you fucking kidding me?"

"Not me. The cops don't give a shit about me. But you know something the cops want to know. That's your play."

"Yeah, and what do I know?"

"Where Sashi is buried."

He seemed not to understand. "Huh?"

"They'll make a deal if you can tell them where Sashi is buried."

Again, he stared at me as if I was speaking a foreign language, but that's where the discussion came to an end. Things happened, everything happened, and, it seemed, all at once. There was a thump at the side door, then loud scratching, howling too, and not from the wind. A dog. The dog I'd heard on the phone the last time I'd spoken to

Jimmy. Paul was shouting at someone in the backyard, "Go! Run! Faster! Run! That's it, run! Faster! Run!" Jimmy's face went from blank to panic to fury. Then a few beats later, the boat's engines revved loudly and it sounded as if it was pulling away from the dock. Palumbo's phone rang and we both startled. It rang and rang and rang.

I said, "Answer it."

Jimmy was frozen, his attention and guts being tugged in a hundred different directions. He reached for the phone. It stopped ringing. Flashing red and blue lights strobed through the front window. The dog was howling louder now and scratching more fiercely. The boat crashed into something, groaning as it broke apart. Jimmy pointed the gun at my head.

"James Palumbo, this is the Suffolk County Police Department ..."

Jimmy turned. I had no chance in a fight with him, but I did have a chance to get the gun out of his hand. I grabbed a crystal obelisk, about eight inches tall, off the end table and brought it down hard as I could on Jimmy's wrist. The bones snapped and the gun fell to the floor. His bloodied hand hung down from his arm at an unnatural angle, exposed bone peeking through the skin. I nearly puked at the sight of it. Jimmy screamed, but didn't freak. This was a man who had played NFL football. Talent, strength, size, and speed were parts of that equation, but the ability to withstand constant pain was another. He reached for the gun with his left hand. I kicked it away before he could grab it.

"You prick! I was her only hope." And with that, he landed a left hook to my jaw that would be felt by generations of Pragers yet to be born. My eyes shut.

When they fluttered open again, I was on the floor, blood pouring out of my mouth, the revolver gone, and Jimmy Palumbo heading out the side door at a run. The dog was yelping and someone was shouting for Jimmy to halt. It was Paul Stern. *Bang!* A shot. *Bang! Bang!* Two more, louder, much much louder than the first. Now I was running, lots of people were running. I got out to the backyard just in time to see Jimmy Palumbo dive off the dock, gun in hand, knocking Paul Stern backwards into the water with him. Cops were all around me, but, crazy and irrational as it was, the only thing I could think about was that I was going to lose Rico again, and that I would lose Sarah again too.

The snow was stained with blood, a lot of blood, steam rising off it. We all ran to the edge of the dock. Three of the cops ran ahead and dived in without hesitation. For reasons I can't begin to explain, I started praying to Mr. Roth, asking him to talk to God on my behalf. Me praying to a dead Jew. Go figure! As Izzy was fond of saying, "God *does* answer prayers, only most of the time, the answer is no." A man who had witnessed the things he'd seen in Auschwitz understood the limitations of prayer. But when I looked down into the water, there was Paul Stern, his arm around Jimmy Palumbo's neck, keeping him from drowning. Then the cops grabbed on and helped.

"Get out of there!" I screamed at him in joy and anguish. "Anything happens to you, my daughter will kill me herself."

Behind me, the dog was at it again, only this time, it was yelping and howling in joy. When I turned to look, I saw McKenna, tears streaming down his face, his shoulders shaking uncontrollably. Then I understood. Standing in front of him was a little girl with green eyes and nine fingers. She was kneeling down to pet her beagle puppy.

I was right to have used Mr. Roth as the intermediary between me and the Almighty, because, this one time, God said yes.

THIRTY-NINE

The minute they brought Jimmy up out of the water I knew I had never really understood anything about the world and thought that maybe I should stop pretending that I did. Sashi stopped petting the little beagle, ran over to Jimmy, crying as fiercely as McKenna had been only moments before, and screamed, "Uncle Jimmy, Uncle Jimmy, please be all right."

He wasn't all right and he wasn't ever going to be all right again, even if he survived. Sashi could see that. That's what the tears were about. That and maybe a lot more. Jimmy's wrist was totally fucked, jagged bone sticking way the hell out, and it was hard to say whether his left thigh was soaked more with blood or water. If that wasn't bad enough, he was crying too. Sashi was holding Jimmy's good hand to her cheek even as the cops worked furiously to stanch the flow from his leg wound and deal with his wrist.

"Don't worry, kid," he said, pulling his hand away from her cheek, stroking her hair. "It'll be okay."

But she knew it was a lie. She knew the shapes and sounds of lies. Her parents had trained her in the art of the lie.

A gurney appeared and Jimmy was on it. As they carried him past me, he said, "You shoulda let us go, Prager. You shoulda let me save her." Then he was gone.

"What was that about?" McKenna asked, more composed now.

"A failed rescue attempt, I think. One gone very wrong."

"What?"

"Never mind," is what I said.

"Come on, let's get you and your partner over there to the hospital." McKenna was pointing at Paul Stern being helped out of the water.

At the hospital, they examined us for hypothermia and frostbite, but both of us checked out okay. Thanks to McKenna's intervention, they got us fixed up with some hospital scrubs to wear under the blankets instead of those ridiculous gowns. You want to suck the dignity out of a human being, make him wear a hospital gown.

"Thanks, Paul. You saved my life."

He was horrified that I said it aloud. Talk about someone squirming in his seat, but he felt compelled to respond. "I did it for me."

"How's that?"

"You're the closest thing I've got on this earth to my biological father. I couldn't just stand there and lose you too. Not now. And then there's Sarah. I never met anyone like her."

"You'll get no argument from me."

We let it go at that for a few minutes, then I started up again.

"How'd you manage to find me in that storm? You don't know the area and you weren't right behind me. The visibility was terrible, sure, but if you were close, I would have seen you."

"Easy," he said. "I tracked you. Footprints in the snow. Remember, I'm from—"

"—Vermont. Yeah, I think I heard that once or twice already tonight."

He blushed.

"So," I said, "you used the dinghy to get across the first channel, huh?"

"Dinghy?"

"A dinghy, it's a small boat that—"

"I know what a dinghy is, Moe."

"Yeah, well, I found one stuck up against a piling and I—"

"I didn't see a dinghy. All I saw was your footprints stop on one side of the channel and begin again on the other side, so I—"

"You swam across! Are you nuts? You could have been killed."

"Well, I thought if a drunk, sixty-year-old man with bad knees could do it, I could."

"Some prosecutor! If you saw me on the observation deck of the Empire State Building one minute and down on Thirty-fourth Street a few minutes later, would you assume I jumped? *Oy gevalt!* I like you, kid, but you've got a lot to learn."

"Never said I didn't."

I changed subjects. "Were you trying to shoot Jimmy in the leg?"

"No. I was aiming at his torso, but I was so incredibly cold that I couldn't stop my hand from shaking."

"Cold, and maybe a little scared too?"

"More than a little, Moe."

When he said those words, I knew that any resemblance to Rico was superficial. Rico Tripoli would never have been able to admit what his son had just confessed. One vote for nurture versus nature. For that matter, Rico would have let me drown and cried about it afterwards from the safety of shore. I didn't tell that to Paul.

We may not have had frostbite or hypothermia, but they kept me in the hospital for two days. They let Paul go home that night. When I asked the doctor why Paul got to go and I had to stay, he mentioned something about the difference in our ages. People seemed to be fixated on my age lately. In the end, I was thankful they kept me there, not because I was worried about my health, but because they kept the press out of my hair and let me get some sleep. I slept for almost an entire day. I had never been that tired in my life, nor had my muscles, the few that I had left, ever felt so incredibly sore. To paraphrase the late great Edmund Kean: drowning is easy, almost drowning is hard.

EPILOGUE

Detective McKenna, who never went to IA, but got a bump up and was now scheduled to receive his department's highest honor, came to visit me two weeks after I got out of the hospital. He came to tell me that the Suffolk crime scene guys had found some curious things in the basement of Jimmy's house. Among other items, they'd discovered four original paintings signed by Sashi Bluntstone. Somewhere Sonia Barrows-Willingham and Randy Junction were having intense, simultaneous orgasms: four of them, to be exact. The cops had also found a cell phone, one of those Wal-Mart jobs that you just buy minutes for as needed. When they checked the records, they found that Sashi and Jimmy had been talking to each other for over a year. I told him what Ben Schare had told me about seeing Sashi on the beach sometimes talking on a cell phone. I could see on McKenna's face that he'd come around to the same conclusion I'd come to the night we found Sashi alive. Neither of us said a word.

The fact was that even if we wanted to cobble together the truth of things, we would have been hard-pressed to do so. Sashi Bluntstone would have been of little help and Jimmy Palumbo none at all. At least Jimmy had a rock solid excuse: he was dead. He had been doing all right at first, huge blood loss and all, and looked like he might make it. Then he contracted one of those nasty hospital-bred bacterial infections that resist every drug known to mankind and lapsed into a coma. He didn't last ten days. Besides, like I said, I don't think either McKenna or I wanted to say the words aloud. What went on between Jimmy and Sashi was something, but it wasn't a kidnapping.

● . ●

I never returned to the house in Sea Cliff. I didn't have the stomach for the inevitably halfhearted thank yous and insincere sorries. I had come into this mess with fond memories of Candy and hating Max. And now, while I didn't hate Candy, I was much less fond of her. Whether or not she was the person who helped Sashi with her paintings, I couldn't say. My guess was it was Max. Yet, at the very least, Candy was complicit in the deceit. Max was Max. I no longer despised him. There wasn't enough there to hate, really. For the most part, I found myself feeling sorry for the both of them, that they had allowed themselves to become so woefully dependent on their daughter. Or, as Candy had put it, slaves to her career. In this case, the child was truly father to the man.

I did, however, have a nice little chat with Sonia Barrows-Willingham and Randy Junction. They had both read Carney's report cover to cover and, in spite of their bluster, were scared shitless at the prospect of my releasing it to the media. Doing so would have ruined their credibility in the art world and decimated the value of their Sashi collections. That was the least of it. If it could be shown that either of them knew the paintings weren't exclusively done by Sashi, it might have led to criminal charges and countless civil suits. And when I pointed that out to them, they were eager to reach an agreement. I proposed a deal: I would sit on the report if they would help pay off the Bluntstones' debts and contribute a portion of the profits of Sashi's resales to a trust fund for her. They couldn't agree fast enough.

● . ○

I never did get an invoice from Declan Carney. I tried, with no success, to contact him. His phone numbers were no longer valid and all my emails bounced back. So after a few weeks, armed with my checkbook, I went to his building in Long Island City. There was a foreclosure notice taped to the front door and there was no response to my insistent buzzing or repeated knocks. I walked around to the back side of the building. There, spray-painted on the back wall, were these words:

GONE HOME

● . ○

Sarah was back in my life and we made a weekly date of meeting at New Carmens for breakfast or dinner. It all depended on her schedule. We talked a few times a week and we even talked about Katy and the stuff we did together as a family. She had forgiven me my sins. Still, the hurt of our estrangement has never gone away. I don't know that it will. There was a seven-year gap between the time we buried Katy and the day Sarah asked me to be a part of the search for Sashi. Those years are impossible to recoup. She had grown into a woman without me there to be a part of it. Sure, I saw some of it at a distance. I'd been like a proud dad watching his kid play in a big game, but from the worst seat in the stadium.

It pretty quickly got serious between her and Paul. Sarah spent her once-a-month long weekends up in Vermont and Paul Stern was down in Brooklyn twice a month. I think I knew where they were headed before they did. It was hard for me not to like Paul, especially since we spent a lot of time together retracing the steps Rico and I had taken decades before. It helped me remember the Rico I had loved without the bitter aftertaste in my mouth. It was harder for Paul because he could only know Rico through me, but, I suppose, second-hand love is better than no love at all.

● . ◉

One icy cold night, long after Bordeaux In Brooklyn had closed for the day's business, I went for a walk along the Promenade to just try and clear my head. It was quite late and the little strip of concrete above the Brooklyn-Queens Expressway was totally deserted. I leaned over the rail and gazed across the river at lower Manhattan. It still didn't look right without the twin towers there. I don't think I would ever get used to them being gone no matter how many years passed. I remembered what my dad's friend Harry would say about the arm he'd lost at Anzio in WWII: "You learn how to work around it, but you never stop missing it."

As far as trying to clear my head, it wasn't working out, so I turned right and walked back towards the store. But before I got ten feet, something slammed hard into my right shoulder and sent searing pain shooting down my back and along my arm. A thousand stars exploded behind my eyes and I lost my balance. A strong arm shoved me down and I landed with a hard thump, the back of my head banging against the concrete for good measure. I tried shaking out the cobwebs, but moving my head at all only made the pain that much worse and exploded more stars. My right arm was numb and useless. I could sense that my shoulder was not where it should have been. Basically, I was screwed.

"I told you you shouldn't've fucked with me, asshole." I recognized the voice, but couldn't quite place it. "You don't remember me?" he said. "Maybe this will help."

Bang! Now my left thigh was on fire.

"David Thompson," I said through pain-clenched teeth.

"Give the man a cigar."

"Nathan Martyr's doorman and all around ass-licker." My eyes were watery but I could see a smile on Thompson's twisted face.

Bang! My other leg was now afire.

"I'm gonna fuck you up and there's nothing you can do about it, because no matter what you think is happening to you, it can't be. See, I'm in Martyr's loft, hanging with some of his friends. Friends that will all testify that I was there with them."

"Then you better kill me, butt-boy, or I'll kill you."

"Thanks for the suggestion, shitbird."

Bang! I heard more than felt my ribs cracking and I started the slow fade into unconsciousness. As I slipped into the darkness, I tensed for the next blow, but it never came. I heard Thompson screaming in pain, then something fell down next to me. Thompson. He was convulsing, writhing, his arms and legs twitching, banging into me. Footsteps ran towards us. Thompson cried out in pain so that it bruised the night. There was a dull thud. The convulsing stopped. Then I thought I heard a woman calling my name, but realized I must have already been unconscious. She couldn't be there.

● .

The woman I'd known as Mary Lambert was sitting at my bedside. I was sore all over and, apparently, a confused elephant had decided to perch on my chest. There was an intravenous drip in my left arm and cold packs on both thighs. My right shoulder and ribs were taped up. There was a sling on my right arm and a brace around my neck.

"Hi," I said in an old man's voice. "Where's Thompson?"

"Under arrest."

"You Taser him?"

"Uh huh," she said.

"I hear those things can be painful."

"Very, but not nearly as painful as when I dug my heel into his nuts."

"Maybe we can discuss that some other time," I said, "like when I can breathe again."

"Sure, Moses Prager. Anything you want." She stood up out of her chair, knelt over me, and kissed my forehead. "I don't think we've been formally introduced. My name is Pamela Osteen."

"Nice to meet you, Miss Osteen," the old man said. "It is *Miss* Osteen?"

"It is." She waved her ringless left hand at me.

"You look an awful lot like a woman I was falling in love with named Mary Lambert."

"I know that broad. Pretty gal, but a liar. I promise you I can be everything she was and lots of things she wasn't."

"Nice to know. Why'd you come?"

She winked. "To save your ass."

"Thanks for that, but—"

"To tell you how sorry Mary Lambert was for lying to you, that it killed her inside to do it because she felt the same things you did, but that she had a job to do."

"And you?"

"To ask that even if you can't forgive Mary, to give me a chance."

"I'll think about it," I said.

She smiled that smile of hers. "Well, then, you won't mind if I stick around while you decide."

"Where will you stay?"

"As close to you as you'll let me."

"That might be pretty close."

"I'll risk it."

That summer, about a week before the grand opening party for Sunrise and Vine, I got one of those postcard invitations in the mail. It was for a showing of Sashi Bluntstone's new work to be held at some gallery in Chelsea. The name of the show was "Art In Captivity" and I wanted to throw up. I had hoped that Max and Candy would have learned something from getting the shit scared out of them. That they might have grown up, but people don't change. It was one of the harsh paradoxes in life that everybody dies, but not everybody grows up. Sashi was back to being the family ATM.

On the front of the invitation was a color reproduction of one of the paintings to be displayed, and on the back, above the invitation copy, was a small photo of Sashi. She looked utterly miserable. She always looked utterly miserable unless there was a beagle licking her face. I wondered if she wasn't destined to die young. I wondered if a cold and random universe was any crueler than a God who had chosen this one time to say yes.

THE END